Praise for Ella M. Kaye

"I always love the texture, dimension, and perspectives in Ella M. Kaye books. Kaye isn't afraid to tackle difficult subjects, and she especially handles social issues with tact and dexterity. This is a riveting read, packed with words to savor."
Author Maggie Toussaint, about Shadows of Rust & Reels

"The author draws rounded characters, with flaws as well as virtues and is unflinching in showing that some of their injuries and suspicions are self-inflicted. ... Like a ballet, the characters unfold to each other and to the reader and when they come together it means something. Ella M Kaye's eye for detail, description and the 'masks' people wear is telling."
Author Lindsay Townsend, about Pier Lights

"Kaye's characters not only come alive, but will jump out and yell at you, pour their hearts out to you, and you will laugh and cry right along with them. The fun, witty banter and the expressive sorrow will keep you on the edge of your seat."
Liz, Reader Review

"You always seem to suck the reader right into the story, which is a phenomenal thing. Leaves the reader wanting more & more.
Annette, Reader Review

"The first few pages caught me up in their story, and I read almost non-stop until I finished."
Rising Star Reviews, about Pier Lights

Also by Ella M. Kaye

<u>Dancers & Lighthouses</u>
Pier Lights
Shadowed Lights
Pieces of Light

<u>Artists & Cottages</u>
Shadows of Blues & Echoes
Shadows of Rust & Reels

<u>Anthology</u>
Music of the Heart from Fire Star Press (2017)
includes the EMK novella *A Melody in the Dark*

Shadows of Greens & Memories

Ella M. Kaye

ISBN: 978-1-948370-03-5

First Digital Edition ©2015 ISBN: 9781310439612

Cover design: LK Hunsaker
Cover photo of Storm Lake, Iowa ©2018 Robin Koster. Used with permission.
Hydrangeas and Greenhouse photos licensed from Shutterstock.
Red Lilies painting by LK Hunsaker.

Elucidate Publishing
PO Box 1262
Hermitage PA 16148

United States of America

One of the wood carvings in Storm Lake, Iowa.

One

"Didn't you used to be Frannie Barrett?"

Francis choked back a sigh at the voice she still recognized from years ago, picked up a couple of not exactly farm fresh tomatoes from the back of the grocery story bin to set in her basket, and gave the woman a half-hearted grin. "How are you, Tana? I'm still Francis Barrett, and I go by Fran. I never did like to be called Frannie, you know."

"Didn't you? But we all called you that." Tana tugged at the bottom of her shirt to pull it out of the indentation between her large breasts and larger stomach as she gave Fran a once-over. "Well, never mind. We all thought you eloped and ran off to ... was it Vegas? Guess that didn't work out so well?"

"Vegas? Is that what people are saying?" Fran perused the bell peppers that were in about the same shape as the tomatoes. Okay enough for salsa, she supposed.

"It's not true, then?"

"Not even close. I've never been to Vegas and I've never been married. I have to run. I'm sure I'll see you around." Making a quick escape from The Third Degree, the biggest thing Tana White Berger was known for throughout Storm Lake after her gossip abilities and the way she'd flaunted her figure, which Fran supposed she no longer did, she hustled with her red grocery basket over her arm to the cashier, paid in cash, and wondered again why she'd decided to move back to Iowa, even temporarily.

Maybe she should have let her aunt sell the darned property as is, contents included, whatever they might be, so she could be rid of it. Most of it, she wouldn't miss. But the little cottage, her father's *escape from it all*, as he'd said so often, Fran couldn't quite let go. Not until she'd come back to see it.

The place was in horrid disrepair. The front porch was unsteady enough Fran tended to duck and move through quickly when she came and went. Queen Anne's Lace and other less pretentious weeds had taken over the parts of the gardens not densely carpeted with dead leaves. The lemon balm had jumped its retainer in the herb garden and filled the whole thing, spilling out into the grass. Even the hydrangeas were messier than normal. Her father never trimmed them back for winter. He waited until summer after the growth returned and only cut those showing decay. That hadn't been done, either, for years, or so it seemed. Pale yellow-brown thin bare stalks stuck out everywhere in different lengths, mixed with gray-black dead wood and withered brown leaves that discouraged the darker brown stalks from regenerating the shrubs with new life. Her father would thrash his hands through what little hair he'd had left if he saw his beautiful gardens in such a state.

So she would at least fix them first. The garden shed would help the house get a better price if it looked tidy and usable rather than a run-down eyesore. The exterior mattered most. If she could fool renters or buyers with an immaculate entrance, they would see the inside as nicer than it was. That's how it worked. First impressions and all.

The place had always been a mess. Except the gardens. The grass was often too long and Fran was never sure if there was much actual grass mixed in with the weeds. If it was green, her father didn't care what was growing out there, outside his gardens. The shed itself had always been a disaster. Mis-matched. Full of stuff. Not even stuff he used, but just stuff. Piles of stuff. Disorderly...

Fran laughed aloud as she stowed the few groceries in the back of her Explorer, shook her head while she got behind the wheel, and sighed as she veered her car onto the little road to her temporary home. She couldn't even call it disorderly. It was far beyond disorderly.

Her aunt had at least hauled out a bunch of garbage. Rather, she'd paid to have it done. She'd also called an exterminator in, to rid it of "rats," she'd said, although Fran was quite sure they were only mice and a cat or two would have worked. Maybe she would get a cat or two. For the mice. For company.

Except she wasn't staying. A few catch and release traps would work for any mice the peppermint plants she had already put around the porch in big containers didn't deter. She looked forward to fresh peppermint iced tea. It would help the summer move along faster.

Not that she generally wanted summer to move along fast. Summer was her favorite time in Storm Lake. Or rather, it was the only time she didn't hate being in Iowa. So she could make do, spend some time out on the beach, maybe go to Lake Fest to see whoever was playing. Give herself time to clear out the rest of the shed. Redecorate. Rent it. Or sell. That decision was still in the air. The only thing Fran was sure of at this point was that she would not stay any longer than necessary.

Possibly, she'd head right back to South Dakota. Or not. Cal was from there. Still there, at least at times. Maybe she'd wander farther. Everything that didn't fit in her SUV plus the rented pull-behind moving trailer had been sold or given away. She could go anywhere, using the house sale or rent as income until she found something to supplement it. And there was a decent amount of money in her savings account, since her mother drummed it into her head from childhood to save part of everything she earned for doing chores beyond the required basics she had to do as a member of the household. That had carried through to every job she had, and she'd always worked at least one job. Often, she'd taken second jobs simply to fill extra time. All of that income had been added to her savings. Nothing was holding her anywhere anymore.

A heaviness descended on her soul as she drove past the tacky bi-level houses in shades of brown and dark green, all pretty much the same, an easy throw-together floor plan that made them not cost too awful much. Despite her memories in her own house, in her parents' old house, she liked the tall stone manor-style structure itself and was always erringly proud of not having the same design as everyone else on the street. Of course it was off the street and behind trees enough it was hard to see until you drove right up in front of it, and she never had visitors of her own there. But she knew it was different, the style was artistic and elegant, and she'd loved it.

The only thing she didn't like was that her mother created the landscaping plan. Symmetrical. Simple. Fake colored wood chips in heavy layers to prevent life underneath from coming through. Made to look like it popped out of a magazine. It was always neat; Fran gave her mother that. But it was boring. Her mother could have let her father be in charge of that one thing with the main house, since it was his thing, after all.

And it wouldn't have been boring.

Turning off the main side road onto a gravel road, Fran glanced over at the big house, still neat as a pin, and kept going to the shed. The work ahead of her made her sigh again. Such a mess. Maybe she'd hire some yard help. She'd far rather do it on her own, though, or as much as she could before she ran out of steam or patience. She knew how to do it. Her father had always pulled her out to his gardens to help, and he always taught her something while she helped. Sometimes it was about gardening. Sometimes there was a point to it. Often, Fran had to bite her tongue to keep from telling him there was no reason she needed to know whatever he rambled about.

At least it wasn't gossip. That was her mother's arena, also, and much of why Fran tried hard to work outside with her father rather than inside with her mother. Maybe there was something wrong with her, as people had always thought, but Fran could not find it within herself to be that awfully interested in other people simply because they lived in the same place she'd been forced to grow up through no choice of her own.

Her father, through his oddities, was at least never boring, and that made him far better company than most people she ran across.

There was, of course, one other shining light in Storm Lake, Iowa. Every day since she'd arrived, Fran had considered driving over to his parents' house and asking how to get in touch with him. She also thought about looking him up online, but that felt too much like stalking. And she was not at all sure she wanted to see him now. Could be, like Tana, he'd put on a bunch of weight and his age was showing hard, and although she couldn't fairly fault him for that, Fran thought it might be better to remember him as he was back in school.

Back in school, when they were in the same class. Eons ago, it seemed. Back when the only time he spoke to her was as a joke, although he often looked like he wanted to talk to her.

Twenty-one years had passed since high school. Twenty years since she'd seen him. Could be he'd turned into a huge ass. If he had, she didn't want to know.

No, it was far better to leave things alone and hope she didn't run into George McKenry.

Two

"Heard someone moved into the old Barrett place the other day. Know who it is?"

The Barrett place? G.F. felt tension flood his body as he jerked his head toward his coworker. He hadn't heard anything about it selling, didn't even know it was for sale. Unless she'd moved home. "No idea." In an attempt to cover his too-quick reaction mixed with too much hope that she might have come home, he grabbed the tamper from Jim and forced the hot asphalt down into the pot hole with a hard shove.

"Practically your neighbor. You haven't checked them out?"

"Other end of the street. And I've got better things to do. Put more in that one."

Dragging the shovel over, letting the tip scrape the surface, which made G.F. cringe, Jim pushed it into the pour pot full of hot asphalt and sand slurry and dumped the mix along the edge of the hole. "Doesn't your old girlfriend own it now that her father passed on?"

Raking it out evenly, G.F. reclaimed the tamper and shoved it down on top of the mess. For the hundredth time, or so, he wiped the sweat from his forehead onto his bright orange T-shirt sleeve. "She was never my girlfriend. Hardly spoke to her."

Jim laughed out loud. "But you were sure mad enough when she took off with that out-o-towner. Went to Vegas, they say. Got married within a week of knowin' him. Musta been desperate. You might've had a shot at her."

"Knock it off and use the energy where it's needed. I want to finish here sometime tonight." Using his foot to help shove the tamper in harder, he inspected the edges.

"Yeah, yeah, big boss man. Think she'd pay more attention to you now that you're doing something productive with your life? Wasn't that her big line?"

"Smooth that out more or they'll have my head. I've got my

hands full enough not to worry about what she'd think, or anyone else, either." One final thud against asphalt and pavement and G.F. stood back to eye his work. Boss man. Right. Boss man enough to have to keep an eye on his old classmate who spent about as much time leaning against the truck sipping whatever he had in his thermos as he did actually working, on top of whatever young loafers and temp workers they sent out on the crew each summer, but not boss enough to not still be sweating like a dog's tongue and ending up sore every night from the grueling physical labor. He was getting way too damned old for this shit.

He doubted Francis Barrett, or whatever her last name was now, would be one bit impressed with how *productive* he was. Fixing roads for Iowa Public Works wasn't prestigious enough to be impressive. Paid good, though. There was that. And with five fast-growing mouths to feed, he couldn't afford to do otherwise. Even if one of them was a mutt he didn't even choose to have.

Not that he chose to have four kids, either. He'd planned on two and had said as much right from the beginning, before the ring, even. She'd agreed, said she had other things to do than *just raise kids*, anyway. Just happened, she said, when she told him about the third one coming. Still, even if he hadn't wanted more than two, the idea of the third coming socked his gut with excitement enough, it hadn't seemed a bad idea. And it wasn't. The kid was worth it.

With the second "accident," meaning number four and twice what he'd bargained for, she'd cried when she told him, apologizing. He'd had to quench his own thoughts to tell her it was fine, that he supposed they needed the one more. And then he'd taken care of it himself to make sure no more would *just happen*. A man could only work so many hours and still have any time left to spend with those kids he worked to support, not to mention their mother who had always been demanding of his time and refused to get a second job on top of being a mother. Fair enough, if she'd spent a decent amount of that time actually being a mother instead of shucking them off on his own mother as much possible.

When he started out with the road crew, G.F. only planned to stay a few years, get his house paid down, some money in the bank, and then move on to something less strenuous, something that didn't leave him dripping in sweat all summer and rubbing his hands for warmth all winter. With two kids, he could have done that. The third made it iffy. After the fourth, he gave up on the idea. He figured it would be worth the sweating and freezing to come home to a house full of arms to hug, after his shower, and a warm body in bed next to him every night, a very willing warm body. Justine had always been plenty willing. She'd hung all over him in public so often they looked like the perfect couple. He figured they were close enough, other than her lack of interest in being with her children as much as with him. So he'd taken the promotions as they came and set his heels in for the long haul.

Then she moved out and took the kids with her, along with half their savings, his savings, what he managed to get her not to spend on herself. Not that he was ever stingy, but there were the four kids and the bills and he didn't want to work on the road until he was sixty. And she had the audacity to demand child support *and* alimony.

G.F. was darn thankful the judge saw no reason for alimony. Wasn't really his choice to break up. She'd taken the step that led to it. He'd done nothing other than not being *available enough*, so she said. How in the hell more available could he have been? He worked and went home, put every dime into his family, didn't throw it away at bars every weekend or even every night like some he knew. He talked with his children, asked about their days, helped with homework, made dinner much of the time so they'd have something decent rather than the frozen things Justine liked to "cook," never went anywhere without her except to work or the store, and never said anything bad to or about the woman in front of the kids. Whether or not he would've had the right. Considering. She was lucky his youngest looked so much like him, or he wouldn't believe she was.

And damn, did he adore the girl. Fortunately, his Lexi was like the good side of her mother, the side he'd fallen for. She was so opposite her brothers, her boisterous all-out-there older brothers who gave her no slack for being a girl.

G.F. did. He tried to watch out for what she might need as a girl that he didn't know much about. The girl's mother sure didn't do much of it. At eleven, his baby would be *that age* soon and it scared the living hell out of him.

At least his kids now lived with him and the money to support them went to direct support and not to her $100 hair appointments. G.F. figured her newest boy toy was covering it. The guy who, a few months ago, made her move out of the little house G.F. was helping to pay for and into his little condo that didn't have room for the kids. He also had Justine eating nothing but health food these days. More power to him.

Either way, he was more than glad to have his kids home full time rather than only on weekends. These days, they went to their mother's every Sunday. He hated even giving in to that, with that man there, but he had no choice in the matter, since she had unsupervised visitation rights. At least they were old enough they could tell him about whatever went on.

Wiping sweat off his forehead onto his clean enough sleeve, he told the crew to wrap it up so they could call it a day. Beginning of May and he was sweating enough to drench his shirt by midday already. Summer used to be his favorite season. These days, it reminded him he wasn't twenty anymore and working on roads under the July and August sun was no joy and no small feat.

He couldn't wait to get home to his plain cluttered chaotic house that was near to paid off, although it needed some work, and hit the shower while he pretended it was just what he wanted. He'd quit telling himself by now he'd ever get the house as in shape as he wanted it. Just too much to be done and he'd rather spend the time with his somewhat undisciplined, but beautiful kids while they were still kids and had to put up with him, like it or not.

Whether or not he wanted to, he found himself thinking of the old Barrett place on the drive home. He'd often thought of buying the place, back before the third and fourth kid came along, meaning sports stuff and scouting stuff and school expenses and food – damn, those boys could eat – for three boys, and dance classes and whatever girl stuff his youngest needed. He often just handed over some dough to a trusted mother of one of her friends since Lexi insisted she could absolutely not go girl shopping with her father, and her mother would not take her. Her grandma was willing, but Lexi was quick to point out her grandma liked "old" styles, not "in" styles. Now and then they came to a compromise, but no matter how much she loved her grandma, it was still *shopping with Grandma*, which was about as uncool as *being seen with Dad.*

They started earlier these days. G.F. didn't remember "cool" making so much difference until at least a couple of years later back when he was still not "old" in Lexi Lingo.

Passing by his own place, he found himself idling in front of the large brick house. It was a light-colored brick, nearly cream if he had to come up with a color name for it, with tall main level windows and jutted out bricks creating a nice architectural detail around the tall door in the center of the front, with no porch, only steps that led from the circular drive, concrete rather than asphalt, and low well-groomed shrubs softening the view only a touch. If he owned it, he'd let the shrubs grow out a bit for a more natural look and add some color, maybe even find matching brick to put along each edge for a built-up flower garden so it was less square.

Still, it was a beautiful house. Different than most in town. Stately. Made to look impressive. And he'd damn sure buy the thing if he could. Except someone apparently had just done that.

A car was out front. A nice one. But bland for his taste. Silver Buick, it looked like. He expected it wasn't Fran. She wasn't a silver Buick type. So someone bought it. G.F. figured that was a good thing. It couldn't sit empty too long without deteriorating.

But who knew when it might come back on the market. By then, he likely wouldn't need a big place. His little chickadees would be flying off to their own nests before too many more years.

He sighed at the thought and turned around to go find them, tamping down his thought of driving just a bit farther to the old garden shed to see if it was still standing. If it wasn't, he didn't want to know.

<h1 style="text-align:center">Three</h1>

Shoving his boots off outside the door, G.F. thought about pulling his sweat-soaked tee off there, too, but his mother had drummed into his head you keep your shirt on inside the house. With three boys, he wouldn't worry about that bit of upbringing, but for his daughter's sake, he listened to his mother.

His head shook when he had to walk around a baseball bat and glove and dirty tennis shoes that left half dry mud all over the entry. "Alright, whoever *left* this mess better come back and *clean it up*." He yelled up the stairs where he heard bits of noise and continued to the living room. Even worse, the dog was on the couch, and both were covered in mud. "Come on, Scruff. Are you serious with this? Get *off* the couch." He encouraged the huge, hairy mutt to listen with a strong push on his behind. "*Who* let the dog play in the mud?"

"I didn't *let* him, Dad. He pulled me into it." His second youngest came down the stairs in nothing but boxers and a dirty face.

"Then why didn't you leave him outside?"

"He didn't want to be outside."

"And you think I want mud all over the house?"

The boy shrugged and G.F.'s anger waned. A pushover. His ex always called him a pushover. Maybe he was, but not entirely. "Come clean up this mess, but put some clothes on first. Your sister doesn't want to see all that."

"She ain't home..."

"*Not*, Frankie. She's *not* home. Stop saying *ain't*. Where is she, then?"

"I don't know. And Mom says ain't."

"You're living with me now. That means my rules, and I want you to sound smart enough you can do better with your life than filling pot holes and near getting heat stroke. Where's your brother?"

"Which one?"

"Oh, for pete's sake. Who do you think I mean? The one in

charge."

"Theo?"

G.F. sighed. Thirteen was a truly horrible age for a kid. He'd thought so when he was thirteen himself and he'd thought so when his older boys were, and he still thought so. They all lost their brains when they were thirteen. Must be 'cause they started getting into girls about that time. "Frankie, let's try this again. Where is Theo?"

"I don't know."

His jaw clenched. *Just a boy. He's just a boy.* "Happen to know where your other brother is? And don't ask me which one. You only have the two, that I know of."

"Justin's still at practice. Like always, Dad."

"Don't get smart. Practice got over forty minutes ago."

The boy shrugged. "Flirting with his girlfriend, probably."

"Girlfriend? Are we talking about the same brother?"

"Justin. Right? I said Justin was probably still hanging out at practice talking to his girlfriend who stays after school to watch him."

"Um, she does, does she? Since when? Why did I not know?"

"You know her, Dad. That one he's always talking to."

"That could mean several different girls. Want to be more specific?"

He shrugged again. "Don't remember her name. Not the one I would pick. She's not as hot as some of them."

G.F. rubbed his neck. "Is your homework done?"

"No, but..."

"Go do it. And then you get to clean the mud from the couch."

"Can I clean the mud first?"

"Whatever. Just put some clothes on and get them both done, sometime before bedtime, preferably. And don't touch that game until they are. Sure your sister isn't upstairs?"

"Wouldn't I have seen her if she was home?"

"Boy, you're trying my patience."

With another shrug, Frank shuffled to the kitchen, for soapy water, G.F. hoped.

Just to be sure, he went up and knocked on his daughter's door. No answer, so he opened it and called her name. Nothing. Not even her school books were dropped on her floor as they normally were. He refrained from cursing and stomped back down the stairs to the phone. Or he would've gone to the phone if it was where it belonged.

"Frankie, any idea where the phone might be?"

"Nope. Should I use this bowl?" The boy sloshed water on the carpet as he tried to balance the large metal bowl between his scrawny arms.

"Could you have found a bigger one, you think?"

"No, we don't have a bigger one."

"I meant... Fine. It's fine. But I did mention clothes somewhere along the line."

"Figured I'd clean first so I don't get it on my clothes."

G.F. sighed and waved at him to go ahead, since he already had the biggest bowl in the house too full of too-soapy water he'd probably spill a few more times before he was done.

Looking under couch cushions and chair cushions and under the couch and under the coffee table, the usual hiding places for the phone, he was nearly at the end of his patience when the front door opened.

"Hey, Dad." Theo dropped his bag on the floor with a thud.

"Where's your sister?"

"Dunno. Haven't been home. Missing again? Try calling over to Eve's."

"If I had any idea where the phone might be this time, I would have done that already..."

"It's right here." Theo grabbed it from atop a book in the crowded shelf beside the door. "Sorry. Forgot to put it back."

"You know, I wouldn't trade any of you for anything, but I sure wouldn't give a wooden nickel for another one."

"You sure? It's getting quiet around here. Might be time for another one."

"Not coming from me. I took care of that..." With a sudden clench of his gut, he stopped in the middle of dialing Eve's mother and stared at the sixteen-year-old.

The boy laughed. "Teasing. Just a joke. Don't have a heart attack."

"Not funny, kid. Not even close to funny."

"The look on your face was."

"Keep laughing. If I ever do have a heart attack, it puts you in charge since you know your mother isn't up to the task." Vindicated by the return look, he scanned the phone's directory for Eve's number. "Hey, before you go anywhere, make sure Frankie is actually cleaning that couch, would you? And put that mutt outside until he gets a bath – your job tonight since you were supposed to be here in charge." G.F. ignored the muttering and hit the dial button. He could hardly blame his daughter for wanting to be at her friend's house where there were only two other girls, quiet girls, than in the madhouse that was his place. Still, the girl knew better than to just take off alone without permission.

Setting the watering pail beside the shed door, Fran wiped her forehead with her sleeve. Enough for the day. The grass, and whatever was mixed in with the grass, was mowed, and her garden wagon was more than half full of weeds. She'd pulled most of the Queen Anne's Lace so they wouldn't take over and set them aside to use the flowers in her salads and the roots in her stews, and left the ones in the back so she could harvest the seeds. She'd long ago learned to distinguish them from similar poisonous plants and more than once wondered if she could get away with accidentally throwing poison hemlock, having "mistaken" it for wild carrots, into Cal's soup. She wouldn't, of course. But it didn't keep her from thinking it now and then.

Coffee grounds were scattered around the base of the hydrangeas. Her father would throw a fit about that, too. He liked them pink. He'd added lime and phosphorous every spring and every fall to make them pink. Fran hated pink. She was not at all a pink person. So she added acidity, in the form of coffee grounds, to their soil to make them blue instead. It could be too late in the season to work, she supposed, but it was worth a try.

Her mother would complain about using those "nasty old grounds" instead of tossing them in the garbage. *There's stuff you can buy for that*, she'd say. *Don't tell anyone your father uses that old stuff from the kitchen in my yard.* But Fran was a coffee addict, no matter how hot the weather, and the grounds were always readily available. Why buy something to do a job she already had the means to do? As for that much, she had to agree with her father.

It was hot for May and she wasn't used to gardening anymore, so she gave herself credit for what was done, even if she'd wanted to do twice as much, washed her hands of the first layer of dirt at the little water pump beside the shed that fed into the fish pond that had no fish but plenty of mosquito larvae – she'd have to go buy pond fish to take care of them – and shuffled in the side door. She tired too easily these days. He'd said, *yeah well, you are thirty. You can't expect to have the energy of a twenty-year-old.* And that was nine years ago. Just before they'd split. Now she was thirty-nine and feeling every bit of it.

"A nice cool shower would be good about now." Talking to herself, she shrugged it off, kicked out of her shoes, and made her way to the tiny bathroom with its claw foot tub. Replace it or update it? She still hadn't decided. She'd yet to de-clutter the room, any room except the little kitchen area since she could not cook in that mess and so had done it the night she moved in, and the tub looked like part of the clutter with its scratched white paint showing the metal underneath. Maybe it would look fine once she cleared stuff out, or she'd have to replace or refinish it. She'd cross that bridge when it was time.

For now, a cool bath had to work since she didn't have a shower.

Soaking in the tub was relaxing, people said. To Fran, it was damned boring. And hard to wash her hair. A shower was much more simple. Maybe she'd put one in. Of course, that, she couldn't do herself, so maybe she wouldn't. The people who ended up buying the place could do it if they wanted. She only had to make it look good enough to sell.

The yard came first. Fran couldn't stand the thought of people driving past the place to get to the fishing hole down the road and seeing the mess it was. Her father would keep rolling in his grave until his gardens weren't a mess. He would likely do the same when she started to de-clutter the house, though, and he'd just have to deal with that.

Fran hated clutter. With a passion, she hated clutter. And chaos. A big reason she'd gone away with Calvin was his laid-back attitude and very together life. His apartment was always clean, with nothing extra lying about, and his car never had anything personal in it other than his phone and briefcase: no garbage, no dirt, no sticky mess in the cup holders. She'd liked that. To her, it looked together, smart, organized, thoughtful.

Well, she'd been part right, anyway. He was organized and had everything pulled together just the way he wanted it. Nice for him, she supposed.

Why she hadn't made the connection between her mother's neat freak tendencies and her control issues to realize Cal's neat freak issues likely meant the same, Fran didn't know. Of course there were neat freaks without control issues. She didn't have control issues. She didn't want to be controlled, but she didn't want to control anyone else, either. She supposed that's what she expected from Calvin, and by the time she was in that far, it felt too late to back out. It wasn't, and she should have, but some lessons took far, far too long to learn.

Four

The end of May. Fran had been in Storm Lake for three weeks already, had the yard cleaned up, and much of the garbage out of the house. Work shed, really. She couldn't rightly call it a house or even a cottage. Even though she could now walk through it fine and see the floors well enough to know they all needed to be redone, the place was tiny. Still, it could be a cottage with some help; it was small, but functional. Enough for her own purposes while she was in town and a nice little getaway for whoever bought it.

Her father had called it his office, but then, he called a lot of things by strange names. It was his garden shed, large for a shed, with a separate space for a tiny kitchenette and a loft overlooking the living area. He'd used the loft as office space. The mud room was big enough he'd added a bathtub and toilet, and then a twin bed against one wall of the living area since he spent more time in his shed in his latter years than he did in the main house next door.

Somewhat next door. The property was large. The shed-office-cottage was a good walk from the house. Fran was unsure whether it was her mother or father who insisted on that much distance. Either way, she'd spent plenty of her teenage years walking back and forth telling her father he should clean up and come back for dinner and often got stuck listening to his latest plant adventures.

She'd yet to step foot inside the attached greenhouse, which was roughly twice the size of the shack. His domain. The last place she'd seen him while he was still fully coherent, or as fully as she'd ever known. They'd argued. Over Calvin. About how he wasn't good enough for her and she was throwing her life away with him. She'd argued vehemently.

A stupid thing to do, since he was right and she'd known it then. Still, Calvin was going away, out of Iowa, and at that moment in time, what Fran most wanted was to get away.

Needing to kick her feet up a while before she could force the energy to go grocery shopping, she flipped through a home design magazine she'd found on the library give-and-take table. Fran liked the library. It was quiet. People left her alone. She didn't have to try to remember what she wanted, like she always did in the store, which caused far too many trips back and forth, which she hated. She didn't have to worry about entertaining herself. She simply planted her rear in one of the chairs beside the magazine stands and grabbed whatever looked interesting. By the time she'd gone through them, there were new editions out. It was always her personal indulgence time and had been since she was young enough to be let out alone.

It was a good walk from their house, her parents' house, to the main part of town, but it was on a small road with a bicycle path wide enough she could step out of the way to let the rare bicycle go past as she walked. Sometimes she'd ridden her bike instead, but she preferred to walk. It had been some time since she'd done much walking. Maybe she'd start again. It wouldn't hurt anything to start losing the thirty extra pounds she told herself over and over to get rid of. Problem was, she didn't care a whole heck of a lot.

Walking more would give her more stamina, however, and that would be a good thing.

G.F. shook his head at his youngest as she sulked beside him. "Horrible thing to be seen shopping with your dad, isn't it?"

Lexi rolled her eyes and dropped her gaze back to the floor.

"I remember being young, you know. Hard to believe, I'm sure, since I'm ancient these days, but I do remember. So if any of your little friends see you, act like you're alone and I'll play along. How's that?"

"They all know you, Dad. Everyone knows you."

"That so? Guess I'm kind of famous, then, and you should want to be seen with me." Again, the rolled eyes. He remembered eleven just well enough to know better than to take it personally. "What kind of cereal do you want this week?"

"I don't eat cereal anymore, remember? It's full of junk. Mom made us eggs and oatmeal or quinoa every morning. Can we get eggs and quinoa?"

"We have eggs, and what in the hell is keen-whaa?" Over-pronouncing it on purpose, he also baited his daughter on purpose, to see if she knew what it was she wanted.

"It's spelled with a q." In her best know-it-all eleven-year-old voice, Lexi spelled it out slowly, as though he was actually ancient. "It's a whole grain and super healthy. And we have eggs, but not enough for all of us every day until you go to the store again."

"Fine. Get eggs and whatever. But I can't exactly cook for you in the morning when I have to be at work by six a.m. and you don't get up until seven-thirty."

"Yeah, I know. I got it. I can cook my own breakfast. It's not rocket science, you know."

"Watch the attitude, little miss. Your mom might allow that, but I don't, and you know it."

At her shrug, he bit his tongue. They'd get adjusted again. At least it wasn't his doing that they had to adjust again. And at least they didn't have to switch schools when their mother moved out of the district, in with her newest boy toy. It was a good thing Theo was old enough and responsible enough to be sure the youngest two were up in time for school and to drive them in the old clunker G.F. bought him as payment for having the extra responsibility. Justin was fully self-responsible at fifteen, but ask him to do anything for his youngest siblings and it was like asking for a kidney.

Anyway, it was also a good thing he still had the house since Justine didn't want it. He hadn't had to fight for it. The place had been awful quiet the past three years other than on their weekend visits. He enjoyed the regular noise and commotion after so many nights of wandering through the place alone trying to decide what to do with himself.

Giving up trying to joke Lexi out of her sulk, G.F. got through his shopping list far faster than he did if he took one of the boys, since Lexi knew where things were and the boys constantly asked for everything under the sun but never knew where to find what they wanted. He was always glad to get out of the store when any of them tagged along.

He wasn't so glad to see his daughter stare at some woman

unloading her groceries into her trunk. Okay, the woman was dressed oddly, at least for Storm Lake, but G.F. figured he'd taught Lexi better manners than that. "Stop staring."

"But Dad..."

"You know better."

"I like her outfit. That skirt is sick."

"Sick? It's *sick?*"

"You know, nice. I like it."

G.F. looked back at the woman's skirt – a long, flowing thing covered in a vine pattern all the way down to her bare ankles and brown barely-there sandals. "Yeah? Should we ask where she got it so we can look for one for you?"

"Dad, you *can't.*"

"Why can't I?"

"You don't *know* her."

"What does that matter?"

"You just *can't.* You'll embarrass me and..."

G.F. stopped hearing the rest of the rant when the woman turned and he saw her face. Couldn't be. When she caught him staring, he had to scold himself. He knew better, also. But it was...

"Did no one teach you that staring is obnoxious?" The woman called him on it.

It made him laugh. Out loud. Most would give him a dirty look or hurry into the car to get away from his stare. Only she would call him on it, from the other lane of the parking lot.

"Dad. *Stop.*" Lexi pulled at his arm and sent a quiet apology over.

"You haven't changed much at all, other than your style, I see." G.F. hushed his daughter, pulled his arm from her, and ambled across the driving path. "And you don't remember me."

"Should I?" Her expression said she didn't care one way or another.

"We only spent, oh, nine or ten years in the same class."

"Did we?" She raised her chin while she mainly didn't bother to look at him enough to try to remember. Haughty girl, then and now. But still as pretty as she was back then, a mature pretty, not cutesy like Justine used to be. Her eyes looked lighter than he remembered, making them more a hazel than a light brown. The lashes were still dark and long. The lips still softly rounded and natural pink with no added color that he could tell. The face was rounder, slightly rounder, less harsh-looking.

He had a hard time buying that she wouldn't remember him at all with as well as he remembered her. "G.F. McKenry. Ring a bell?"

She brushed a strand of hair behind her ear. "Are you sure you have the right person?"

"Frannie Barrett, or at least it used to be Barrett. Yeah, I'm pretty sure I do. You haven't changed too awful much."

"I suppose that's meant to be a compliment. G.F.?"

"George. But I don't go by that anymore. Guess I shouldn't be surprised you didn't recognize me. Wouldn't talk to me back in school. Why should you now? Thing is, my daughter was wondering where you got that skirt because she thinks it's *sick*, which is obviously a good thing – got me on why it is…"

"New lingo. You never know how they come up with it. Interesting though, isn't it?"

He tilted his head in a grudging acknowledgment. "Right. The language geek. How many do you speak now? Wasn't it four way back when?"

"It's still four. I've been busy. And you never talked to me, either. I was a language geek and all, you know." She looked past him, a curious, somewhat sad expression crossing her face. "Your daughter?"

"Yep." He turned enough to give Lexi a sign she could join them and wrapped an arm over her shoulder. "Lexi, this is Frannie Barrett, an old class mate. So you don't have to worry that I'll embarrass you asking a stranger where she got her clothes."

Fran threw him a glance, but focused on his daughter. "It's very nice to meet you, and I got the skirt in South Dakota. A private shop. I think it was hand made exclusively for that shop. Sorry I can't be more helpful. If you'll excuse me, I need to run." Without looking at him again, she turned and escaped into her car. Brand new Explorer. Green. Probably with all the bells and whistles. Figured.

"Does she really know four languages?"

G.F. rolled his eyes. "You heard us from over there?"

"Not much. Only that. And that you wouldn't talk to her in school. Why wouldn't you? You talk to everyone."

"That wasn't quite the whole story, and it's not your concern, but yes; she couldn't throw a ball straight even a short distance to save her life, but she was always correcting everyone's grammar. Used to irk the hell out of us."

"You correct mine."

"I'm your father, not your classmate."

"So?"

"What do you mean, so?"

"If she knows it better, what's wrong with being helpful? Isn't it good to be helpful? You do. You help anyone who needs help with stuff you're good at. What's the difference?"

"Because it's ... it just is."

"So I shouldn't help Frankie with his math?"

"Not the same thing, Lex. Let's go before the groceries get warm."

Of course it wasn't different. But how did he explain to his eleven-year-old daughter that when others in the class made fun of the grammar geek, he'd done nothing to counter them, although he knew he should? Peer pressure at its worst. It still bothered him that he hadn't. Why should she want to talk to him? But she was wrong; he had tried. He tried several times. She'd shut him out. It was too much an insult to his pride to admit it to his daughter.

Some things you didn't grow out of, even if you should.

As he pulled into his drive in front of the big old forest green and brown split-level house that looked like every other house on the street, except a little more messy in front, G.F. tried to make himself tell Lexi she was right. It wasn't different. He'd been an ass to Francis Barrett just because she'd hurt his pride. No wonder she didn't want to speak to him.

"What does she do?"

"Huh?" He looked over at his daughter who usually jumped right out of the car nearly before it was stopped. She was sitting still, looking at him. A rare thing.

"Frannie. What does she do?"

"No idea. Haven't seen her since graduation or just after. And she doesn't like to be called Frannie. You call her Ms. Barrett as I've taught you."

"Is that her real name? I mean before she got married, or her after-married name?"

"It was her name when I knew her. Not sure what it is now. But that'll do unless she says differently."

"You mean you plan to see her again?"

G.F. released an inaudible sigh at the girl's teasing look. "Small town, Lexi. If she stays around, I imagine it'll be hard not to."

Five

"Found out who's in the old Barrett place."

G.F. wiped dirty sweat from his forehead as he surveyed the newest road patch.

"Don't even want to know?" Jim rested his arms atop his shovel and grinned. "Bet you do. Frannie's back in town. Wife seen her the other day and said she's snooty as ever."

"You saw her. You didn't *seen* her." One of Fran's biggest pet peeves. He remembered well how often she'd corrected someone. Never use *seen* unless it's with *have* or *had*.

Jim laughed. "Good imitation. Remember her well, huh?"

"This one's good. Let's move on." He walked away from his coworker and grabbed a good swallow of lukewarm water. *Snooty.* He'd always hated when people called her that, and again, he said nothing. Maybe she was, but then, maybe she had reason. And maybe she wasn't and they just didn't get her or who she was. Maybe she didn't want them to know who she was. Most had called her father crazy, also, but he wasn't. G.F. knew better. He had spoken up for the man at times but people didn't listen, so he stopped bothering.

Why wouldn't she have moved away?

But with that guy? G.F. still thought that was a bad move, but maybe she'd been happy with him. He hoped she had been. Maybe she still was. He hadn't thought to check her hand for a ring.

What in the hell was wrong with him? Why did he even care? She'd hardly glanced at him when he tried to talk to her back in high school, and she'd done the same in the parking lot. What difference did it make to him if she was happy or not?

Somehow it made a difference. And maybe he'd make an attempt to run into her again. Without Lexi, this time.

Anyway, if she was living in her old house and driving a new Explorer, she was doing well. He was glad to know she was. He'd heard the place had been rented out even before her father died, but he could be wrong. Or she'd kicked them out.

Who knew? Fact was, if she could afford to live in it and pay the real estate tax and all, she was doing well enough.

The Buick in front of her house... It wasn't hers. Her husband's, maybe? Somehow, he had trouble seeing that sleeked-back, wily kid growing up and owning a silver Buick. She could have dumped him for someone else, though. He had no trouble seeing her hooked up with a man who drove a new silver Buick.

The thought annoyed him, for no good reason, and he used the action of shoving the tamper against the asphalt to smooth it down as a frustration release.

Fran stood at the door leading from the little shack into the greenhouse. She had to go in. She couldn't sell the place unless she at least went in to see if there was something she needed to save of her father's. It wasn't too likely, she supposed. His whole world was plants, and plants didn't live if they were neglected inside a building. Anything he'd wanted to save would be out in the gardens. If he'd still been with it enough before they shipped him off to the retirement home. That was a big *if*.

"Get over it, Francis. It's just a building." Biting her bottom lip, a horrid habit she'd picked up and needed to stop, she took a deep breath, opened the flimsy homemade wood plank door that joined the shack with the greenhouse, and was nearly knocked over by the scent of plant decay and dusty, old air. Had no one been inside since they took him away nearly two years ago?

She had to pull her T-shirt up over her nose and mouth to be able to breathe in the heavily scented stale air. As she expected, the greenhouse was a rotted mess. Old containers of every type and size were scattered around the cracked wood makeshift tables with peeling paint – mainly dumped wood her father had found along roadsides from peoples' construction projects, to include old doors and pallets – a menagerie of old unwanted junk topped by dirt, and dried plant remnants drooping and dried over the sides of well-used containers.

With a shake of the head, Fran went straight to the side door to shove it open. It resisted stubbornly. Wood and weather and neglect.

An apt metaphor for her father. Such a shame. The man had such potential. Near genius, her mother said. She'd said it was his downfall: he knew too much and worried far too much about it.

Just as Calvin had said about her.

Using her shoulder and hip, she shoved into the door and cursed at the pain, but the thing opened.

First, she gasped at the fresh air and let her shirt drop to breathe it in. Then, she gasped at a sight she'd never seen.

The neglect showed: weeds were overtaking the circular raised-bed garden surrounded by a circular path of flat stone with moss now nearly smothering the stone. It needed to be swept back some. The stone was a beautiful color. She'd never seen it. Last she knew, it was a dirt circle with a few dirt pathways her father used to get to the herbs he'd been trying to get going. Evidence of the herbs were there from last summer. Most wouldn't survive an Iowa winter outdoors, but it looked like parsley was trying to come back, and a bit of thyme. By the looks of the dried greenery, he'd had quite a lush garden, enough to cook with all summer and to dry and store for winter meals.

Flat moss-covered stone also filled in the center of the circular area, inside the raised garden, and a stone bench sat exactly in the middle. She guessed it used to be a stone table since it was round. It looked well supported by mismatched bricks, and sturdy enough to sit on safely. Fran brushed aside an old cobweb and lowered onto the bench, supporting her own weight while testing its strength and balance. Luckily, the thing held. Had he used it as a bench? Or maybe it was a cutting table? A drying table for his herbs? It was low, though, so he would have had to lean over to use it. Or sit on the ground.

Someone would have had to help him get it there. Likely several someones, with as heavy as it would be. Or a piece of machinery. It had to have had a particular purpose to go to that much effort. Maybe whoever helped him do it could tell her.

Hollyhocks bordered the outside edge of the raised stone wall and bees happily buzzed around them. Fran never minded bees. They were a gardener's best friends, her father said. Treat them well and they'll return the favor. And ladybugs. Her mother had thrown a hissy when he'd bought bugs, but not just any bugs, garden helpers, her father said. They kept the aphids away. And Fran had loved them. She hoped they were still around, as well.

So much going for him. And when her mother died from a heart attack, he declined fast, so she heard. Faster, anyway. He was already declining the last time Fran visited only as a visit, before the last time she'd been home, out of necessity. Why would her mother's death have such an effect on him when they were already living apart? Except for his mind, he'd been fairly healthy. It didn't make sense. Even before, they'd hardly spoken to each other in a lot of years.

"Oh, Dad. What happened? And how do I keep it from happening to me?" She allowed herself a rare sulk in the form of bending her elbows to her knees and burying her head in her hands. She didn't sulk. Almost never. No point in it, as her mother always said. It helped nothing.

Fran wasn't sure it didn't. It felt good to sulk outside in the once-thriving circle garden her father had obviously loved.

And she had reason. She deserved a good sulk.

Six

Unable to go back into the greenhouse, Fran focused her attention on the little shack. Why had she let her aunt rent out the main house? She could be staying there and taking showers and living comfortably instead of curling into a ball on her father's old bumpy mattress trying to avoid the bumps and waking up sore and grouchy. She'd thought about a hotel but she hated hotels. She'd rather live in the little shack.

Since it would take longer than she'd expected to fix it decently, she wanted it comfortable. So, first thing after three cups of strong black coffee and half a whole grain bagel with local honey, she slipped into her cleanest jeans – a small stacked washer and dryer set was a must, as well – and a loose T-shirt she generally only wore around the house, and headed out to find a mattress store. First things first: she had to start sleeping better.

Amazed at how the prices of the things had jumped since the last time she'd had to buy one, Fran overlooked the saleswoman's attempt at the whole shebang, fancy headboard and high box springs, and ordered only a pillow top mattress. A double, since she moved a lot in her sleep, though it would make close quarters in the small space. She couldn't get around the $50 delivery fee since she wasn't sure it would fit in her Explorer, and even if it did, she couldn't very well carry the thing herself.

"I can pick it up for you."

She started at the voice behind her and turned to find George, this time with a young boy.

"Won't even charge you."

"Why would you do that? And..?" She couldn't quite ask why he was there. Storm Lake was small but not that small.

"Quite a coincidence running into you again so soon, and in here." He gave her a half grin, a cocky grin. "Another store, I mean."

She was quite sure that wasn't what he'd meant. "Yes. Very

coincidental."

"The boy outgrew his bed like he's outgrowing everything else. Crazy how fast they grow. Never thought much about it when I was his age."

"Your son?" A stupid question, since the boy looked like him, although far less sturdy than George's football star build that had filled out even better now. The boy's hair was darker and rather messy looking, which she supposed was a purposeful style. His face was more pinched than George's nice square face. Fran could easily see where that came from.

"Yep. This is Frankie, my youngest boy. He's just thirteen recently. Lexi, you met her the other day, is the baby of the group at eleven."

Group? "How many do you have?" Since his son was with him, she kept herself from asking if they were all from the same mother.

"Four. Other two are fifteen and sixteen, and they're strong boys. They can help me move that to wherever you need it."

"I couldn't impose, but thank you." Fran said hello to Frankie and turned back to the saleswoman. Four kids. The man had four kids and still looked like he was fit enough to be a football star.

"It's no problem, Fran. We'll be coming for his, anyway. Staying at your old place? It's just down the road from us."

"No. Yes." She was flustered enough without having to deal with that amused grin. "I am, but not the main house."

He looked confused. "Camping outside? That mattress'll get wet."

And he still thought he was too funny for his own good. "Thanks for the offer, but I'm fine. Nice to have met you, Frankie."

"Frank. I hate being called Frankie."

"Don't be rude."

Fran cut his father off. "It's not rude at all. Thank you for telling me. I hated to be called Frannie, but people still did it. I'll remember not to do the same." She spoke to the boy, purposely turned from his father.

"That's a cool band. You listen to them?"

Band? The Maroon 5 T-shirt. She'd forgotten to change. "I saw them years ago when they were still mostly unknown. I haven't kept up, though."

"Cool. I could let you borrow my CDs. I have them all."

With a grin instead of an answer, she excused herself, finished with the clerk, and told them to have a nice day. She had too many errands to stand there chatting with someone who hadn't bothered back when she'd cared more than she did now.

Let the woman be angry. G.F. brushed off his son's objection as he told the clerk to subtract the delivery fee from Fran's order and he'd pick it up. The clerk knew him well. They'd dated. Briefly. And parted friendly. So she gave in to him as he knew she would.

Outside the store, Frankie stopped him. "What's up with that woman? Another old love?"

"Your mom talks too much. And no, just went to school together."

"Gotta be cool to like Maroon 5 at her age."

"Her age? Not like we're ancient, you know."

Frankie shrugged. "To me, you kinda are."

"Wait till you get there, boy."

"Is she the one Mom says I was named after?"

G.F. stopped in his tracks from the other side of the truck. "Your mom said what, exactly?"

"That I was named after an old love. It's why she hates my name so much and won't use it. Thanks for that."

"Your mom is..." He stopped himself and shook his head. "A bit misguided at times. You were named after my great uncle, as I told you. And she was not an old love, as I also told you. Clean the wax out of your ears and let's get going."

While they headed to pick up Lexi from Eve's, G.F. couldn't quite push away the thought that he'd darned near lied to both kids in a few days' time, both times about the same woman. He did have an uncle Frank. That was true. He wasn't terribly close to him, though. He told himself he liked the name. Truth was ... it wasn't the name itself, or even the uncle, no matter how much he'd insisted, when it was his turn again to pick the first name of the newborn, that he was honoring his uncle. Even if she didn't believe him, there was no need to tell their son quite that much. She told them far, far more than they needed to know. The woman didn't ever shut up.

He'd liked that at first. He always knew where he stood with her. No guessing. She said what she thought with no qualms. At seventeen, that was refreshing in a girl. As they got older, it wasn't so much. Not that he was ashamed of how much he'd dated, but he would've preferred his kids be older before knowing he had a fair reputation as a ladies' man. Even if he wasn't so much as she made it sound. Yeah, he dated a lot. Just didn't settle well. No harm in that when you were young.

Until you let it go too far and got caught, anyway.

"Alright, enough. You two get dishes tonight since you want to be so full of yourselves." G.F. saw the sighs from Lexi and Frankie, but during dinner, the boy had told his siblings about seeing Fran and repeated what his mother told him and Lexi wouldn't stop the third degree, including about what she'd been wearing which led to music and how "cool" and "sick" Fran was and how he'd been an idiot not to ask her out back in school, never minding how they wouldn't be there if he'd hooked up with Fran instead of with their mother.

Not too late, Theo said, since he was free now, if she was, and he should ask.

The woman didn't want to talk to him. That much was clear. Why embarrass himself by asking her if she was free to ask out? Not likely.

Still, he looked forward to going out to her place and seeing what she meant by staying there but not at the main house. Maybe it meant the garden shack was still standing, but she surely wouldn't be living in that. Was she that short on funds? Her father had done well, despite what people thought of him, with his own garden and lawn care business he went into after leaving Des Moines and a high pressure design job of some kind to move his wife and daughter into a smaller area. Wouldn't he have left it to his only child? Could be the old man had truly lost his mind enough he put it elsewhere, or it was eaten in medical bills. Sad, but possible. Maybe he'd see what else she might need when he stopped by with the mattress.

She had to sit for only a few minutes. Nearly midnight. Too much shopping, which she hated. Too much cleaning, which she was fine with but not in shape for well enough. But, she had the loft cleaned out to make space for the mattress, and the rest of it uncluttered enough she wouldn't be mortified to have the delivery men see it. She'd told them to bring at least two men for delivery. She hadn't thought to tell them to not be afraid of heights. They could very well refuse to take it up there, she supposed, or charge her more. If they wouldn't do it, maybe George and his boys would.

She couldn't ask them, though. She could find a couple of other young men looking for quick money. Maybe she'd hire them to take a bulk load of garbage to the recycling center, as well. The newspaper stacks, she kept. They were in a corner of the greenhouse to use as mulch. Everything else had to go. Why her father kept paper bags full of tin cans, she couldn't guess. A few to use as seedling support, fine, but more than ten bags of them? And in the shack in pathways instead of in the greenhouse? He'd cleaned them carefully, taken off the labels, cut off both top and bottom. Apparently he'd meant to use them. But ten bags full? The man had been either extremely hopeful as to how long he thought he'd live or he'd lost it sooner than she realized.

He could have, she supposed. Not Alzheimer's, they said. Just dementia. *Just.* A ridiculous word.

And it scared her.

How often had Cal laughed when she went to the kitchen and forgot why she went to the kitchen? Or to the store and forgot half of what she wanted. Making a list wasn't helpful when you forgot to take it to the store. She placated herself by saying she'd always been that way; she was *just* busy and thinking of other things. Still, since they'd had to take her sixty-seven-year-old father to a nursing home because he kept wandering around town not knowing how to get home or remembering that he'd driven there, and then started to forget his name, she nearly panicked every time she forgot anything.

Keep active. Read plenty. Socialize. Dance. Her research told her how to help prevent it, if that was actually possible. On good days, she made herself believe it was and followed the research suggestions, at least the first two. On not so good days, she buried herself in her oil paints and sketched out vivid, disturbing, worried paintings on completely innocent canvases. Then, when dry, she pulled them off the frames and hid them in her large black leather portfolio. One of the few things she'd saved to bring with her to Iowa. Her furniture was all sold off. She wanted none of it, nothing that reminded her of Calvin in any way. Some of it, she lost a bunch of money on, but she didn't even care, even if she did get her mother's thrifty side. She didn't want it. She wanted as clean a start as it was possible to get.

That did not include George McKenry, whatever he went by these days. Or his whole group of children.

Seven

Fran jumped at the loud knock rattling the dilapidated screen door and grabbed the rusted putter her father had kept under his bed. Shoving her free hand through her messy bed hair, she debated whether to check or to ignore it and hope they went away. The clock glared 8:17. She'd been awake to see 2 a.m. and again later to see 3:30 and it was an ungodly time to be startled out of bed, considering. When she was twenty, she'd hardly needed sleep. But, as he'd said, she wasn't twenty anymore.

Another knock made her curse, and with a glance to be sure she was decently covered, Fran shuffled over and cracked the main door that was nearly as dilapidated as the screen door.

"Good morning. Delivery boys are here." George grinned while moist, cool air streamed in around him and brought his scent with it. A soft scent that reminded her of her visit to Massachusetts. "The other two are in the truck. Looks like you need this mattress, too."

Fran wanted to slug him right across the jaw. She thought about putting the putter down and then changed her mind to move it where he could see it. "Why are you here?"

"Brought your mattress. Saved you the fifty bucks. Gonna rain soon so didn't want to wait till later. Have a leak in the bed."

She felt her eyebrows raise. "Maybe you should fix that before *you* need a new mattress."

"Yeah, when I get to it." Suddenly, he got her meaning. "The bed of the truck, that is. Nothing wrong with my own equipment, if that's what you were hinting."

"I'm sure that's nice for your wife. And I turned down your offer, so, again, why are you here?"

"Used to be nice for the wife. Now someone else's equipment functions for her. We divorced a few years ago."

Divorced. George was divorced. "Should I say I'm sorry?"

He snickered. "Why? I'm not. Kids are doing okay with it. I'm sure a hell of a lot happier without her, though I still have to see her at times."

"Guess you should have stayed single forever like you always said you would."

With a grin flickering the sides of his mouth, George leaned against her door frame. "So much for not remembering me."

"I never said I didn't remember. You can leave it on the porch."

"What?"

"The mattress. Since you brought it. Unless you'd rather take it back to the store since I paid for delivery."

"On the porch? Gonna rain soon. And this isn't..." He cast a quick look around the slanted decaying overhang that somewhat shielded the arched and swollen wood planks that made up the shack's front porch. "No offense, but it won't stay dry here."

"I'll get it."

One finger scratched the skin alongside his eye. "You know it's gotta weigh about fifty pounds, not to mention the bulk of it. Or, sorry, maybe you have company in there to help you out?"

"Don't worry about it. I'll manage." Not that she had a clue how she would and of course she couldn't get it up to the loft.

"Your damned pride was always getting you in trouble, you know." With his voice lowered, he eyed her and stepped closer, as close as the mostly closed door allowed. "If you're worried about me being alone with you in your place, I have my kids here to help, so no need to worry, not that I'm that type, anyway."

Setting the putter aside, she folded her arms in front of her chest. "I didn't say I was worried, and I didn't ask for your opinion about my pride."

"Yeah well, what else would keep you from letting us bring this thing inside for you since we're here?"

Embarrassment, Fran wanted to say. The place was still a mess. She supposed that was pride and it was silly not to let them bring it in. Why did she care what he thought, anyway? "Fine. But whatever it was that made you pick it up after I refused your offer is something you might want to work on before you worry about my pride." With some hesitation, she opened the door.

"Guess that's fair." He headed back to his truck, an old truck in faded black, but large, a dual cab. "Come on guys, let's bring it in."

She found it impossible not to admire the bulge of George's arms and muscles of his back as he carried one end of the thick mattress and let two boys, Frank and another, carry the other end.

He introduced his fifteen-year-old, Justin, a sturdy boy with shoulders nearly like his father. They would be in time, she expected. Other than that, he didn't look much like George. He looked like Justine Haden. Fran tried hard not to hold it against the kid.

"Where do you want it?" There wasn't even struggle in George's voice, which again made her want to slug him.

"Up there." She pointed at the loft and shrugged at his raised eyebrows. "That's why I was willing to pay for delivery. You can prop it against the wall if you want."

"Yeah? How do you plan to get it up there?"

"I'll hire someone, of course."

He gave her a sly grin. "Good luck with that." He told the boys to set it down a minute and turned back to her. "I tell you what: Lexi's doing her best to grow herbs indoors and getting frustrated with the lack of results. How about we get this thing up there for you in exchange for you helping her learn how to do what she needs?"

"What makes you think I know?"

"Figured you picked up a few tips from your father." He propped an elbow on the edge of her mattress.

"Quite an assumption. Did you? Yours was a carpenter, wasn't he? Did you pick up his skills?"

"Sure did. Want help with that, too?"

"I wasn't..."

"I'm not certified, but I know what I'm doing."

"Hey Dad, would you flirt later? I have practice to get to."

Fran found herself surprised by Justin's impertinence, but she supposed she shouldn't be. Most kids were these days.

"Mind the manners I taught you. Offering help isn't flirting. Come on, let's get this up that ladder. I'll go up first. You two support it and push from below."

The boys grumbled and Fran tried to object, but George hushed his kids and said it was no trouble; if they could climb pine trees to the top against his orders, they could do this well enough.

She stood at the bottom of her ladder steps to do what she could to break a fall if needed until George told her to move away because she'd get more hurt than they would if they were silly enough to lose their grip. With luck and muscle and some pretty good teamwork, she had to admit, they got the thing up there with no incident. She couldn't help watching him make his way back down the ladder.

"Thank you." She spoke to the boys, not to George. "Can I pay you for your trouble?"

"No, ma'am. Thank you, anyway." Justin glanced at his father.

"Are you sure? That was a heck of a job."

"Nah, it's fine. Good workout before practice." He tapped his younger brother on the arm. "Come on. We'll be in the truck."

George shook his head as they left. "Left me alone to *flirt*, I suppose. Never mind them. Their mother's influence. I do what I can to counter it. And it was only an offer for an old classmate."

"Offer?"

"Construction on the front porch. Looks like you could use help, unless you have someone already."

"I can do what I need done." She bristled at his raised eyebrows. "I've done a lot by myself. I manage fine."

"Have you? Rumor was you ran off and got married. And I know I'm being rude now, but guess I have to wonder why you had to do so much by yourself if the story is true."

"Only half true. I never married." Fran caught herself looking away from him as though she was embarrassed to admit it, as though she had any reason to be embarrassed.

"Guess I can tell Lexi to call you Ms. Barrett, then. Wasn't sure."

"She can call me Fran, if I run into her again before I leave."

"Leave." He nodded and his chest rose and fell hard. "I see. Just came to sell."

"Or rent. I haven't decided."

"The main house or just this?"

"Both together. The house is rented temporarily, but they're only waiting for their own house to be built. The timing works well, since I intend to have this place cleaned up by the end of summer when they plan to move out."

"Shame to sell that house. It's a beautiful place. If I had the money, I'd buy it." He glanced around the shack. "If you change your mind about needing help with this, let me know." Pulling a card out of his pocket, he handed it to her. A handmade, or rather home computer made, card read *McKenry Contracting* with a phone number.

"Just my general labor card, a side job for the boys and me, and sometimes Lexi, depending what it is. They get whatever they can do and I get the rest. "

"A family business. That's nice."

"Well, more a way to get them to feel better about themselves like kids do when they earn their keep. Too many don't anymore. Hate to see it. They only accept the jobs they want and have time to do around school and their activities. I'm not slave driving them."

"I didn't assume you were. They look like good kids. And they respect you. It shows."

"Does it?" George scratched his head. "Gotta wonder at times. And I better run. J has practice." He let himself halfway out the door. "Nice to see you again, Frannie, since I haven't said so. I was sorry to hear about your parents."

"Thank you." She wished he hadn't said it. As far as she knew, he was the first to bother. It was easier to take when they didn't. "For the delivery, as well. I'd be glad to help Lexi with her herbs if she'd like to come over."

He smiled, a genuine smile. "Great. Have a number we can call?"

Flustered about saying yes, about admitting she'd learned gardening from her father after making a fuss about it, and even more flustered by that smile, Fran sifted through the stacks of junk on the makeshift desk for something to write on and with, jotted her cell number, and handed it to him. She knew darn well the touch of her fingers wasn't accidental.

When he nodded and went out the door, she stepped out behind him. "It was nice to see you, too, George. Never thought it would be, to be honest."

"I understand that one. And it's G.F. I hate to be called George."

"I know. You always did. Call me Fran instead of Frannie and I'll do the same for you."

That smile again with a tip of the head. "Call if you need anything, Fran. Have a nice weekend."

G.F. tried to pay attention to Justin's soccer practice since the boy wanted pointers on how he could improve, but he kept seeing Fran disheveled, just out of bed, and not quite as all together as she always had been. He was sure she'd been braless under the big tee and he knew he shouldn't focus on that detail, but it was damned hard not to. The woman was built well. Not skinny. He didn't like skinny. He liked substance. He liked roundness, enough, not too overmuch. She'd been skinnier in high school. It made her look too sharp. He liked her looks far better now. She looked all around more real.

And he sure as hell liked her attitude better. It was less sharp, too. Maybe all of that doing so much herself had done a good job of rounding those edges. The edge was there, but it was less scary than before.

Or he was only old enough now not to be scared off so easily.

He'd wanted to object to her staying in that old garden shed, with as much work as it needed, and with that pathetic excuse for a lock. The golf putter could be an effective weapon under the right circumstances, he supposed, but he didn't like the idea of that being her only defense. And she wasn't the type to want to live in a dusty old shack cluttered with everything under the sun.

Her father's things. He knew them for what they were and had to feel for the girl having to sort through that stuff. Maybe the boys could at least help with that. What could he ask in return? He didn't want her paying them because it was too much like asking her for work for his boys and it felt wrong. Or desperate. He was far from desperate, and he wouldn't have her think otherwise. Truth was, he could swing the house payments on her parents' place if he wanted, but he didn't particularly want that much of a mortgage. Still, she was far too prideful to accept help for nothing. He did have to appreciate that.

She hadn't married that guy. In a way, he was glad she hadn't...

"Dad." Frankie tugged on his arm. "Can we go mini golf when J's done? You said maybe next weekend last weekend and now it's next weekend."

"Maybe doesn't mean yes." G.F. flinched when his second oldest was knocked to the ground, hard, and breathed again when the boy jumped right back up. He'd done it himself often enough during his football games and practices, and it hadn't bothered him an ounce. Different when it was your kid, though.

"But can we?"

Mini golf. With the kids. It would different if... "Maybe. I'll be right back. Keep an eye on his technique for me."

"I don't know soccer. Why isn't Theo here?"

"Theo earned the weekend off by watching over all of you maniacs during the week. I'll only be a couple of minutes." He jumped down off the bleachers and pulled his phone from his jeans pocket, her number from his shirt pocket, and before he could change his mind, he dialed her.

She took forever to answer and then sounded rushed.

"Did I interrupt?" He paced in between somewhat watching practice and keeping an eye on Frankie.

"Who is this?"

"Don't have caller ID? Should have come up."

"Didn't look. George?"

"G.F."

"Right. What do you want?"

He bristled. She still had plenty of sharpness, apparently. "Guess I called at a bad time."

"I'm working."

"My apologies. I'll let you go." He hung up before he came to his senses enough to realize he shouldn't have. "Hell." He called right back. This time she didn't answer and he couldn't blame her. But he left a message: "Look, I'm sorry. I just ... uh, well, the kids want to go play mini-golf in, oh, about an hour and a half or so and Lexi hates to be the only girl there, so I wondered if you wanted to tag along and then you could talk to her about the herb thing. Ignore this message if you'd rather, as though I have to tell you you should. Anyway... let me know, if you want, or drop by. We'll be at Pirate's Pointe." Hell. Stupid message. He hung up, sighed, and went back to the bleachers to tell Frankie yes about mini-golf. Whether or not she called back.

Eight

Insufferable man. He didn't used to be, not that she'd been able to tell. To hang up on her just because she was busy and he interrupted?

Stepping back up on the ladder, Fran clenched her jaw as she balanced the knick-knack shelf she'd bought at a craft store and painted soft teal, marked where the hangers would need to go to make sure it butted right up against the side of the small window, then moved to the other side to do the same. It would have been far easier to hang the things with help, but as she told G.F., she was used to not having help. She managed just fine.

Moving off the ladder and away from the window, Fran surveyed her work. It looked better than she'd hoped, and once the valances were done and hanging over the whole thing, it would look even better. The wall was now a cream color. Adding teal accents beside the far-too-small window made it look bigger. She would add her bird figurines to the shelves for the illusion of a window and do a venetian blind in matching teal fabric that could be pulled down over the actual window for privacy.

So far, only one wall was painted. She wanted to see how the window illusion would work and couldn't make herself wait until the whole place was painted first. It gave her the impetus to keep going to have that small part of the shack look so nice.

The big sectional couch her father claimed for his shed when his mother insisted it leave her house would have to be replaced. It was light blue microfiber with several rips or cuts from her father's carelessness, and stained because he often sat on it after leaving the greenhouse, before cleaning up. Fran agreed with her mother on that; the man had been far too much of a slob. The shack was the one place he wasn't nagged, and so he did as he wished.

Maybe she'd cover it instead, with darker teal fabric in some kind of texture to make it look smaller compared to the light walls. The place already looked bigger with one dark-paneled wall painted cream. The couch could work if cleaned and covered. And with pillows to match the curtains.

She sighed as her phone beeped to remind her she had a message. George, she assumed, asking her again to come play mini-golf. She used to love mini-golf. Wondering how long had it been since her last game, she decided to at least see if it was him or something important.

Ignore this message if you'd rather, as though I have to tell you you should. Anyway... let me know, if you want.

Fran chuckled. Maybe not insufferable. Maybe just ... unsure. Was he? She'd never seen him that way, but he did tend to look as though he was falling all over himself trying to... To what? Why was he bothering?

Old thoughts of him flickered through her tired brain as she poured more coffee and let herself sit for a couple of minutes. Football star. With thick wavy light brown hair brightened by hints of red that he'd kept longer than most of the team. Thick shoulders. Strong hard calves and thighs. And an honor student, though he didn't look it or act like it. Flocked by girls who ignored that he was an honor student and instead focused on his build, his sports ability, his friendliness. Including that ditzy little Justine who wore her shirts too tight and talked like a low class uneducated girl from the city 'hood instead of the small town girl she was, despite how educated and successful her parents were. Fran rolled her eyes at how kids too often tried to be what they weren't, trying to look too "cool" for their hometowns. She wondered how many of them grew up to realize how silly they'd looked.

She'd been one of them. An embarrassing admission, but at least she recognized it in herself by now.

That was something she'd always liked about George. He was comfortable where he was and with what he was doing. He never insulted Storm Lake, never talked about being somewhere "better" or of doing something "important" or other such nonsense. By now, she knew it was nonsense. Back then... What a silly, impertinent thing she used to be, and he had to have known she was.

Let me know, if you want.

She laughed. Such a change from Cal who never asked, always insisted. Heaven forbid she insist anything, but he insisted everything. What a horribly silly, impertinent thing to leave her parents and friends for that.

A deep sigh mixed with a shudder, and Fran got up to throw herself together. She had to run get fabric for the couch. She had to finish the cottage and get it rented so she could go find a new start. She'd burned too many bridges in Storm Lake. Some bridges just couldn't be rebuilt. And she had no energy left to try.

Her truck.

G.F. did a fast U-turn, probably illegally, and went back to the shopping center he'd just seen her pull into. Could be someone else, he supposed. Explorers weren't rare, but there weren't too many nearly brand new dark green Explorers in the area, that he'd noticed.

"Wow, Dad. Something on fire?" Justin's hand was shoved against the dashboard. Exaggerating, of course.

"It's Ms. Barrett. *Look*." Lexi pointed at the woman in a long flowing skirt that nearly dragged on the pavement with a loose top that covered her backside. Gray. Up and down. Darker on the bottom than on top, but all gray. Still, she looked awfully colorful to him, with her pale brown hair kind of the color of sand when it's been wet and is mostly dry again pulled partly back into a clip. The rest fell over her neck and just reached the low rounded neckline of her shirt.

Justin laughed. "That's why the sudden Dale Earnhardt move? Got the hots for her, huh?"

"Mind your manners." G.F. slowly pulled alongside Fran and she startled, then stopped.

"*Hi*, Ms. Barrett." Lexi had rolled the window down. "Dad saw your car and nearly wrecked us turning around."

"Lexi. Don't exaggerate." Doing his best not to look as flustered as he was, he tried to come up with an excuse as to why he'd pulled over in a sudden *Dale Earnhardt move* just to talk to her. "Just a sec. Let me park."

Not at all sure she'd stay put, G.F. backed up into an empty space, left the truck running, and told the kids to stay right where they were. He was glad to find Fran had stayed put, but she gave him a *what the hell* look, which he couldn't fault.

"So I uh … just wanted to apologize. For hanging up on you earlier. Kids were distracting me. Most I know are used to that by now and don't think anything of it, but I thought you might. As you should." He tucked a thumb into his front jeans pocket and pulled it out again. Last thing he wanted was to look like a shy teenage boy hitting on a girl above his league.

"It was my fault, I think." She glanced behind him. "I didn't mean to be abrupt. I get very focused when I'm working."

"A good thing. Too many haven't figured out how to focus on work while they're working. Sorry I bothered you. And I'll go now. Just wanted…"

"Hello, Lexi." Fran looked past him. "Nice to see you again."

"Hi, Ms. Barrett. Are you going shopping?"

"Thought I told you to stay in the truck."

Lexi shrugged at him. "I wanted to say hello. It's the polite thing to do, right?"

"Not when you're disobeying orders. Go on."

"But I…"

"Go." He watched her sulk as she said goodbye to Fran and shuffled away. "Sorry about that. She likes to shop. Not with me or my mother since we *don't understand girls her age*. Her mother won't hardly do it, although, since she still acts like a girl Lexi's age… Sorry. Shouldn't talk about her that way."

Fran propped her thumb over the long strap of her small handbag. "I heard you'd married Justine Haden."

"Yeah. A couple of years after high school." He noticed her try to hide her thoughts. "You remember *her* fine, I see."

"It would be hard not to."

"Right. You were kind of enemies, if I remember."

"I wouldn't call it that. We just didn't see things much the same. But then, I was used to not seeing things the same as others. Anyway, you're on your way somewhere, so don't let me hold you."

"That's something I always liked about you, you know." His voice came out softer than he'd planned, and he'd never planned to say so much, but it damned sure caught her attention. "That you didn't see things like everyone else. Thought it was kind of cool. Anyway, we're going to mini-golf, as I said. I'll probably be on my own since the kids went behind my back to arrange to meet friends there. Guess I'll sit and sulk about them being old enough I'm now uncool to hang out with, and indulge in too much iced coffee until they're done."

Fran glanced over at his truck. "I thought parents just dropped their kids off these days and went back to pick them up."

"Yeah, I will with the two oldest at times, although Theo's driving now, so it's more gritting my teeth and letting him head out on his own, often with J tagging along, but I don't tend to do it with the two youngest, particularly with Lexi. She talks to anyone and everyone with no discretion." He knew he was talking too much, but he couldn't make himself stop. Nerves. Which annoyed him.

"Like her mother." Fran didn't look one ounce nervous, which also annoyed him.

"Yeah. That's much of what scares me."

"You married her."

"Kinda had to. Which is why it scares me. Hypocritical, I know, but I'm older and wiser now. Don't really want Lexi to follow her mother's path, or mine. Anyway, if you get bored, we'll be at Pirate's Pointe and I'll be at the entrance pouting in my coffee."

She grinned. "If I didn't have so many errands..."

"Yeah?" He stepped closer. "How about you let them wait and come sit with me a while? In return, I'll help you with them, as much as I can."

"I'm not much of a sitter. Drives me crazy to just sit."

"Then come play a round or two with me. As a warning, I cheat when I get frustrated about not being able to get it in the hole."

"Is that so?" She somewhat held back a grin. "Anything to do with your marriage breaking up?"

He felt his jaw drop and forced it closed, which likely made him look like a bumbling baboon. But he'd had no idea she would turn something so innocent into something so sexual, much less say it aloud, especially to him. "I only meant the game." Stepping just a touch closer, he tilted his head down beside hers. "I never cheated on

Justine. Before or during marriage, not even while waiting for the divorce to be legal. And inability was never an issue." He stepped back again. "In case you wanted to know."

The glimmer in her eyes said she appreciated him playing along. "Well. Like I said, if I didn't have errands. Another time, maybe."

Rubbing his chin, trying hard not to look flustered, between her subtle flirting and the way she smelled of something fresh and somewhat spicy, he figured he better just take what he could get. "You're on. Have a good rest of the day, Fran."

Nine

Fran wasn't sure why she'd veered her car toward Pirate's Pointe after she grabbed the fabric she needed. She also needed to get home and get busy, but something about G.F. sitting alone at the mini-golf course while his children abandoned him made her feel just sorry enough for him to see if he was actually doing so.

The man was trying to connect with his kids, to spend time with them. For her, that gave him high marks in the parenting department. Not that she knew much about parenting. Except her father had constantly tried to spend time with her in the only way he knew how, and she'd never appreciated it enough. It was an acknowledgment to him, she figured. Her father had always liked George. At football games, Virgil Barrett cheered heavily for the defensive end guard and often talked about him on the way home. Fran had listened politely and shrugged when asked her thoughts.

She caught a few stares, at her clothing, she supposed, from women in unattractively tight jeans in a size too small which they expected made them look smaller, she figured, or in skinny jeans over toothpick legs. Fran told herself to stop being petty. Her figure was no better than either, but she did cover it up decently instead of broadcasting it.

Walking shoulders straight to the side of the little building where a few metal benches sat along the mini golf course, Fran found him easily. But not alone. A redhead in tight jeans and skinny tank top sat close, talking to him. So much for hanging out alone. She told herself not to make assumptions. Girls had always thrown themselves at him. It was no surprise they still did, with as good as he still looked, when most men his age had let themselves go and had beer bellies spilling out over top their jeans. It could be he had actually planned to be alone.

He looked either bored or annoyed, so Fran kept walking toward him. When he saw her, he jumped up, knocking a drink on the bench beside him all over his jeans, and on the girl, too. The skinny redhead jumped backward and yelled at him for being so careless.

Fran veered toward the little building, asked for a handful of napkins, and made her way over. "Need these?"

He gave her an embarrassed grin. "Yes, sadly. One of my klutzy days. Thank you."

"No problem. I have them a lot. It's a distraction issue, really..."

He stopped sopping up the wet spot on his thigh and met her eyes. "Do you?"

Flashes of her father leapt in, maybe to his thoughts, also, and she tried to shrug it off. "I tend to go too many directions at once and they interfere with each other."

He grinned. "Better than not going any direction."

"Well, look who dragged her snooty ass back to town." The redhead stared, hands on her skinny hips that showed bare saggy skin between her low cut jeans and high cut tank.

"Justine, be polite for a change." He gave her a few of the napkins.

Fran never would have recognized Justine Haden, now Justine McKenry, she supposed. She'd lost a good twenty pounds or so, about as much as Fran had gained, but the woman looked far older than herself and George. A good ten years older. Fake tanned. Dyed hair – she'd been a brunette back in high school. Her face looked old and worn. Leathery.

"Why, G.F., you *do* still have the hots for her. How cute. And convenient, I suppose." Justine glanced at Fran's left hand. "Single, I see. How very convenient for you, *honey*."

"Knock it off."

"You know he named our son after you, right? He never liked that uncle much, although he thought he could fool me..."

"*Justine*. Leave our issues private, if you would. Fran, I'm sorry. Can I get you anything while I replace this?" He motioned to the nearly empty plastic glass.

"Thank you, maybe after our game." She took his arm and addressed her old nemesis. "You'll understand if I don't stay and chat. We have a date to play golf." Fran too much enjoyed the look on the woman's face as she nearly pulled him away.

"Sorry about that." George paid for the game and handed her a ball and club.

"Not your fault. Is it going to be uncomfortable playing that way?"

"After the ex embarrassed the hell out of me, you mean?"

"No. I mean the cola all over your jeans. You have no reason to be embarrassed."

"I'm too used to being drenched in sweat all day for this to matter. At least it wasn't a couple of inches higher. And honestly, it was worth it to see her freak out about getting a few splashes on her clothes."

"Other than her yelling at you?" Fran placed her ball on the little indentation that marked the start of the course.

"Hell, that was nothing. That woman would make a screaming banshee look tame. Too used to it to think about it. Sadly. Want me to give you more room?" He was standing close enough she'd brushed his arm while placing her ball.

She met his eyes. "In that case, I'm not at all sorry you're divorced, George. And no, I'm good in tight places." Aiming toward the curves on the little path to try to get it beyond both, Fran was satisfied enough when the yellow ball bounced against the far curve's edge and stopped in what should be a good path to the hole.

"Nice shot. And I'm tempted to take that the way you didn't mean it." With a slight grin, he bent to place his ball and moved around her, brushing her arm when she barely moved.

"Are you sure I didn't?" She laughed when he hit it way too hard and it bounced over onto the mulch.

"I think that was a purposeful distraction and not entirely fair."

She gave him a soft shrug. "Well, you did warn me you cheat, at the game, so I expected I should offer a counter to that."

He stepped closer. "You're a hell of a lot more fiery than you used to be."

"Not true. We never actually talked before." She went on ahead to where her ball had stopped, aimed, and putted it right into the hole.

George grabbed his, set it on the course beside where it went out, and took three tries to get it in. With a sigh, he pulled the scorecard from his back pocket and started to mark it.

She took it from his hand. "No scores. I'm only keeping you company."

He stared for some time, as though trying to decide something or the other, and started to speak when a *Hi, Fran* interrupted.

"How are you, Lexi?"

"I won! Can I watch your game? Are you good at this? Because Dad's really good. He always wins when we all play together, so we don't let him much anymore."

George rolled his eyes. "So much for teaching you to be good sports. You're done already?" His boys came up behind their sister.

"Just now." Justin nodded a hello to Fran. "But we can hang out here. No hurry. Unless I can have the keys to your truck so we can turn the radio on and..."

"Um, no." George pulled out his wallet and handed the boy a twenty. "You can play again. Just behind us."

To their credit, they did stay one hole behind, although there was plenty of harassment from the boys whenever their father missed an easy shot, and Lexi was constantly cheering Fran on.

"Respect?" George rolled his eyes as he propped a hand on the side of the fake mountain. "They respect me, you say?"

"Yes, very much. They wouldn't dare tease you like that if they didn't." She stepped up to the hole just inside the cave of the fake mountain. Thrown off by the sudden darker playing field, she hit it against the wall and nearly back to where she'd started.

"This one throws me, too." He came up behind her, close enough his soft masculine scent drifted into her heightened senses, and putted the green ball nearly right down the middle, almost a hole in one.

"Does it, really?" Fran positioned her club to aim at his ball, but hit the side again and only made it halfway through the cave.

He stepped in front of her, with a glance back toward the entrance. "So, I have to ask, since you kind of brought it up. Was ... inability an issue with ... hell, I don't remember his name right at this moment."

"Cal. And no. It was more disinterest."

"You're kidding, right? Or you mean on your part."

"Not on my part. He wasn't around a lot. A very busy, important man, Cal was. Quite frankly, I didn't see him often enough to get disinterested."

"That's why you left him."

"I didn't leave him. He left me. Nine years ago." Swerving around him, she went to find her ball, putted it too hard so it again bounced off the wall, and cursed.

"Sorry." He touched her arm.

"You weren't trying to rattle me on purpose?"

"No." He leaned his head down and held her eyes. "I knew he wasn't good enough for you. I'm sorry I was right."

"Guess I should have listened to my father." Wanting away from the conversation, she went to her ball. She added so many strokes before she hit the hole, if they'd been keeping score, he likely would have caught up with her.

George motioned for her to start the next one. This time, it was a good shot and he told her as much. "So." He putted his ball close to hers. "You found someone else in between, I'm guessing. Someone you plan to go home to when you're done here?"

"No." She shot it past the hole. "I dated a bit. Nothing serious."

With a nod, he put his ball in the hole. "No kids?"

"No." Flustered, she hit it too hard, and his kids caught up. When the next shot nearly went in but stopped on the edge, George nudged it with his foot and gave her a wink.

Justin teased about flirting and trying to let her win.

"We're not keeping score." George spoke to his son, but then caught her gaze. "Just hanging out. Why don't you guys go on ahead of us and we'll harass you for a change?"

Playing along with his kids' comments about Fran winning, no matter how often they both said they weren't keeping track, he told them to go on and get in the truck, and he saw Fran to her Explorer. Very neat inside, he noticed when he held the door. "Can I ask why you got such a big vehicle when you don't have kids to cart around?"

"It hauls more than kids."

He leaned his head to look inside. The seats were all laid flat. But nothing was in it.

"I packed it full instead of renting a truck or moving company. And I'll do that again when I move."

Move. Again, that word. "Where are you headed next?"

"I don't know yet. I'm taking one thing at a time these days."

"Well." He scratched his chin. "Thanks for keeping me company. It was much nicer than sitting on that bench. Who knows how long she would have stayed if you hadn't come. Wouldn't mind if *she'd* pick up and move. Anywhere. Away. A long ways away."

"Wouldn't that make it hard on the kids, or ... on you having to go visit? Do you get them for weekends?"

"Nope. I have custody. Her choice, which works for me. And I think they'd be all right with it. I'm not the only one she yells at. Theo and Justin don't go to her place unless the younger two are there, since they're old enough to choose and she's not willing to fight about it. They do it to watch over Frankie and Lexi. Sucks for them, but makes me feel better. So, yeah, since I have custody, if she moves, it's on her to come back and visit. My guess is she wouldn't bother much."

"That's sad."

"Yeah, but they're smart kids, and strong. They'll be fine."

"And you'll be more careful with your next choice."

"Oh, for damned sure." He stepped back. "Guess I'll let you get going since I've taken enough of your errands time."

"It was fun. I'm glad you did." She brushed hair from her face and didn't make a move to get in her vehicle.

"Yeah? So... How about coming for dinner, in that case?" He knew he was pushing it, but she'd been great with his kids, Lexi in particular, even with the girl sticking to Fran much of the time, asking twenty questions, times twenty, until G.F. told her to hush.

And she did well with him, not getting bent out of shape by his flirting, as the boys called it, even throwing it back at him, but casually. She hadn't even cringed at the way he'd said he was used to being drenched in sweat all day. "We're just grilling hot dogs and hamburgers. Nothing fancy. And the house is pretty much always a mess. But you're welcome, if you can ignore it."

"Thank you, but I've already wasted a half day of work…"

"Play time is never wasted. It's good for the soul."

"Yes, I meant… Well, your children might prefer I not tag along again, you know."

"They won't care in the slightest." When she looked like she might argue, he called over to the truck. "Anyone mind a dinner guest?"

The boys either shrugged or said it was fine. Lexi jumped out and came over. "Please, Ms. Barrett. Come eat with us. *Please.*"

"That's just not fair. And I do have plenty of work I should be doing." Fran scolded him with a look.

"Okay, Lexi, don't beg. Go back to the truck. It was nice of Ms. Barrett to spend this much time putting up with us. She has other plans for the rest of the day."

"Fran. Please. I'd rather they call me by my name."

Damn, she had beautiful eyes. Round. Light brown, nearly hazel when the sun hit them right. Long thick lashes. He nearly told her they were beautiful. Instead, he nodded. "If you'd rather." He offered his hand. "Thanks for coming to my rescue. Give us a call if you get bored out there alone and would like to join our chaos."

She accepted his hand, held it a moment, which made his gut tighten, then moved her gaze from him to Lexi. "If you're free tomorrow, I have more shopping to do, and I hear you enjoy shopping."

"Oh. *Yes.* Can I?" The girl turned expectant eyes up at him.

"Tomorrow is your mom's day."

"But…"

"Sorry. It's out of my hands. She'll have a conniption if I don't get you there."

"I'm sorry. I didn't know." Fran took Lexi's hand, cupping it in both of her own, a protective move. "How about another day this week, after school? If it's okay with your father."

Of course he agreed. On Monday. Kind of a reward for having to go to her mom's, although he didn't let himself say as much.

Getting the excited girl into the truck, he waited and watched

Fran pull out and back up, and then flagged her to stop and jogged over to her window.

She gave him a questioning look over the top of too-big sunglasses. "Forget something?"

"Yeah. I'd really like you to come for dinner. Not sure I sounded enough like I do. Unless you have plans other than errands that might wait? A date, maybe?"

"I have no plans other than working on the property. And I haven't dated in ... far longer than I want to admit."

"Then follow us home. I'd love to not be the only adult there."

"You know..." She removed the sunglasses. "I've been wondering about Frank's name. Is your ex right?"

"She's only part right, but it's a respect thing, not a teenage crush thing. I always respected the way you were just yourself and did your own thing despite the crowd or peer pressure. I've always hoped my kids would do the same. Some do. Frankie does, so far. It's respect, not lust, as she was hinting."

"I'm very horribly flattered about now. I never realized..." She looked into the rearview as a car behind her honked to get out of the way. "Thank you. Another night, maybe. For dinner." Fran touched the hand he had set over her door's window frame and moved to pull away.

G.F. stood back and let her go and threw a wave at the car behind in an apology. He should have told her back then. Maybe she would have talked to him instead of turning to that fly-by-night Calvin. He hoped to hell the asshole hadn't hurt her, other than leaving her, and not being available enough for her.

He thought of her soft touch all the way home and through grilling burgers and hot dogs for half the neighborhood kids and one of their mothers who invited herself with the purpose, again, of hitting on him. He couldn't stand the whiny little brat she was "raising" and he sure as hell wasn't about to hook up with her. He'd made it clear often enough.

When the mess was cleaned up and the kids were playing lawn darts in the dark under his big yard lights and the woman had gone on home and taken the brat with her, he picked up the phone and leaned against the kitchen counter. She answered much more friendly this time and he had to get it out fast.

"Hey Fran, sorry to bother you again. Making sure you got in okay since I didn't earlier. Getting your work done? Am I interrupting?"

"Honestly? I've been lazy tonight. I guess I don't feel a huge rush to rent the place now that it doesn't look as bad."

"Making progress, then?"

"I am. And thank you."

"For?"

"Checking on me. Not necessary, but thank you. I'm not used to having anyone bother."

"Small town folks, you know. We do that."

"No. Most don't."

G.F. pushed himself from the counter and paced. "Suppose that's true these days. Anyway, I wanted to invite you, just in case you need a break tomorrow from all that work, well, the community band still plays in the square on Sundays. Thought you might be interested. I know you used to go at times, with your father. Maybe it was just for him, though."

"It wasn't for him. He went for me because he didn't want me there alone. Silly man. No one would have bothered me. Nice, I guess. At least by now I think so. What time are they? The same?"

"Two o'clock."

"The same."

"Yep. Some things don't change, thank goodness."

Silence crept over the line. "And some do, thank goodness. Thank you. I'll think about it. I suppose you're going?"

"Every week."

"Maybe I'll see you there. Thanks again, G.F. Good night."

He barely made himself return the wish and paced more after he hung up. Stupid, to let himself start getting hooked. She was getting the place ready to rent. To move away. Where, she wasn't sure.

At least she was in less a hurry to do so. Could be a good thing.

Ten

G.F. spotted her from his position in the third row of the band shell. She was easy to spot, again in a long skirt, straighter this time and blue instead of gray, with a different long shirt over top, in tan. She walked slowly, looking around, for him maybe, up toward the green benches in neat rows in front of the shell. He should have suggested she bring a chair. The benches were full since they'd started already. Folding chairs of all kinds were scattered around behind the benches, near to filling the open grass area.

She stopped just behind the chairs, gave up looking around the crowd, and focused on the band. He watched until she spotted him. A grin flirted around her lips, or at least he thought it did. She was farther away than he liked. But she'd come.

He supposed he should have told her he was part of the band, lead saxophone. Justine hated the sax. With a passion. Maybe it was part of why he'd taken it up again.

Fran started away and his heart nearly stopped. She couldn't leave. He tried hard to keep focus on his music as she ambled back, away from the band. But then she stopped, turned, and lowered onto the grass. He could barely see her back there, but she stayed. Sitting on the grass in that skirt. Something about it was too endearing.

For the first time, he found himself wishing the concert would end. With any luck, she'd stay right there and he could go to her.

Fran knew some of those who stopped to say hello didn't recognize her and some of those who recognized her didn't bother to say hello. Both were fine. It wasn't really her town anymore. In some ways, it always would be. In others, it never had been. It didn't matter. She was there only for George.

She loved that he'd joined the community band. He was good on that sax. Always so talented. She'd always admired his talent. A shame he'd quit playing the piano once they reached high school and peer pressure got too much for him. He'd switched to sax, which was fine, nice really, but she'd loved to hear him play piano the few times she had.

Disappointed when it was over, she stayed where she was, under shade of a distant tree, out of the way, and watched people scatter or mingle. She saw it with fully different eyes than she had when younger. She'd been so worried about what they thought, despite how much George admired that she did her own thing. It didn't keep her from worrying about what they thought. She no longer cared. At this point, Fran watched, studied them, those she remembered and those she didn't, some newcomers, young kids who likely belonged to some of her classmates, with disinterest.

While George headed her direction, he paused a few times to return a hello to someone, sometimes more than a simple hello. Otherwise, he headed straight to her, gave her a grin, and lowered to the grass beside her. "Hey, Fran. Glad you came."

"So am I. It sounded good, even better than I remember."

"Yeah, we seem to be more interested in this stuff as we age, don't we?"

"I always enjoyed it. More now, though."

"It's my sexy saxophone, right?" He grinned, teasing.

"I would say it probably is." Okay, she was definitely flirting. Fran was surprised at herself, but not at all ashamed by it. He looked nice in the band's uniform. They were all in a white shirt and black pants or skirts. He had his shirt sleeves rolled up, and he smelled incredible, like ... like a very sexy mixture of Iowa boy and something much spicier and impossible to pin down. "You're still good with that thing. I always enjoyed that, too."

He stared, his shoulders pulling back in surprise.

"Didn't know that, did you?"

"Had no idea. My turn to be flattered." He stared a bit longer. "Are you up to a walk by the lake? Seems we have things we could talk about."

"Can I ask you something first?" She studied his large strong hand propped in the grass and played with the green blades close to it.

He leaned closer. "Anything. Honestly."

Anything? Was the man truly that open? Fran looked out at people, mostly older people, folding up their chairs and heading back to their cars. Most were couples who looked like they'd been together nearly forever and likely felt like it had been forever. She often wondered what that would be like, to be that fully connected to another person.

Allowing a deep breath to push her on, she gave her attention back to him. "That day in the hallway, and this will likely sound ridiculous since it was so long ago, but ... the day you were standing around with a couple of your friends, and you asked me out in front of them, although we'd never even talked... You probably don't remember..."

"I do remember. A stupid thing to do. I've always regretted it."

She met his eyes, the deep, dark brown eyes speckled with bits of lighter brown. "Because you didn't mean it. I figured you didn't."

"No." He shifted, drawing closer. "I meant it. I damned well meant it. But I was afraid you thought I was..."

"Teasing. As everyone else teased the *uppity Barrett girl* with the crazy father. Weren't you? Tell me the truth. I'm not sixteen anymore. I can take it."

"Frannie." He took her hand. "I wasn't teasing. I did mean it. I regret doing it in front of those guys, because when you turned away, I had to play it off. Grammar geek girl snubs the football player. That would've been..." He stopped and his chest rose and fell. "Look, I know I was a huge ass back then. I was. Things have changed. And I am sorry. But I absolutely meant it and it hurt my pride ... no, it hurt my heart when you turned away and acted like I was dirt beneath your feet. I had to salvage what I could."

"I did not act like you were dirt. I only brushed it off as the joke I expected it was."

"Yeah, well, kinda felt the same."

It hurt his heart? "It wasn't my intention."

"I know that now. Like I said, I'm sorry I did it that way."

"You honestly would have dated me back then if I'd said yes?"

"Absolutely."

"Why?"

He raised a hand to her face. "I have always found you interesting. Sweet but strong. Intelligent. Always questioning everything, with a look if not otherwise. You weren't caught up in the whole game playing popularity contest thing. You were different. I liked that. Still do."

"You know I couldn't risk saying yes in front of them just to have you laugh and say you weren't serious. I wasn't concerned about popularity, but I did have my pride."

"Yeah, I get it. But you know what? I'm asking again. No one listening. I'm not jerking you around. Come walk with me. And then have dinner with me, if you still want to have dinner after we walk a while. Gives you time to think about it."

Dinner. Dinner was a date. Maybe. His children ... with their mom. He'd said she had them on Sundays.

"Hey, G.F."

At a male's voice, he took his hand from her face and looked up at the guy. "Stan, how was it this week?"

"Good as always. Who's your friend?"

He stood and offered Fran a hand to help her to her feet, then introduced her. She knew the guy to a small extent and could tell he recognized her name. *The daughter of the crazy Virgil Barrett.* The look was all over his face.

"If you'll excuse us, we were headed for a walk." George grabbed his sax case in his other hand and kept her fingers.

He wasn't teasing. For years, Fran had thought of it too often – that moment when the one boy she had a true interest in had asked her out and she'd never been sure if he meant it. How would things have changed if she'd taken a chance and agreed? Would he have married her instead of that silly little Justine? Would she have children instead of looking at happy couples with precious little ones and forcing herself to believe she didn't really want that?

Not that it mattered now. It wasn't possible for her anymore. Not since the scare when she thought she was pregnant and Cal had gone off like she'd just told him he had to go live in a poor house and share a cot with a stranger or some such thing. He'd avoided her completely until she took care of it, to be sure she couldn't.

She'd believed then it didn't matter.

And it didn't, really. She was nearly forty. Getting closer to grandparent age than parent age. She was set in her ways, selfish with her time. Fran believed she'd earned the right to be selfish with her time at this point. She'd given enough. She'd put herself last enough. Maybe too much. Maybe once the house rented, or sold, she'd travel. Anywhere. Alone. Have a fling with a foreign man in a foreign country like they did in those movies and be smarter than the women in those movies and not fall for them, only enjoy the moment and come back home with no regrets.

She could.

George set the saxophone case in the back of the truck and locked it again. A sexy man, really. Not gorgeous. He'd never been the cutest of the bunch. If not for football, he likely wouldn't have attracted girls at all. Well, his build might have. Otherwise, he was closer to homely than to gorgeous. Just kind of normal looking, like she was. Still, there was something about him she'd always enjoyed watching.

"Ready?" A question on his face said he caught her thinking too much about him, studying him.

"You don't have to pick the kids up? How long do they stay there?"

"I took them her way. She'll drop them off tonight after dinner. Theo has the key to get in if I'm not there, but she usually pushes it until bedtime or later. Just to push my buttons, I'm sure."

"She only gets one day instead of the weekend?"

"Her choice. Someone always needs transported somewhere on Saturdays. She hates to do it, says she's done it enough, which is fair, I suppose, so she only takes Sunday because it's easier for her."

"Ouch. They're okay with that? Is Lexi?"

"Lexi's fine with it. She and her mother never got along, from the time she was little. Frankie has issues with the whole thing. He's closest to her. Theo goes over and helps her folks pretty often. He's saving for a better car and they pay him for help with chores whenever we don't have side jobs he wants to do. Guess it's something. They've never done anything else for them. Barely ever spoke to me."

Fran hardly realized they were walking already, toward the lake. He was easy to talk to, which surprised her. "And Justin?"

His chest rose and fell. "J hasn't spoken to her since she left me, well, since I made her leave after finding out what she was doing. I keep trying to tell him it's between the two of us and shouldn't affect his relationship with his mom, but I can't get through. Thing is, she was always smothering him. Her favorite of the kids; sad to say she has a favorite. She lectured the boy like crazy about how to best get along with girls, how to attract the 'right' kind of girls, good enough for him. I think he's finding it too hypocritical that she screwed around on me after all that talk. He's a smart kid. Good sense of justice. Always did have."

"So he's disappointed."

"Yeah. My guess. Not sure what I can do about it. As much as I can't stand the woman these days, it doesn't feel right to have the kids feel the same. I'm always careful what I say around them. Doesn't seem to help."

Fran rubbed a thumb along his with the somewhat uneasy realization they were holding hands like teenagers, out where anyone could see they were. "It's not up to you. She'll have to do it."

"Right. Fat chance. I can't even get her to see that it's wrong to talk bad about me in front of my own kids. Fairness means nothing to the woman. He can't relate."

"Some things can't be fixed. You have to just let it go." She heard herself say it. Her dad's words. She'd disagreed at the time, but he was right.

"Straight from Virgil Barrett's mouth." He gave her a grin. "Your father was a smart man, you know."

Fran stopped walking and stared at him.

"Yeah, I know." He stepped closer and squeezed her hand. "Not what most thought and I'm sure you had an earful of the rest. I've wanted to tell you for years how much I respected him. He was a smart man. Such a shame a man like that had to lose his senses when others who have no sense in the first place walk around like they know it all. Your father was a good man, Frannie. You should be proud of him."

She started walking again. Silent. She swore she'd probably go home with George and stay forever just for that, for those words that affected her far too much. Her mother had been far too much like his ex. She'd said too much negative garbage about Fran's father. The problem was: it backfired. She lost far more respect for her mother than for her father. Maybe she should warn Justine Haden McKenry about that.

Probably wouldn't do any good.

After a mostly quiet walk along the lake where he enjoyed watching little ones playing along the thin beach, running in and out of the water squealing while Fran focused out at the boats, especially the sailboats, G.F. took her to the Regatta Grille for dinner. They talked about anything except the big things, mostly about local events, what had changed and what hadn't, how she was coming along with repairs to the shed. Sounded like she was turning it into a small house, which he figured was a good way to go. He wanted to know what she did for a living and half hoped she either wouldn't ask him what he did or wouldn't try to hide an *I figured* attitude. More than that, he wanted to ask about Calvin whatever-his-last-name was. About what happened between them other than the *disinterest*, which he found hard to believe. He was also wondering why she never had kids, and why she avoided them as well as possible while they ambled.

Too soon. She was still trying to decide whether to trust him. So he avoided talk of jobs and relationships in favor of letting her get to know him as he was, not for what he did, or what he'd done back in school.

Again, she focused out on the sailboats. With a thank you to their server for his water refill, he decided that was safe enough to ask. "You like boats?"

"Oh, I like the looks of them. I haven't been on one to know whether I like it. Mom was terrified of water. She hardly let me take a bath when I was little. It was usually showers instead as far back as I remember."

"Ah. So that's why you didn't come to senior day at King's

Pointe?"

Fran looked back out at the lake, the boats. "No, Dad insisted she let me do that."

"Then why didn't you?"

"What does it matter?"

Figuring he'd gone that far, so should answer her fairly, George leaned in somewhat, his voice low. "I'd finally screwed up the courage to ask you out again, without anyone around to hear. And you didn't come."

She held his gaze for some time, then pulled back to sip her coffee.

"Fran?"

A sigh raised her shoulders lightly. "One of my friends warned me you intended to ask me out. I expected it was a prank, that maybe it would be around even more people, so a bigger joke. I couldn't face it."

If she'd punched him in the gut, it would have felt better. His head shook. "Never would have imagined you'd care what I thought or did anywhere near that much."

She caught his eyes. "I did."

"That's why you avoided me the rest of the time you were still in town."

"Yes. Another mistake."

"Seems we both did plenty of that. I'm glad you came back home so we could at least clear the air."

"So am I. It changes all of those memories to see them differently."

"Sure does. Interested in dessert?"

"No. Thank you. I ate far too much already."

He patted his stomach. "Same here. We might have to jog back to the cars instead of walking."

"I don't jog." She finished her coffee and leaned back against her chair. "I hated running back in school and haven't done it since. It probably shows, but I don't even care."

Letting their server know they were done, he looked back at her. "You look nice. No reason you should care."

"Thank you. Still the charmer, obviously."

"I mean it, Frannie. You look great, but not real happy, if I can say as much."

"I miss my father. I hate that I stayed away from him for so long. The longer I'm here, the guiltier I feel. Going through his things and getting rid of a lot of it... It has to be done. Still..."

"Can I help?"

"You already are. Without your company, being here would be a lot harder. Thank you for that, too."

She tried to pay her half of the check but he said it was his invitation and he wouldn't have it. If she wanted to ask him out, he'd be fair enough to let her pay. Although he didn't intend to give her the chance. She'd likely get so sick of him she wouldn't want to add on to their time together. Of course, that depended on how often she'd agree.

They ambled back as slowly as they'd come and he appreciated that she wasn't in a hurry to get away from him. Traces of red appeared over the water through the dusk, reflecting in the lake, and a nice breeze played with her hair. She didn't seem to mind that, either.

Since she'd had to park a distance away, he gave her a lift to her Explorer and saw her to the door, holding it open as he blocked the small bit of traffic buzzing fast from getting too close to her. "Mind if I trail you home?"

"Why?" She stood close enough her skirt swept against his legs.

"To see that you get there fine."

"No need. I'm used to..."

"Taking care of yourself. Yeah, I got it. But I won't have to worry about keeping you out so late if I see you home."

"I'm not still sixteen, G.F. And it's not even nine o'clock."

"Guess I can't help but still see you that way to some extent."

"I suppose I'll take that as a compliment, even though I know I don't nearly look sixteen, either."

"A hell of a lot closer than a lot of women our age. And that is a compliment. You've taken care of yourself well."

"Not as well as you have. Whatever you do now, it must agree with you."

He laughed. "Well, I can't say that. Every night when I get home, I tell myself I'm too damned old for the job, but every morning, I go back."

"Thirty-nine isn't old."

"Tell my kids that."

"Right, I'm sure we felt the same about our parents." She brushed hair behind her ear. "So, what is it you do that's so hard on you?"

There it was. Might as well get it out of the way, he figured. "Road construction. Supervisor these days. Not impressive, but it pays."

"You didn't want to tell me."

"Not so much."

"Why?"

He shrugged. "Figured you were doing something with your brains as Mom always said I should."

"It's an honest job. Do you enjoy it?"

"Most days. Always liked being out and about and doing something with my hands."

"Then it sounds like a good choice, and the rest of us would be in a world of hurt if someone didn't keep the roads decent. Maybe you could tell me more about it someday. About the process. I wonder now and then when I drive past construction."

He chuckled. "Always curious, even about mundane stuff. Another thing I've always liked about you."

She leaned in to give him a quick hug. "Thank you for today, and yesterday. I enjoyed myself thoroughly, and it's been a long time since I have."

"Frannie." He caught her eyes enough to be sure she knew he wasn't calling her Frannie as an insult at all. To him, that's who she was. "I could say exactly the same. And I'll feel better if I can follow you home. Just down the road from me, anyway. Not a big deal."

Fran hoped he would simply pull in her drive, wave as she went in, and leave. He didn't, of course. He got out and walked her to the door. At times, there was such a thing as being too much a gentleman. It was nice, she supposed, but awkward.

A cool breeze made her nearly invite him in, but she didn't want him inside. "I'll plan to be in the park earlier next Sunday so I can sit closer. I did enjoy the concert, even more than when I was a child."

"I'm glad you did." He leaned against the old post with bits of white paint still clinging to the weather-worn wood holding the dilapidated porch roof.

"I'm not sure how sturdy that is."

"Doubt I'm that heavy." He grinned and patted his stomach. "Even if I have put on a few pounds."

"Haven't we all? Or at least most of us. Your ex managed to go the other direction."

"Yeah well, guess that happens when you only eat rabbit food and bar smoke. I don't think it looks good on her any more than the bad dye job, but guess she's happy with it." He straightened and came up close. "You look a hell of a lot better than Justine. Always did. And with that, I should go."

She didn't particularly want him to go. "I'd offer coffee, but the place isn't decent enough yet."

"I don't care about that."

"I do." And his nearness was getting to her. The man was a good several inches taller than she was, and meeting his eyes when he was so close tilted her neck back too far.

"Ah, okay. Women and their abodes. Something we men don't quite get. But I'll respect your wishes. See you later, Fran. Have a good night."

"You too." She watched him shamelessly as he started away. The few pounds looked fine on him. They were only a few. He had nice thighs. Full. Firm...

"I've been meaning to ask..." He turned back. "That mattress okay sitting on the floor? I've been wondering if it doesn't make it too hard."

"A little, but it works. You've been wondering about my bed?"

He opened his mouth, closed it, and ambled back to her. "You keep flirting with me that way, and I'm bound to take it as an invitation of sorts."

"Who says I'm flirting?"

"I say you are. Am I wrong?"

She studied the play of his lips, the way he was trying not to smile, the sparkle of his eyes showing an attraction, the way his bangs shifted in the breeze, highlighting his dark eyes.

"Frannie?"

"George?"

"You know I don't mind it so much when you say it." His fingers brushed her leg. Barely. "How about letting me in for coffee?"

"I don't think so."

"I would never push anything you don't want."

"That's not what I'm worried about."

"No?" He lowered his face.

It would be so easy to reach up and kiss him. But if she tied herself into a relationship, she'd have to stay long enough to see how it worked out. She'd have to at least know...

His lips touched hers. Barely. Cautiously. Nice. It was nice. A glorious way to end a beautiful day in a place she didn't want to be.

She pulled back gently. "Hm. You should go now before we get ourselves in trouble."

"Trouble isn't always a bad thing." His voice was low and hoarse.

It made her want to touch him, his large shoulder, his soft nape. "Oh, I don't know. Doesn't seem like it worked very well for either of us before."

"Okay. You win." He lifted her hand and kissed her fingers. "But realize I plan to see you again long before next Sunday. Good night, Fran. Call if you need anything."

She watched him again while he ambled to his truck in no apparent hurry. With his backside in his truck and the engine started, she gave him a wave and closed the door behind her, the screen door. She wanted the fresh air, to enjoy the night and the crickets and the thought of his lips on hers. She didn't want to tell him he couldn't come in because she had paintings on and beside her desk. Just as well. Letting him in could easily lead to trouble.

Changing into old clothes, she settled at her desk to work on the current painting in progress, but set it aside. With the image of the sailboats in her head, and thinking of how it reminded her of one of

Van Gogh's milder works, sailboats on the shore all in a row, Fran grabbed a new canvas, spread white, turquoise, cerulean blue, and a touch of light gray on her palette, and began to etch in the sky and lake, leaving space at the bottom to add the sand. Her sailboats, vivid in deep reds and greens, would be out on the lake. The foreground would capture a couple walking hand in hand.

Perhaps she would leave it as a gift for George when she moved away to wherever she was going.

Eleven

Wiping sweat from her forehead onto her T-shirt, Fran surveyed the garden. The iris she'd put in just after clearing the weeds out were poking up through the composted and mulched dirt. The hydrangeas were filling in with dark green leaves. She nearly trimmed off the bare dead branches, but her father always left them, so she left them. There was a beauty in the long pale brown sienna stalks acting as a place keeper of sorts, a way of saying they still mattered even if they didn't have life anymore. She liked the mix of bare and full, of brown and green. Soon, the leaves would be large and buds would open into huge tufts of flowers. With any luck, they would be deep blue on the edges of both sides beside the porch where she'd put the coffee grounds and pink at the center of each side where she'd spread the ashes of fallen branches she'd burned, as a nod to her father. She could end up with a purplish mix instead. It was impossible to tell so far.

She'd found a load of deep red iris at a good price since they should have been planted last fall, and stuck them in the refrigerator for a week or so while she got the weeds cleared out and the ground ready. Color in the yard attracted attention. A bright door also attracted attention and was good for sales. Or for renting. The shack was close to the main road, on the opposite side of George's end of the road, and would show before the main house came into view, so its outside mattered a great deal.

Her mother had always said as much as she complained about tall grass and the ramshackle look. Her father said he didn't care what people thought and he didn't want them there if they were going to be that persnickety. Fran agreed with both, if that was possible.

After lunch, since the forecast was clear for the next few days, she would sand the peeling yellowed varnish off the front door. It was entirely possible she wouldn't have energy left to paint after the sanding was done, but she expected it would be fine to wait until morning.

Sliding her dirty hands down her jeans to rid herself of the first layer of grime and pulling the bottom edge of her T-shirt up to wipe her forehead again, she heard a car coming. Not a car. Too loud. A truck.

She turned toward the road, the path off the road that led to both the house and the little shack. He was at work. It was Monday. Just someone...

The front of a black Chevy inched through the gravel and peeked its nose out from the shrubbery guarding the house. George. And she was covered in dirt, her hair an unmanageable mess, with sweat streaking her shirt underneath her soaked bra. She pondered whether to duck inside the house and refuse to answer the door, but it was too late. He saw her.

What difference did it make, anyway? He might as well see her as she was outside of the skirts and fixed hair. At home, she was a mess. Always. She had no plan to change that. He didn't need to keep coming around if he was going to be too persnickety about her looks.

She ambled over to the gravel parking spot where weeds poked through and waited for him to descend from the heights of his truck.

"Hey, Fran. Am I interrupting?"

She held her hands up to show him. "I would have washed at least, if you'd called."

"I did call. You didn't answer. Actually, I kind of had to come since you didn't answer. Lexi isn't up to shopping today. She hated to cancel, but she's..."

"Sick?"

"Well, not contagious. She often feels that way on Monday. Can't tell you how much school she's missed."

"Why?"

"Nerves. I've taken her in to the doctor. Nothing actually wrong, thank goodness. My guess is it's spending Sunday with her mother and the boyfriend. She swears nothing happens. She just doesn't want to be there." He shoved a hand through his hair. "If it keeps up, I'll have to go back to court and ask them not to force me to send her, since her mother won't give in."

"Poor baby. Justine should have to visit at your place where Lexi is more comfortable, in the least."

"Yeah. And as much as I don't want her there, I have offered, even said I'd get out of the way. She won't do it. Anyway, is your service that bad out here?"

Her phone was inside. She hadn't expected to get a call. "I'm not even sure I've turned it on yet today. I tend to forget since I don't use it much, and because I don't have great service in the middle of the trees."

"Yeah, us, either. Have to keep a house phone for that. You might need to hook one up."

"I'm not staying..." At his look, she thought maybe she might. For a while. "But it could be more rentable with a phone hookup, I guess, since I'm turning it into a cottage instead of just a shed."

"And safer for you. If you ever need it."

"I'm fine here, George."

"Okay. Well, since I had to come out, I thought you might join me for lunch. We can eat outside. I wouldn't dare go in your place like this." He looked down at his sweat-streaked work clothes. "Especially since you don't want me in there." With a teasing grin, he raised a plastic bag. "Grabbed sandwiches and chips from the store. Two kinds. You can choose. Unless you'd rather not."

"Actually, that saves me from having to find something, and I'm not particular. Whatever you have is fine."

"Good. Porch step work okay?"

"If you can stand me that close."

"I can if you can. Honestly, I'm glad to find you outside working so I don't feel like an obnoxious pig coming over like this."

"You're fine. Honestly. I don't think there's a sexier thing in the world than a working man who looks like a working man." She was flirting horribly. Fran knew she was. But she'd thought about that kiss all night until she fell asleep sometime early morning, and then woke thinking about it. It was hard not to flirt.

"That so?" He lowered the bag and came up right in front of her. "I did wash my hands. And I washed my face."

"Then you're ahead of me on both counts."

"I don't mind." Leaning closer, he raised his free hand, cupped his fingers around her ear back into her messy hair, and brought her mouth up to his.

A beautiful soft sensual kiss. Not too far. Not as light and brief as the night before. Soft. Sensual. Perfect for a lunch break come as you are kiss. Short, though.

She rubbed her lips together when he released her, soaking in the moisture, the thought of it. His gaze was soft, seeking. And she wanted more. So she wrapped her arms up around his neck, brought him back to her lips, felt the heat and sweat of his hard strong neck and shoulders, and raised to her toes when his arm wrapped around her waist, pulling her in.

"Mm, now that was a kiss." He spoke beside her ear, still holding her. "Guess you must be hungry."

She couldn't help a chuckle as she met his eyes. "Do you mean for lunch or are you flirting?"

"Which do you want me to mean?"

"Hm. Lunch." She trailed her fingers back down his shoulders and released him. "For now. Since we both have to get back to work soon."

A luscious woman. G.F. gave her another quick kiss before climbing back in his truck, after she agreed to come by his place for coffee after dinner. The kids would be there. A casual thing, so as not to chase her off. Anyway, he hoped the commotion wouldn't chase her off.

She wouldn't agree to come for dinner. And she wouldn't let him come pick her up. Independent. Nice, he supposed, after his leech of a wife. If it didn't go too far.

He'd at least half expected her to rail on him for just stopping by her place, particularly with her so disheveled. He liked disheveled. Normal. Everyday. Her nails were unpainted. Her shoes were old and starting to come apart at the toes. And her hair... G.F. chuckled to himself at the thought of her hair sticking out from an absently wrapped band in the back only part holding it up off her neck. It wasn't silky smooth. It wasn't perfectly curled and pinned. It was a mess, and had often enough been a mess in school, though she looked like she'd tried to make it behave back then. These days, she let it go, let it curl messily. He preferred it that way.

I'm not staying. So she said. After that kiss, though, the luscious kiss when she raised to her toes to get closer and held him in with both arms around his shoulders, her breasts pressing into his chest, and with the way she'd been flirting, he thought maybe she might change her mind with a bit of persuasion.

Fran sighed as he left. She had no further interest in working on the garden, or on the house. She wasn't about to sand the door. It could wait. She was in far less a hurry to be finished with her project than she had been only a couple of weeks ago.

But she wasn't staying. Storm Lake hadn't been all that friendly to her. Why should she stay? Of course, South Dakota hadn't been much better, not after those she'd started to get friendly with met Cal and backed away.

Stupid woman. It should have been warning enough. But he was fire. He was always smoldering, often burning hot and fast. She'd liked that, had gotten caught up in it. He was a fast-building, fast-moving whirlwind of a man who, once he got you ensnared, didn't let go. Until he was spent and wanted new ground to sweep off and away.

"You were only a test, Francie." She hated Francie even more than she hated Frannie, but he never stopped, never considered what she wanted, other than him. *"I gave her my promise years back and I can't break it. Just wanted to be sure I was doing the right thing, that I could leave someone I lust after greatly for her when it came to it. Seems I can."* He'd shrugged. And left.

A test. He'd taken her innocence, swept her away from home, made her break from her parents, from her few friends. And then he dumped her like a greasy fast food bag that no longer held any importance once he'd emptied it of its important contents.

What if she was a test for G.F.? What if he was only looking for a fill-in while finding something different than his ex? Maybe she didn't care. She could use him the same way. And then she could leave.

What did it matter?

Refilling her glass with tepid water, she drank half of it down and wandered through the little shack. Not so much a shack anymore. Nearly livable. The clutter was all stacked in the greenhouse waiting for someone to ship it away. The light shades of teal and cream made it look less tiny, less claustrophobic. It needed something on the walls still. Not too much. Not enough to look wall-cluttered. Just enough to look homey.

Instead of working inside or out, Fran grabbed her sketchbook and colored pencils and a small wooden folding chair that had the local school's imprint on back, and planted herself in front of the hydrangeas. Since they weren't blooming yet, she had to use a combination of the broad pointed leaves and empty stalks in front of her and her memory of the blooms to get the image she wanted. It didn't look half bad when she finished.

Flipping to a clean page, she did the same with the iris. This time, she went to find the empty bulb packages she'd kept to remember which variety she'd planted and used the picture on the front to fill in the details.

On a third page, she combined the two, creating the look on paper that she hoped she would get in the garden.

Wiping sweat again, Fran went back inside to her water glass and the scratched up desk, cleared the surface, and pulled out her oils. The main reason she didn't want George in the house was the prepared canvases sitting around, along with a few she was still working on: scenes from South Dakota. A beautiful place. Except for memories of Cal.

And the one of the lake that kept her up far too late the night before. The sky and water were done. The sand was in its beginning layers. The outline of three sailboats were in place. She hadn't done anything with the couple yet.

She'd have to find a place to store the canvases away from where George would see them before she could let him in. Her art was only for her. No one knew she'd been working at it for years, since her first high school art class and that first grid drawing that received praise from her teacher.

With far too much pride, she'd bragged about it to her parents. Her mother said it was nice and to go do her homework. Her father pointed out a couple of things that didn't look quite right. Expecting praise and getting ambivalence and criticism, Fran tore the thing to pieces.

A couple of weeks later, she tried again and showed no one.

Twelve

G.F. paced the kitchen. The woman changed her mind about coming over for coffee. At least she'd called. But damn, he'd been looking forward to it since lunch. He even broke his own rules and cleaned up messes the kids were supposed to clean to make sure the place looked good.

Got busy, she said. Hell, he was always busy. Still, he'd made time and energy to clean the kids' messes.

On top of it, they'd harassed the hell out of him for being so worried about what his *girlfriend* would think. Frankie told him she shouldn't come to the house, just in case "mom might stop by," like she ever did. He'd told the boy over and over he and his mother were not getting back together, whether or not she ever stopped by, even if she quit seeing the current guy. Wouldn't happen. He was fool enough to do it once but not nearly fool enough to do it again after he was out of it. He didn't say that much. He only said it just didn't work and sometimes you had to let things go.

Frankie answered he could let Fran go just as well.

Yeah, maybe he could, but he sure as hell didn't want to.

Stopping his circles of the kitchen, he looked at the coffee pot set up and ready to turn on. He'd wanted it fresh when she came and so waited instead of starting it at the beginning of dinner like he usually did so it would be ready when he finished eating. Switching it on, he rifled through cabinets to find the other coffee thermos, the one not stained from tar and such that he carried to work every day.

Finding and rinsing it, and getting it filled with mostly coffee and a decent amount of milk since he didn't have cream and she'd added plenty of cream at dinner the other night, G.F. found Theo to tell him he was in charge for a bit and to stay home and *be* in charge this time, then went out to the truck and drove right on down to her place. She'd said yes to coffee. If she didn't want to go out, that was fine. He was flexible. But he didn't take no well after he'd been given a yes.

She was outside the door, looking at him like he was crazy, by the time he got up to her porch. "What are you doing?"

He raised the thermos and two mugs. "Bringing it to you since you're too busy to come by."

"I'm a mess and I'm working."

"Always time for a coffee break when you work hard. And I don't care, Frannie. Never did." He moseyed up close and stood directly in front of her. Her move. He'd leave if she said to leave.

"You showered, though. Not fair since I haven't and you look better."

"If you wanted fair, you should have come on over as you said you would."

"George, I wasn't blowing you off. Like I said, I lost track of time and I wasn't going over there like this." She motioned at her worn, dirt-smudged T-shirt and faded jeans that were either stained or muddy.

"Fine. So I came to you. We'll try the other again another night."

She set her hands on her hips. "You don't give up easily, do you?"

"No, ma'am. That's something you should know about me."

Her head shook softly. "Just a second. Don't move." She disappeared through the door, closing it behind her.

He had to wonder if she'd found a better weapon than the putter by now and would come back with it. He half hoped she would. Just so he'd know she could, and would, if she felt the need.

When the door opened again, she shoved three wooden folding chairs at him and went back in. He opened them up and set two of them close together with the other in front to be a table of sorts, set the thermos and mugs on it, and turned to find her holding a paper plate covered in plastic wrap.

"Brownies to go with the coffee. From the bake sale I ran into. I don't want to eat them all on my own. Do you eat sweets these days? I know you didn't use to. Sour was your thing, wasn't it?"

A grin spread across his face. "I love sweets these days since I'm not still in sports training. And you remember a heck of a lot about me. You remember all those details about everyone?"

She set the plate on the chair beside the coffee and stepped close to him. "No, actually. Only you. No one else was all that interesting that I could tell. But then, I'm not easily impressed. In fact, I've been told I'm very hard to impress."

"You know, if you use that line to flirt, you might just get us both in trouble tonight."

"You're as bad as a teenager, George McKenry."

"Yeah, I've heard. As the song goes, I might be a bad boy to some extent, but, well, guess I won't call myself a *real* good man, but I wouldn't mind trying to convince you I am, however you want to take that."

Her attempt at a scornful expression didn't work well with the bit of a grin mixed in. "Have a brownie and cool down. You're not coming in tonight."

"Didn't expect I would." He sat to pour them both coffee.

"Just pushing to see how far you get?"

"Might be. You've surprised me already." George handed her a mug, trying not to comment on the fact that she was still on her feet, watching him, debate all over her expression. "Guess it's more that I'm trying to figure you out. Hard to mesh the image I've had of you since our school days with who I see now. You've changed a good deal."

"How do you know?" She tested the coffee's heat level and took a good swallow. "You didn't know who I was then."

"Probably true, but I think I could say the same. To less extent, I suppose. I've always been pretty open. Still..."

"We didn't talk then to know each other much at all."

"No. A shame. Glad you're giving me another chance."

Fran lowered onto the chair, picked up a brownie, and studied it for some time. "Truth is..." She met his gaze. "I have changed in some ways. I would have been far harder to talk to back then, so it was maybe just as well you didn't try. It never came out right when I did, so I covered that with ... well, with an attitude that looked like who I wasn't. I do realize that by now, that people were justified for thinking I was snooty."

"Got some edges knocked off through the years." Grabbing a brownie, he took a good bite. Store mix. Common. Still, decent enough to enjoy. His mother's brownies spoiled him for all others.

"To say the least."

He washed it down with coffee, and shrugged. "That happens. Life. Adulthood. Always heard it did, but it's hard to believe when you're still young and know everything."

She paused from taking a bite. "Did you really?"

"Did I what?" He set the thing down to chase a fly away from the plate.

"Think you knew everything when you were younger."

"Oh yeah. I had it all figured out. Except I didn't, of course. Took some hard knocks to tell me I didn't. Didn't you?"

"No."

"No? Serious?"

"Not at all. That's why I was hard to talk to. I didn't feel comfortable talking about stuff I didn't really understand, which was most everything. Still is, although I've tried harder to understand things. I know what people thought, and what they still think, that I feel above them all. Not true. I never thought that. I just didn't understand what they all seemed to understand and so I kept my distance to try not to appear stupid. Guess it worked."

Leaving the brownie on the plate, he leaned forward to rest his elbows on his knees, the hot mug in both hands. "We all thought you were too smart to talk to us plain folks."

"Please." She took a small bite of the chocolate, studying it again, avoiding his gaze. "I was the plain one and I know it. Everyone else was vibrant and confident and I ... just couldn't keep up with that."

He felt himself pull back in surprise. "That's how you saw yourself? Honestly?"

"Of course. I might not understand much of anything else, but I know who and what I am. The biggest change is that I don't apologize for it or hide from it any longer." With a shake of her head, she returned her brownie to the other side of the plate. "I'm not sure these are worth the calories. Sorry. I should have tested them before offering."

"Yeah, they're not like Mom's. I'll have to bring some over sometime." He looked out over the yard, listening to the crickets and to an owl in the distance while he thought about what she'd said. Plain. He never guessed Francis Barrett would ever see herself as plain. "You know, I kind of think you have that backwards."

"Backward. No 's' on the end." She flashed an apologetic glance. "Sorry. Habit."

He chuckled. "Okay."

"I have what backward?"

Propping his elbows back on his knees, he looked up into her strong almond-shaped face. "I think you know a whole heck of a lot about a lot of stuff and not enough about yourself. You're far from plain." He reached over to touch her fingers since they were within reach. "And you know what, Frannie? All of us who talked about everything as though we knew everything and understood it all had it *backward*. Why doesn't that sound right?"

"Because most people say it wrong. In British English, it's *backwards*. In American English, it's *backward*. I can't tell you why, just that it is."

"Interesting. Anyway, we big talkers didn't know jack shit and didn't much care that we didn't. We could have learned a hell of a lot from you, to be honest. That's how I see it."

She stood and went to the edge of the porch to pinch off a yellowed leaf from a hydrangea, her back mostly to him, her coffee mug in one hand. "Would you have listened to what I thought?"

He nodded, although she wouldn't see it. "Yeah. I think I would have. But the rest of the crew? Probably not. They're kind of surface level, and I don't mean any offense by that, 'cause most people are, I think, at least at that age. But you're not, and I try not to be."

Turning to stare at him over her mug as she sipped her coffee, Fran looked every bit like she didn't believe he would have listened back then, or maybe now, either. Her eyes moved to the side of his head and she came to him, reached out to touch his hair ... and showed him a ladybug crawling on her hand.

"And I hoped you were just playing with my hair." He threw what he hoped was a charming grin.

"My father ordered these. Not this one, I'm sure, but probably one of its predecessors."

"Yeah, so I heard."

She caught his eyes.

He shrugged. "Small town. Hard to order bugs by mail and not have people know."

"They're good for the garden. He used them instead of chemicals to control aphids."

"I know that, too. Like I said, he was a good man. Smart."

"How did you know him so well?"

Her nearness as he sat on the little wooden chair and she stood in front of him within an easy arm's reach, plus her scent mixed with some kind of plant, basil maybe, made it hard for him to think about her father. "I brought extra stuff from Dad's jobs over to him that would have gone to the scrap pile. He held me talking every time."

Fran rolled her eyes. "You could have said you didn't have time."

"Could have, but I enjoyed our chats." He reached out to take the little red bug and let it crawl on his hand. "A lot of it was about you. He adored the hell out of you. And he worried about you."

She looked out over the yard.

"Did he have need to worry? Were you okay?"

"Apparently I'm fine."

G.F. got up to take the little bug to the nearby hydrangea, then came back. Except she set her mug down and walked out into the yard, so he followed. "Didn't ask if you were fine now. Cal... Was he good to you? You stayed with him a long time, right? If he left nine years ago and you took off with him when you were nineteen...."

She ran her fingers along a dark green broad leaf, her back to him. "Eleven years. I'd been with him for eleven years when he just walked out. It devastated me for a while, but it was for the best."

"For the best. Does that mean he wasn't good to you, or for you, but you put up with it?" He stood close but didn't touch her. "Not trying to be insulting. I put up with plenty myself. Way too much. People do."

She turned to him, but he could barely see her face from the glow of the yellow porch light. Her eyes glistened. Again, she raised her hand to his hair.

"Another bug? They must like my aftershave."

"No bug this time. And I don't know about them, but I do." She slid her hand through his hair to the back of his head. "I lost myself trying to be what he wanted, which, of course, was a pointless undertaking. For the past nine years I've been trying to fix that. I'm not sure it's worked yet. I can tell you I don't want to be in Storm Lake right now. I needed more time to brush off the teenage version of me I wasn't ready to deal with. But things work as they work. I have to take care of this stuff now before I can..."

"Leave again."

"Yes. I stayed away once I was away because I don't want to be here. Coming back only reminded me of why I didn't."

He allowed himself a large sigh. "Okay, Frannie. I got it." Lowering his head, he stroked fingers alongside her face. "And I understand."

"Have you ever thought of moving out of here?"

"No." He cupped her head below her ear. "But you never know what's going to happen from day to day."

She met his lips, carefully at first, then stronger. Her fingers wove through the back of his hair, keeping him pulled in. Her warm, soft body pressed up against his, her arm wrapping around his waist, her hand clutching his shirt at the small of his back.

George wasn't sure if she was trying to change his mind about staying in Storm Lake or if his answer felt like a safety net, like she could play with him a while and then walk away since he wouldn't follow, but whatever she was doing, it sure as hell felt nice. He had to fight to control himself, since as close as she was to him, she'd darn well feel it if he didn't.

Suddenly, she released him and backed away. "You should go."

"Why?"

With a shake of her head, she half-jogged back up to the porch and gathered the mugs.

He caught up and took his from her hand. "Haven't finished my coffee."

"Take it with you. You can bring it back." She folded two of the wooden chairs with one hand and set them next to the door.

"When?" He ambled closer, sipping from the mug, eyeing her

over top of it.

"Whenever. I'm usually here. If you call first, I'll clean up a bit."

"So you're not giving me the brush off?"

She stopped and turned back. Stared. Started to talk and then didn't.

Taking a chance, he closed the distance and touched her face. "I don't care if you clean up first. Tell me I can come by as I please."

"I'm not always home. Usually. Not always."

"I know. And you know what I'm asking."

She shrugged. "You've already seen me like this. Doesn't get much worse."

Before she could get away, he wrapped his free arm around her, holding his mug to the side, and claimed her mouth. Only for a second or two. "Okay." He kissed in front of her ear. "I'll go. For now. If I don't come back as soon as you like, you can call and say so. Or drop by my place. Whenever. We're usually home evenings other than sports events and such."

Taking a long swallow from his mug, he handed it to her. "Night, Fran. Thanks for having coffee with me. Be sure to lock that door."

Fran watched his backside sway just so slightly in the glow of the not strong enough porch light, then set the mug on the chair and caught up as he opened his door. Letting herself not think, just react, just do as she wanted without thinking, as she never did anymore, she wrapped her arms up around his neck and pulled him down for a kiss, a very deep kiss, long, lingering. Toe curling. The man knew how to kiss. And he gave in to her, wrapping his strong arms around her waist and pulling her in next to his body.

Her fingers gripped onto his shoulders when she felt him get hard against her hip.

He released her, looked up at the sky, and grabbed a deep, fast breath. "Now that was a hell of a good night kiss."

"Sorry. I..."

"You're kidding, right?"

"I mean for... You're still not coming inside."

His eyes sparkled with a grin. "I'm going to assume you mean inside your house, although…"

"Either."

"Didn't expect I would. Either. But in case you want to know, I fixed any issue that might come with that after Lexi was born."

"What?"

"Protection, Frannie. No need. If it ever gets that far. I'm safe."

"Oh. I didn't… I meant…"

"And I didn't plan to try to stay. Gotta get home to my kids."

"Right." She pulled back, partly, letting her fingers skiff down his shoulders to his arms.

"Forgot about them?"

"Yes. Sorry again."

He chuckled deep from his chest and kissed her nose. "Don't be. So did I. Only for a minute or so. Don't tell them."

"I wouldn't dare. And I just wanted to be sure you know I'm not giving you the brush off. Night, George. You do smell good, by the way." She made herself release him and stepped back.

"Not leaving till you're inside with the door shut and locked."

"There's no one out here."

"Won't help to argue."

Of course she gave in. A shadow of Cal giving her orders came to mind, but it wasn't the same. George was only being a gentleman, making sure she was safe. She couldn't fault him for that.

Grabbing the mugs and thermos, she fumbled through the door, gave him a wave, then closed and locked it. As she watched out the window at his headlights disappearing, a sigh escaped. "Might as well get cleaned up, I guess." She spoke out loud to fill the silence and then looked at the things in her hands. They weren't hers. They were his. Had he realized he was waiting to finish his coffee so he could leave his own mug with her? And the thermos. Why had he..?

He made an excuse to come back? Or was he as befuddled as she was and… She sincerely doubted it.

Setting them in the kitchen, Fran shoved a hand through her messy hair. He was probably laughing at her now, wondering if she'd realized what she'd done. There was one way to find out. She grabbed her phone and dialed his number, waited through three rings…

"Yeah, I know they're mine. You can bring them this way for coffee tomorrow night. Or I'll come sit on the porch with you again. Your choice. Night, Fran." With humor in his voice, he hung up.

Insolent man. Maybe she'd just wash them and set them on the porch so he could grab them and go.

Although probably she'd let him in if he came. But she'd have to hide the canvases first.

Thirteen

"Herbs need plenty of sunshine." Fran set the potting soil in between her clay pots and Lexi's. While mixing it together, she explained the purpose of the vermiculite, peat moss, limestone, and phosphorous fertilizer. The girl had mentioned while shopping the day before how much she hated science, so Fran was gently working into showing her how much science knowledge would help with what she wanted to do. Her father had done the same for her. Unlike her mother, who only said she had to know it to pass her tests with good grades, her father put it into real life and made it make sense.

"We're starting them inside until they get some height to them, and then we'll put them out in the garden."

"But we don't have a garden. Where will I put mine?" Lexi dipped her hands into the little utility wagon full of potting mix and dumped it into her pots.

"You can keep them in containers on the porch, but you'll have to move them to bigger ones. That's why we put the coffee filters in first, so you can just dump the plants gently into your hand and move the whole thing into a bigger prepared container."

"Why didn't you just use new filters instead of those dirty ones?"

"They aren't dirty. It's only coffee grounds. Look." Fran took her to the far shelf where used grounds were spread out to dry. "I'll use these to add nitrogen to my plants. The hydrangeas love them. It turns them bright blue if you add enough grounds early enough in the season. Your herbs will like them, also. Just dry them so they don't mold and work them into your soil about once a month. Whatever you don't need for your herbs, since you don't want to overdo anything, throw out in the grass, especially in any spots that need some help."

"Like the places Scruff digs up."

"Scruff?"

"Our dog. Frankie's dog, really. Dad didn't really want a dog since we're messy enough, but Frankie found him abandoned as a pup. He was wet and scroungy and packed with mud. It was just after Mom dumped us back at Dad's, and Dad couldn't say no to Frankie when he cried about wanting to keep him. He's not so cute anymore, though. He's big and he doesn't listen and he still loves to be dirty. Dad about kicked him out the other day when he flopped on the couch full of mud."

"I can imagine. Here. Add some extra vermiculite for your basil. It loves water."

"I want a kitty, but Dad says five animals in the house is about enough. He said I could have another fish, but they die too easily."

"Five animals?"

"Yeah. Scruff and the four of us."

Fran had to keep herself from laughing. "Well, how long fish live depends where you get them and how you take care of them. Of course, they're also easy to replace if you don't get the expensive ones. Which reminds me, I need to get a couple more for my pond and then put a barrier around it. Something keeps taking them out."

"A cat?"

"Possibly. I haven't caught one at it yet."

"You wouldn't hurt it?" Lexi stared, wide-eyed.

"Of course not. I'll just have to take measures to keep them out of my pond so the fish can keep the mosquitoes away."

"Mosquitoes don't like fish?"

"The fish eat the larvae mosquitoes lay in any standing water they find. They'll reproduce by the thousands right in your yard if you're not careful. Science, Lexi, is important. Everything works together. If you understand how it works, you don't need things like harsh chemicals that pollute our water and our bodies."

"Like planting marigolds with herbs to keep pests away."

"Exactly. Speaking of, that's what we're planting next. Marigolds are simple to grow. Preferably, you want to do this in very early spring or late winter, but we should still get some decent growth this year. Then you can make your dad a fresh garden salad with Lexi-grown herbs."

She smiled big. "He'll love that. He's always picking up fresh stuff from the farmers market in town. Can I go with you to help you pick out fish for your pond?”

"If it's okay with your dad."

Cursing while he rubbed his sleeve over his burning eyes, G.F. thought again about a different job. Damned near anything. Anything that would support the house and four kids, anyway. Heading to rinse them with water, he heard his phone ringing on the truck's dashboard. The kids' ringtone. He had a separate one for them so he could ignore spammers and still be reachable for his kids. They knew not to call him at work if they didn't have to.

With the thought that something was wrong and he hadn't been there, he pulled off the thick leather gloves as he jogged over to the truck and yanked the phone out with sweaty, sticky hands. "What's wrong?"

"Dad?"

"Lexi. What's wrong?"

"Nothing. Can I go shopping with Fran?"

"What? You called me at work for that?"

"She's going now and I have to have permission. She won't take me unless you say it's okay. She's getting goldfish and..."

He grabbed a deep breath while nodding at his new young coworker that everything was fine. "Fine. Go ahead. Let her know she can take you to town whenever. Just have her text me so I know where you are. Okay?"

"She's right here."

"Lex, I have to..."

"Hey, it's me. Sorry. Did we call at a bad time?"

"I'm up to my eyebrows in asphalt that's dripping back into my eyes with the sweat pouring off my head. Damn, it's hot today. Make sure she's drinking water if you take her out. She doesn't do heat real well."

"Okay. So, iced coffee tonight? I have a special blend I've been wanting to try."

Even with his burning eyes and pounding heart, he couldn't help but grin. "Sounds fucking amazing right now. Excuse the language."

"Don't worry about it. I'll let you get back to work."

"Hey, you can take her out when you like. Just send a quick text to let me know. I don't freak out about texts."

A pause. "Sorry we freaked you out. I'll make it up to you later. Bye, George."

Make it up to him? He grinned, and shook his head.

"All good with the kids?" Jim propped a gloved hand on his hip.

"Yep. All's good." Iced coffee, special blend, and making it up to him. Definitely all good.

"Great. How about calling it an early day? It's gotta be at least ninety."

"Eighty-nine, and only if we get enough done first."

"Fucking close enough, I'd say."

"Yeah, well, they didn't make you supervisor for a reason."

"Fran let me pick out *five* goldfish. One of them is white and black and gold and even has a streak of silver. She thinks a cat is catching her fish, so we put an old door over the pond and tomorrow, we're going to build a barrier to protect the fish..."

"Lexi. Can you give me one minute to get inside first?" G.F. kicked his boots off on the porch and scratched his head while nudging his daughter through the door enough he could get into the house. "Why is it so hot in here? Someone turn the air up again?"

"Theo said it isn't working." Lexi trailed him into the living room. "We put fans on. Tomorrow, we're building a little wall around the pond with a mesh fence she said they wouldn't climb over because their claws would get stuck and I'm going to try to catch the cat and make friends with it and..."

"We're not getting a cat, as I told you. Where's your brother?"

"I know, but Fran said..."

"Alexis. *Where* is Theo?"

"He's not home. He was, but he went out. He should be back..."

"Out? He's supposed to be in charge." G.F. stomped back to the stairs. "*Justin.*"

"He's getting ready for practice."

"Season's over."

"Special one, with a meeting, he said. He's about to leave, just waiting for you since Theo's not here, but Frankie and I are okay by ourselves. We're not babies."

"Isn't it your turn for dinner?"

"Oh. I just got home. Fran dropped me off like two minutes before you got here, maybe five. Anyway, she said I could keep the cat..."

"*Stop* with the cat, would you? I said *no*."

Lexi got that look on her face, opened and closed her mouth, and ran upstairs to her room.

He sighed and scratched his head. His eyes still burned. He'd lost probably ten pounds of sweat, ran out of water in his big thermos since the new guy hadn't thought to bring any and downed it like it was 200 degrees rather than ninety. The back of his hand burned where the asphalt slipped past his glove and shirt. And he was starving since he hadn't gone to Fran's for lunch since she had errands that wouldn't wait, so he'd made do with the trail mix he carried and took a short lunch to make up for the longer ones he'd been taking.

And Theo wasn't home. And no one had done anything about dinner.

Going to grab the phone, he cursed when it was again not on the charger, searched a bit, halted Justin when he tried to run out the door with a quick "be back later" to question him about the special practice and to ask where the phone was, which the boy didn't know, and yelled up to Frankie.

He appeared at the top of the stairs. "Yeah?"

"Yeah? You mean, yes, dad? how was your day, dad?"

"Okay."

Gritting his jaw, he forced a deep breath. "Have you fed the dog yet?"

"No."

"Are you doing your homework?"

"No."

"Is it done?"

"No."

"Any idea where the phone is?"

"Yeah."

He waited. And gritted his teeth again. "Where is the phone, Frankie?"

"I have it."

"You know, I don't want to know why. Just bring it to me, feed the dog, and get on your homework."

"It's hot in here."

"Thank you for the observation. I'll look at it. Bring me the phone."

The boy sighed hard and disappeared, came back with it in his hand, and trudged down the stairs as though he was the one who'd worked out on the road all day instead of sitting in the air conditioned school staying late for makeup work since he hadn't bothered to do his work the past few weeks. "Understandable," the school counselor said, with the "marital issues" that threw kids off, *having* to move back in with him after being with their mother for so long, with the woman looking at him like it was his fault.

First things first. He called the pizza place for delivery, offering a nice tip if it was fast, then went to look at the A/C unit. With any luck, he'd be able to fix it. And then he'd deal with his moody daughter. Before he did, he had to prepare himself for her tears so he wouldn't give in and let the kid bring another animal into the house.

Fran smiled when she heard his truck pull in and went out to meet him.

He slammed the truck door, opened the one behind him, pulled out a pizza box, and slammed that door, too. "Hey, sorry I'm so late."

"Bad day?"

"Won't even go there. At least the house is cooling back down. A/C had to go out on the hottest day of the year, so after sweating my ass off all day, I had to spend an hour fixing that, yet. Brought dinner since Lexi didn't bother to do anything about it, although it was her night."

"Oh, that's probably my fault. I didn't get her home as early as I planned."

"It's fine. But about the cat you said she could try to make friends with... I can't have one more animal in the house. Can't do it."

"I didn't tell her she could take it home. I said she could make friends with it here if it was willing and it could hang around and keep mice away for me."

He shoved a hand through his hair. "Hell. No wonder she got so upset. I didn't give her time to tell me all that."

Taking the box, she set it on the little wrought iron scrolled table she'd bought, along with the new fish and a fish pond barrier, and slid her arms over his shoulders. "I was thinking about you out in this heat all day."

"Yeah, my eyes are burning like hell from the sweat mixed with chemicals dripping into them all day, and I burned the back of my hand. I'm getting too old for this by now."

"Old?" She pulled back enough to scan his close enough to perfect body. "You're not nearly old. But since you've had enough heat, come inside and cool off and I'll do what I can for your eyes..."

"Cool off? You don't have an HVAC in this thing, do you?"

"No. There's a small wood stove for winter and I picked up a portable A/C unit for the worst of summer. I don't mind heat unless it's close to a hundred, or far too humid, but I figured you might appreciate not being too hot tonight. Come inside, George."

His head tilted. "You're letting me in?"

"For the cool air. Don't get any ideas."

A slight grin said it was too late for that. He picked up the box. "I'm starving, so I'm not going to fuss. Nice table. New?"

"Yes. I figured it would be nicer than using the chair as a table when I'm entertaining outdoors."

"No room on your porch for that."

"Not yet. But Lexi said she knows a couple of strong boys good with a hammer that could come help me out this summer while they're off school and need to stay busy."

"Fran. You don't need to hire my kids. I already appreciate that you're spending time with Lexi..."

"I know darn well I don't have to, but there are some things I can't do myself and I'll have to hire someone."

"I can..."

"No. I will not take advantage. I'll pay them. If they're interested. If not, I'll find someone else."

"They'll be interested. I may have to supervise that kind of a project, though. And you'll need a permit..."

"Already have that. Supervise as you wish, but it's your boys I'm hiring. Before you say anything else, I'll feel much better having them out here working than someone I don't know at all."

"Yeah. Me too."

With a grin, she ran fingers down the front of his clean T-shirt, grasped his hand, and led him to her door.

"Let me call Lexi real quick." G.F. pulled his phone out as Fran held the door to allow him in to ... not a shack. A cottage. Sticking it back in his pocket, he scanned the whites, creams, and teals, the new shelving on the walls, the plush pillows on the oversized couch he would have thrown out if it was his place that was now covered, small vertical blinds that matched the shelves beside the windows, extending the look of the windows, bird figurines, not cheap ones, but real-looking beautifully painted figurines, and paintings of birds and flowers hung on the walls.

"Um, I'm ... speechless. You did all of this yourself?"

"Well, I have stacks of stuff in the greenhouse I need to get rid of and I haven't finished the kitchenette and bathroom yet, but yes."

"How'd you get everything to match like this? I can't even find the right pillows for Lexi's room, so she says."

"I made it. It's easier to find just the right fabric than just the right pre-made store-bought things."

"Didn't know you could sew."

"There's a lot I can do you don't know about. I'll be back in a minute. Make yourself comfortable."

With a grin, he wandered over to a painting featured on the main wall. Hydrangeas and lilies. With the texture of an oil painting, but not signed. When she returned, standing close, he shook his head. "Beautiful artwork and perfect with everything. Doesn't look commercial."

"It's not."

"You had it done to match."

"Something like that, and it's not fully dry, so don't touch it. Let me see your hand."

He tried to tell her it was fine, but she took it and rubbed something lightly over the burn from a white plastic jar. "Should I ask what that is?"

"Aloe and Frankincense in coconut oil, for healing and soothing. It should help with that burn pretty fast."

"Already feels better."

"Good. Come sit down and lean your head back." She showed him a clear dropper bottle with a label he couldn't read. "For your eyes."

"What is it?"

"Distilled water and green tea. Don't worry. I use it all the time when I come in from the garden. It won't hurt."

Obeying, since he figured she knew what she was doing, George lowered onto the old couch, a comfortable thing he could nearly fall asleep on, and leaned his head back. From behind, she held one eye open to apply the rinse, then the other, and blotted them with a tissue.

"Better?"

"Amazingly? Yes."

"Good. Take it with you. I have another." She capped it and handed it to him. "So, iced coffee? You want it with your pizza or after?"

"Whichever you want." Finally calm enough, and cool enough, he caught her hand and pulled her around in front of him, between his legs. She was dressed nice, in a pale yellow sleeveless blouse over a yellow and rust striped flowing skirt. "You always dress so nice to go shopping?"

"No. I changed. Showered, and then changed, so I wouldn't smell. It is hot today."

"You smell pretty damned good, actually."

"Good. So does the pizza. And I'm starving, too."

"Guess I won't ask for what. Yet."

She reminded him that he was going to call Lexi, but he decided it would wait till he got home and could apologize in person. Instead, while they ate, he asked about her day, if his daughter had behaved well, and offered help with her fish pond reconstruction. She planned to put up a chicken wire fence and surround it with small shrubs and flowering vines. He figured it would work if she could get it to stay up well enough without adding a top post that a cat could jump up on and then over. She was still working on that part of the plan and said she'd gladly take suggestions.

"Let me think about that a bit. This is incredible." He took another good swallow of the iced coffee. "What's in it?"

"Homemade lavender syrup."

"Really?"

"And real cream."

"Nice. I may come over every night for this."

With a smile, she got up to clear the little square table just outside the kitchenette and planted a quick kiss on his lips. He caught her hand, pushed his chair back, and pulled her onto his legs. Dropping the plates she'd picked up back onto the table, Fran wrapped her arms over his shoulders and let her body melt in against his. A luscious, sensuous, lingering kiss. The woman was driving him nearly insane with her flirting and resisting, the way she let him see her dirty and wind-blown and then dressed up for him smelling of ... something floral but not frilly.

"Hm. Okay." She gave him a curious, teasing look. "I have dessert. Ready for that now, or you want to wait until dinner settles?"

"Frannie, the places my mind is going right now, you might want to clarify."

"Dessert, George. As in homemade apple raspberry pie. We stopped at the store on the way home, which is why we were later than we should have been. You have a couple of bins of raspberries at your place, too. Lexi said you like them."

Speechless for a moment, he stared until he could sort his thoughts well enough to find his tongue. "I have to ask. Why are you doing all of this?"

"All of what?"

"Oh. Treating me like I'm... like..." Like she had to bribe him to stay, but he didn't want to say that.

"Like I enjoy your company? I do enjoy your company."

"Okay, but... hell, only my mother has ever spoiled me like this, and the kids get most of that by now. So..."

"So maybe it's time someone did. And, just because I want to. Because you've made me not detest being here again while I have to be, as I did before you decided to force your presence on me. No other motive than that. Dessert now or later?"

Unable to answer, he pulled her back in against his body and kissed the side of her head. Move away? No. She could not.

Fourteen

Fran wandered into the greenhouse, out the side door to the little garden, and lowered onto the stone bench in the center. Why had her father put the bench in the center and the fire pit to one side, between the raised planters? It would make far more sense to put benches on the inside of the planters, letting the planter walls be back rests as they faced the fire in the middle. It would be a nice conversation center that way.

But her father had never been a big conversationalist, other than when he was trying to teach someone something, whether or not they wanted to be taught. And he'd never done things the way others did. He danced to his own tune, as people said when they were trying to be nice about it.

George had talked with her about him the night before while they had coffee with dessert, this time a strawberry banana bread made with buckwheat in place of half the flour and honey rather than sugar to keep it healthier. It was nice to bake for someone who truly appreciated the effort.

When Virgil Barrett heard George was doing construction work on the side, with his own father, he'd walked up to the door, refused to go in since he wasn't invited, and asked for any scraps that would get thrown out otherwise.

Fran shoved a hand through her hair with a grimace. The nerve of begging. She could just hear her mother throwing a hissy. And Fran agreed. George only shrugged and said he was far happier taking it to Virgil than dumping it off somewhere to be burned. She told him he probably burned some of it, anyway, since hardwood ash was good soil additive for certain plants. He'd laughed, said it was at least still useful.

He hadn't minded doing it. Not only that, but he'd enjoyed talking to her father. He'd offered to tell Fran what her father said when he spoke of her, but she refused. It was between them. Not her business.

Probably, a lot of the ash from wood George had carted to the shack was now in the soil helping the flowers and herbs.

Sipping her first cup of morning coffee while she pulled a few new weeds, Fran considered the way he hadn't tried to come into her place since the other night when it was her idea. He was always content sitting on the front porch talking. That was something she and Cal hardly ever did – just talk. They communicated as needed but hardly more than that.

George was a talker. About anything or about nothing. She imagined it might get on her nerves after a while. For now, it was nice. His voice was soothing, deep and soft but not so soft she had trouble hearing him like she did with Cal. Maybe that's why they hadn't talked much. It was annoying to both of them, her for not being able to hear him well, although her ears were good, and him for having to repeat himself so often.

Nine years, Francis. Let it go already.

George had asked what she'd been doing since she left home. She'd skirted around the question, mentioned some translating jobs. That was all from the W.C. era ... *With Cal.* A joke she'd come up with to try to laugh off how much of that time was down the toilet. She shared with it with George and he got a kick out of it, but he also eyed her as though wondering why she would have thrown all that time away. He had the kids, he'd said, which made the Justine years not all bad, and they weren't all bad, anyway. They'd had fun times. Play times. Family time. Much of the time they got along fine.

Fran couldn't quite say the same. She kept busy. Worked a lot of hours. Made good money as a translator, part of the time in D.C. at an embassy since her French and German were perfect and her Italian was decent. Her Spanish was good, but there were plenty of fluent bilingual English/Spanish speakers, so she focused on the others.

Cal got her into it. When he left, she quit.

The rest of it, she hadn't admitted to George yet. Even Cal didn't know her secret passion. She was awfully glad now she hadn't shared it with him. He'd laughed enough about her *farm girl* skills.

"Stop reminiscing and get to work, Fran. Too much to do to

lollygag." Her father's voice came to her as she said it. His word. He loved to lollygag, but only after his work was done.

The weather had cooled and felt like rain, so she decided to work inside instead of in the gardens. The main area was all painted by now, leaving the kitchen spur, as she'd taken to calling it, the little bathroom, and the loft. She was doing them all in cream to keep it open and light. And she found herself picking up only teal in different shades for accents and decorations. She'd have to choose one more color. Two didn't work. Any decorating plan needed three.

G.F. shucked his soaked jacket onto the front porch along with his soaked boots and walked in on a yelling match between Frankie and Lexi. "*Knock it off.*" His voice boomed through the room and he was infinitely thankful for the silence it brought. For about three seconds.

Rolling his eyes, he went in farther to find the perpetrators and pulled the boy out of the girl's face. "What's going on?"

They both answered at once, about some stupid television show or the other and a video game, and he lost all patience. "Fine. No TV and no games for either of you this weekend. Problem solved." Of course it brought whining and arguing until he took each one by the shoulder and sent them up to their rooms until they could talk like humans instead of cawing crows.

He'd had enough cawing from Jim all day at work. Every freaking time it rained any little bit, the man threw a shit fit all day long. If it was up to G.F., he'd fire the whiner and put someone in the job who actually wanted it. But it wasn't. Yet. He was thinking of putting in for the boss man's job when the guy retired in a couple of years. He'd earned it. He figured it was his if he wanted it, even if it meant a desk job which he thought he didn't want. Maybe he did. At least he wouldn't come home soaked and chilled or soaked with near heat stroke. There was that.

After a quick shower, he threw dinner together since it was his turn, and listened to more bickering along with a request to please not leave Theo in charge again because he was more interested in talking to his girlfriend on the phone than...

"Wait." G.F. set his fork down. "Why are you on the phone when you're supposed to be in charge?"

His oldest shrugged. "You won't let me have her here when you're not and you're never home anymore, so I have to at least talk to her during the week."

"I'm home every night…"

"Yeah, to rush through dinner and rush out to your girlfriend's. Not that I think you shouldn't have one. You should. But really, Dad, you still have us, too, and I'm going to lose *my* girlfriend if I can't ever see her." Theo shoved mashed potatoes from a box into his mouth.

"Go ahead. See your girl tonight if she's free. I'm not going out."

Lexi looked up wide-eyed. "You didn't break up with Fran already?"

"Nope. Just admitting Theo is right and I need to stay home with my beautiful children." He saw the eye-rolling, except from his daughter who said he should invite her over instead of just ditching her, that they all had their chores done and the house looked okay and…

"Alright. I'll ask her. If, by raise of hands, or shrugs of shoulders, none of you will be offended about sharing your Dad time." He listened to the murmurs that sounded like agreement or disinterest and asked whose turn it was to do dishes as he got up to call her. Before he walked away, he told Theo he wanted to chat about this girl of his before he went anywhere.

"Come on, Dad. I know the rules. I'm just gonna invite her to play disc golf and then grab a sundae at DQ. In a group. Just Paul and Billy and their girls and us. Call their parents if you want. Not like they don't already know how overprotective you are."

"Alright, don't get smart. Heaven forbid I want you to be smarter than I was."

"You just contradicted yourself, you know."

"It was an expression, boy. Go on and have fun, but not too much fun. Just remember…"

"She's not that kind of girl, Dad."

"Good. Maybe you should bring her over this weekend. To hang out. I'll do a barbeque. She can bring her parents, if you want."

"Yeah? Sounds good. I'll ask. It'll have to be tomorrow since we have to do Mom's Sunday."

"I remember. See what she says and we'll go from there." Shaking his head at his son getting so old overnight, he rang Fran. She didn't answer, so he left a quick message with an invitation to come over and went to get his chores done before she came, if she did.

Fran stopped waiting for his truck to pull in sometime before nine. The rain, she supposed. Not a good night to sit on the small dilapidated front porch. She would have let him in, though. She'd even put her canvases and paints in the greenhouse so she could let him in.

She fought disappointment at losing the excuse to let him in, and to show him how much more she'd done with the place in the past three days. It was looking pretty cozy, she had to admit.

Figuring she'd earned the right to sit and relax on the old soft couch with its new dark teal slip covers and overstuffed cream and light teal pillows, Fran started water for tea. Getting up again, she went to her little shelf stereo and wished it had better sound as she loaded Stevie Ray Vaughan's *Texas Flood*.

It was nice to sit alone and immerse herself into the downpour of Vaughan's rich emotions and gorgeous guitar work.

For the first time since leaving South Dakota, she missed having a piano available. She hoped her renters were taking good care of her old spinet, a rather inexpensive little thing more valuable for sentimental reasons than otherwise, but it was hers. Her father bought it for her when she expressed interest. Finding practice time when her mother wouldn't have to hear it had been a challenge, but she managed.

George didn't know that yet, either, that she'd expressed interest because she'd heard him play. She was still frustrated that she couldn't make it sound like he did, that it sounded more like technique than like art, but still, she was fairly proficient with the technique. Enough to teach piano for the past ten years after leaving the translator career. At the local grade school. On the cheap light-stained wood upright that was more functional than beautiful.

Fran scanned the cottage for any possible space she could put the little spinet. It could go where her father's cot had been, she supposed, but she'd have to rearrange the furniture, pushing the couch nearly against the wall. While she pondered, she found herself moving along with *Love Struck Baby*, since it was impossible not to move along with it.

At the song change, she went to get her tea and sank down into the sofa, closing her eyes to shut out the rain and the fact that George hadn't come over, and absorbed into the blues.

Fifteen

With Buddy Guy playing in the background, Fran lost track of time as she worked on her newest canvas: a piano with a boy propped on the bench, his fingers on the keys. From memory. The boy's hair was giving her the most trouble, possibly because she couldn't pin down the color of George's hair. Brownish blondish reddish ... depending on the light source of the moment. These days the blond showed more, highlights from working in the sun, she expected. At night on her porch, though, it looked very dark. Barely touched his neck. His chin was always smooth, although when he came for lunch, she could see the start of whiskers growing back. His small mustache was always carefully trimmed.

Of course the boy in the painting didn't have whiskers or a mustache. He was a Freshman. The last time she'd heard him play.

Stopping for a moment to stretch, Fran looked over at the wall clock, one with actual hands and no numbers, then looked back at it. Ten till two. Sunday. "Hell." She was covered in paint and hadn't bothered to shower yet and his concert was about to start.

Saturday morning she realized she'd forgotten to turn her phone on the day before and found his message. She'd called and he didn't answer. He'd called later that night and said they'd had practice and errands and such all day and he was barbecuing for the kids and some of their friends who would likely stay too late to allow him to leave, but she could come over and join them. After his Friday night message about hanging with his kids to catch up on time with them, Fran decided to leave them alone Saturday night, also.

But she wanted to go to the community concert.

Rushing through the shower with her hair up to keep it dry, Fran threw on the most wear-ready thing she could find and dashed out the door. Again, she had to park farther away than she would have liked. The music grew louder as she walked closer. Passing the picnic table off to the side of the shelter, she got a whiff of pizza from the table full of kids sitting there and realized she hadn't thought about lunch, either. Her stomach growled, but she wasn't leaving until he was done.

She sat in the same place as the week before, under the same tree. George didn't notice her that she could tell. And that was fine. There wasn't much better than sitting out on the vivid green grass under shade of an old bent oak listening to luscious music, especially when you had a very special interest in one of the musicians to make it more personal. It did feel very personal. Even if George didn't know she was there, it felt like he was playing for her.

A self-centered thought, she told herself. Still, the saxophone's rich flavor sank deeply into her soul. It did belong to her since she felt it so deeply. It belonged to anyone who truly felt it.

George didn't quite belong to her, but she did have those incredible kisses in her forever memory, or so she hoped, at least as long as she had memory, and his arms – his very strong sexy arms that surrounded her when she allowed. She hoped she would never forget that.

It ended far too soon since she'd arrived so late and Fran sat watching him as he packed his instrument and talked with his fellow musicians and as he was stopped a dozen times or so, lingering with smiles or laughs, or trying to brush them off; it was easy to see who he liked and who he didn't and she put that in her to-remember cap.

Finally, he headed off toward his truck, so she got up to intercept. It took her some time, since he walked faster and was either avoiding more talk or had somewhere to be. Fran hoped he didn't have somewhere to be. It was supposed to be his day without the kids, and selfishly, she wanted the rest of it with him if possible.

He was looking at the ground while he walked, unusual for him, so she touched his arm to get his attention.

He startled slightly and recovered quickly. "Didn't know you were here."

"I was late. Got busy working and lost track of time. I wish I hadn't. It ended far too soon that way."

With a slight nod, he opened the back door and put the

instrument inside.

"In a hurry to leave?"

"Nah, just … figured I'd get some work done on the house today since I have time."

"And no kids."

"Right. For a few hours yet."

"How about dinner first? We can make it quick. My treat. Or if you want an excuse not to work on the house…"

"Maybe another time." He opened the front door.

"Are you angry with me?"

He paused, then turned. "What are we doing here, Frannie?"

"What do you mean?"

"I mean if you're going to avoid my children like they have the plague or something, other than Lexi since she's throwing herself at you, this isn't gonna work. So let's call it like it is…"

"I'm not." She ambled closer, watching him. "I'm not avoiding them, George. I'm trying not to interfere."

"Not interfere? Too damned late for that." Without warning, he leaned down and kissed her hard. Then he caught her eyes. "You know how much they ask me about you? You know how much I think about you? How, Friday night when it was storming and I was pacing all over the house because Theo was out with his girl and driving and I was a nervous wreck until he got home … how I wished you were there pacing with me and telling me I was being ridiculous and overprotective and … and you wouldn't even answer your damned phone, how irked I was?"

"I forgot it wasn't on. I told you that."

"Yeah well, the fact that you can forget tells me you're not thinking half as much about me as I am…" He stopped and grabbed a deep breath. "Like I said, what are we doing?"

Fran held her tongue for the few moments she needed to gather herself, as she'd learned to do instead of saying something stupid or saying nothing at all. This time, though, saying nothing seemed the best thing, so she turned and walked away.

She was halfway back to her car, fuming to herself, ready to finish what needed to be done so she could get the hell out of Storm Lake and find somewhere else to be when strong fingers gripped her arm and she turned, ready to...

"I'm sorry."

He looked sorry, but she waited. Silent.

"Frannie, I..."

"I hate being called that."

"We're back to that now?"

"George, what do you want?"

"I want you to stay. I want this to matter to you enough you'll even think about staying."

"Stay? We've had a few lunches and a few cups of coffee together. How does that constitute me changing my plans?" She had been considering it, though. Briefly. Off and on.

"We've had a bit more than that." He kissed her. Softly. Only for a second.

"Only a bit." She met his eyes. Daring him. People wandered around them. People he knew. A few she did, but she didn't care. George cared about this place, these people, a lot of them, anyway...

"Maybe we should work on that. I've missed you the past couple of days." Returning to her lips, he slid a hand around her head, the other around her back. A longer kiss, still decent for being in public. "Better?"

"People are staring."

"Don't care in the slightest."

"Well, that's nice, but..."

"But?" He was close, holding her gaze, calling her dare, or her bluff.

"But ... you can't just expect me to play happy step-mother to your kids I hardly know because it's what you want. You can't expect me to be at your beck and call twenty-four hours a day. I've done that. I'm not doing it again. If I want my phone off, that's my business. We're not..."

"I know. You're right. That's why I caught up with you. To tell you I was wrong..."

"Yeah? Because this sure feels like I'm being blamed for just... I'm not sure exactly. I haven't lied to you. I haven't tried to make myself look like someone you want or need or..." She paused when someone she barely recognized came over and told him how great it sounded and how sad they'd be when the summer concerts ended.

He brushed them off as soon as he could do it politely and slid his fingers down to hers, gripping them gently. "I know. I just think we've wasted too much time already. Years. With the wrong people. I'm too old to waste time these days."

"That doesn't mean I'm okay with being rushed."

"I know that, too. And Mom told me to back off, to not get pushy, as I tend to do..."

"Your mom? You told your mom ... what, exactly?"

"That we're seeing each other." He shrugged. "Aren't we? They wanted to come today, by the way, but she's fighting some summer virus and didn't want to spread it."

His mom. His parents. Fran felt her head shake. Too much too soon. He was revving his engine far too high too fast, as he so often did after school while showing off. Her father often said the boy was hard as salt on steel when it came to vehicles, that he'd have to learn to settle himself down before he was fit to ... to be tied down to a decent girl.

A warning? Fran had taken it that way. Maybe it was.

"Your offer of having dinner with me still good?"

Fran startled out of her thoughts. Dinner. "I don't know. Maybe you should get your housework done like you planned and..."

"Come on, Frannie. You offered." He leaned close and squeezed her hand. "We can grab chicken salad from Grand Central and a couple of cups of better coffee than I make and head down to Circle Park to eat. Casual enough?"

Sandwiches and coffee outside. That was more like it, more fitting for where they were in the relationship. "Do you mind wandering the tree museum since we'll be right there? Don't laugh. I know there are trees everywhere, but..."

"Fine with me. I'll have to admit I've never bothered."

"I think most local people haven't, and yet tourists come just to look at them. Sad, really."

"I'm sure every place has the same kind of thing."

"Maybe, but I don't understand it. I always explore everything interesting I can find wherever I'm living."

"Well. As I've said, you're different than most. So maybe you'll have to be a tour guide to my own hometown, if you can stand it."

"Which? Touring the place I don't want to be, or spending that much more time with you?"

A chuckle came from deep within his chest. "Touché, mon ami. I suppose we'll just have to see how it goes."

"Exactement comment je vis ces jours-ci." At his raised eyebrows, she started walking toward her car.

Fran stopped in front of a rather plain-looking tree, as far as he was concerned, and he checked the sign. "Kentucky Coffee?"

"Ornamental, though, or possibly male."

"Male?" He couldn't hide a smirk. "How do you know a *tree* is male?" He made a show of scanning the trunk looking for proof of its maleness.

"You're being a teenager again. There's no fruit, in June, a good thing with this one since the pods and seeds are poisonous." She caressed a long, thin leaf. "I should put a couple in the yard. Females, though, so they'll bear fruit."

At that, he stopped. "Who do you plan to poison?"

She looked over him as though just realizing he was there after hardly saying a word while they ordered their sandwiches and coffee barely before Grand Central closed – Sunday hours, he'd forgotten – and as they wandered the little park. "They're not poisonous when they're roasted right."

"So you want to grow your own coffee beans?"

"It's not actually coffee, just a kind of seed that can be used as a substitute. A legume. Not a great substitute, I've heard, but..."

"Then why not just plant real coffee?"

"In Iowa? I could do it in the greenhouse if I was going to be here for a few years, but it still wouldn't be great coffee with artificial conditions. Kentucky Coffee trees are rare. Planting them helps the species survive."

He didn't quite get the point of planting something in your yard that had poisonous fruit, or why it mattered if such a thing survived, but he left it alone as she started walking again.

A shiver ran through his spine at the thought of her wanting to plant a poisonous tree in her yard. Could be he should be more wary. As she'd pointed out, he didn't know her well yet. *Exactly the way I live these days.* She'd said it in French and George knew she didn't realize he understood, but he decided to keep that information to himself for the moment. She lived day to day? Seeing what would happen? He couldn't imagine. He had to have specific goals and plans in order to get anything done. What had she done other than what she'd admitted so far? He knew there was more. He also knew she didn't want to say.

The *Little House* tree was kind of cool, he supposed, as well as the Bunker Hill tree and the Isaac Newton apple tree, if the story about the apple falling on Newton's head was true, and he had his doubts. A lot of it was kind of cool, or at least the stories of where they came from were, if you chose to believe them, and obviously Fran did. Maybe her father believed it, in which case, George might have to reconsider. He'd have a hard time not believing Virgil Barrett about trees, or history.

He checked his watch when she moved back to the path. "I'm going to have to head over to pick up my kids in a few."

"I thought Justine dropped them off."

"Supposed to. Said something about car issues. Not worth the argument."

She nodded and lowered to a bench, her coffee between her hands. He'd finished his long ago.

"Fran." He crouched in front of her and rested his forearms over her knees. "How about coming over tonight?"

"Don't you need the time with your kids?"

"Did that all day yesterday and the night before. They'll be sick of having to be with their parents by tonight and they'll all scatter up to their rooms or somewhere. Unless you come. Then they might stick around out of curiosity. So you'd be helping me out."

"Well, that's an interesting line." She looked up at a couple of birds chasing each other until they landed on two different branches close together. "Listen to me talking about planting trees. Why would

I do that here?"

"Yeah, I was wondering that myself. Maybe you're part thinking about not leaving?"

She met his eyes. Quiet. Thoughtful. "There are too many bad memories here, George. I don't..."

"Memories don't leave because you move."

"Yes, they can, actually. Try it."

Try it? He shrugged. "Guess I don't have any bad enough to make me want to leave them and run, or to make it worth uprooting my kids. Couldn't go far anyway, without permission from the court. Custody issues and all."

She nodded again and stood, heading back to their separate vehicles. He couldn't get a straight answer about whether she'd come over, so he left it as an open invitation.

<h1 style="text-align:center">sixteen</h1>

His boys were doing an amazing job on her front porch. They'd started right after school let out for the summer and had been there every day it wasn't raining. George had come by every day for lunch to supervise and help with pointers and he went straight to her place when he was off work to see how it was going.

In the meantime, Lexi was helping with her pond and came up with the idea of making a clothesline-like rope a couple of feet outside the edge of the pond that would be tied to the chicken wire to hold it up. The wire wasn't attractive, but Fran already had vines planted around it. When they filled in, it would make a nice little sheltered area for an outdoor reading nook.

It was a little tricky to do, but George helped them out and got the lines tight enough on the posts he helped dig into the ground, with just a touch of concrete to hold them, that it worked. He'd also put in the post holes for the porch, helped Theo and Justin mix the concrete since it had to be just the right amount of mix and water in order to set strong enough, and did much of the roof work himself. He did it during lunch and after work and Fran fussed at him about needing to rest on his time off, but he assured her he was just fine.

He talked about the idea of putting a back porch on the place, also, and screening it in for more living space, to make it more rentable, so he said. Maybe she would. That would take more time, though. She wasn't sure about going all that far.

She'd picked up a small bag of cat food to help Lexi in her quest to befriend whatever stray was getting into her pond, but so far, although the bowl was empty every morning, neither of them saw whatever was eating it. Fran suspected it was more likely a possum or coon, so they stopped feeding the thing.

By Friday, her porch was together enough to put the little table and chair set on it, with cushions for the chairs and a glass top for the metal scroll-work table, so she and George could sit more comfortably and not worry about falling through. Theo and Justin were out on a double date, and George was nearly beside himself that both boys were now dating. Frankie and Lexi were staying over at their grandparents.

For herself, Fran was simply glad to have him to herself for the night without worrying about taking him from his kids.

"How about this tonight instead of coffee?" She set a couple of bottles of Dunkelweizen on the table and offered an opener.

"Beer? You drink beer?"

"Only select varieties. This one's German. Dunkels means dark wheat. It has kind of a clove and banana flavor to it. Want to try mine first?"

"Nope. I trust you completely." He popped the lid off her bottle and handed it to her, then did his own.

Fran felt her eyebrows raise. "Ich bin mir nicht sicher das ist eine gute idee."

He paused on the way to taking a swallow and scratched his chin. "You know, when you correct my grammar in English, at least I understand what you said." With a good swallow as though he knew he'd like it, he nodded. "Yeah. I could get used to this okay, too."

"Not terribly particular, are you?" She sipped her own.

"Why? Is this Germany's version of a cheap college kid's drink?"

"No. It's a good one. I wouldn't serve you cheap stuff."

Studying her face, he took her hand and kissed her fingers. "Actually, I am pretty particular these days. Always was, really. Before you mention Justine, I never intended to get stuck with her. Just happened."

"She planned to get you stuck. It was fully intentional on her part."

"Probably. Either way, I got four great kids out of it, so there is that, and they're worth the rest of it."

With a nod, Fran took a larger swallow.

"So." He released her hand and kicked back, with one ankle over the other. "You never wanted to have kids of your own?"

There it was: the conversation she didn't want to have. With a shrug, she took another swallow. "Never got married. And I know that's not a prerequisite, especially these days, but I've kept busy and, well, it didn't happen."

"Guess it would be less likely when he wasn't so available."

"And when he tried so hard not to. Not once did he forget to ask if I'd used my protection, along with his."

"Can't say I could see him as a father type, not that I saw him much at all."

"No. Not something I'd want to do to a child. So it was mutual, in a way."

George stared a while, as though wondering if he should say whatever he was thinking.

"I know. I shouldn't have done it to myself, either. Still, it wasn't all bad. I got to travel a lot. His business took him everywhere. I even spent a good bit of time in Germany, which was nice. Technically, I was his translator. The company paid me to be there. Die Deutschen machen viel spaß, die meisten von ihnen. Sie sind geradlinig und haben einen sinn für humor, den sie nicht erraten würden."

"Okay. I caught *German*. Deutschen is German, yes?"

"Yes. I said they're a fun people, straight-forward with a heck of a sense of humor. I met a group not related to his company that was glad to let me hang out with them when I wasn't working. We went to a kegel club, which is their version of bowling. Personally, I like it better. The balls are smaller and easier to hold onto. And of course, you can't possibly kegel without a pint in your other hand."

He threw her a smile. "Never would have guessed you were running around Germany drinking and bowling."

"I never would have expected it, either." During a short lull, Fran set her gaze out on the horizon. Red lines shot through the low clouds, leaving pink traces filtered through the fast-darkening sky. A light breeze tossed the scent of her peppermint up around them. It had filled in nicely, enough she'd be able to freeze some in ice cubes to use during the winter... or to leave with George so they could use them during the winter.

"So where did you live when you weren't traveling? Vegas?"

Fran nearly choked on her beer, between her suddenly interrupted thoughts and the notion he might actually believe the rumors. "I have no idea where that rumor came from. I've never been there."

"No? That's where Cal said he was taking you, according to your father."

She stared until she could find her voice. "He told my father he was taking me to Vegas?"

"To elope."

Her head shook of its own accord. "Maybe he expected my father would let it go if he thought Cal was making me honest, so to speak. No, he's from South Dakota. That's where I've been most of the time. Beautiful place, not as green as I like, but the rock formations are just incredible. I got to see Mount Rushmore and the Crazy Horse memorial. They're both indescribable."

"Yeah." He took a couple of large swallows.

"You've been?"

"Years ago. Family vacation. I should take the kids."

"You should. Be sure to take them to a Pow Wow on one of the reservations while you're there. It's quite an experience."

He was silent for some time, looking out over her gardens and watching a passing car until he couldn't see it any longer. Then he heaved a deep breath. "You plan to move back there?"

"I don't know."

He looked over, waiting.

"I'm ... I brought everything with me that I wanted to keep. I haven't decided yet where I'll go next. I might wander a while."

"Alone."

"Yes. As I have been the past nine years."

"You don't get tired of being alone, Frannie?"

"Of course. But I'd rather be alone than to fall into another trap. I'm too old to do that again, as you would say."

"Thirty-nine isn't all that old. I know I say it, but..."

"Old enough to know better. Unlike nineteen when you feel your whole life ahead of you and..."

"And want to run from what's behind you."

"Right." She took a long swallow from the bottle and set it down. "I think I'll switch to coffee. Want a cup?"

"No, I'm good with this. Thing is..." George bent forward to prop his elbows on his knees, his beer in both hands in front of him. He stared at it. "When you're nineteen, it makes some sense to get out and about and see what else might be there waiting. I get it. Thought of it often enough myself before I got tied down. When you're nearly forty, though, and you're still running from your past, seems to me it's not working well. Maybe looking forward would be more helpful."

"Might be." She stood and picked up her bottle. "But I can't see forward, and when I try, it's far scarier than what I see behind me."

"Why?" He raised his head to meet her eyes.

"Because of my father. Because too many signs point to too many similarities."

"Fran..."

She shook her head and went in to ditch the beer in favor of coffee. Even if he didn't want it, she brought out two mugs. Instead of sitting, she set them both down and moved in front of him, making him sit up, and stroked fingers along his hair. "I'm a 'live in this moment' type, G.F. I know you aren't. I know it would drive you crazy long term. But while I'm here, I very much value our time together. Can you deal with that?"

"Guess I can, since I am. Not like you haven't warned me." He pulled her down onto his leg. "You're not your father, Fran."

"Not yet."

He ran fingers, rough, work-hardened fingers, along her forehead and back into her hair. "Well, as I said, I liked your father a lot. Respected him as much as I do my own. So that's not scaring me."

"That's all fine, but..."

He kissed her. Gently. "And you're a hell of a lot nicer to look at than Virgil was, no offense to him. This..." He met her lips again, teased, then deepened the kiss. "You're definitely not your father."

"Why? Did you kiss him, too?"

"Funny girl." Caressing her head, his chest rose and fell hard. "At least consider that this might not be such a bad place to live now that things have changed. You can still wander. Sometimes we can wander together. I'd love to travel more."

"You're tied down."

"Yeah well, it wouldn't hurt them to get out and about more, either. Haven't done that enough. Not that your kind of wandering fits having four kids tag along. Still…"

"At least my vehicle will fit six people."

He grinned. "It would. Only question would be if you could handle it."

"That, I'm not so sure about. Especially with the dog Lexi talks about."

"Can't even say I blame you. And the dog could stay with my parents while we travel. So it would just be me and the kids till they're old enough to head out on their own."

"They're great kids, George. Still…"

"They are great kids. Still, they are kids. They love to bicker about stupid things. They love to make messes and leave them. They love to harass the hell out of me. And of course in August, they start school again and that pretty well curtails travel for much of the year. But…" He picked up her hand and caressed her fingers, her work-roughened fingers. They weren't pretty and smooth like most women's hands. "My folks would be okay with keeping them for a week here and there. We could still wander a bit. Alone. Together alone."

"George…"

"I know. I'm getting way too far ahead of things. Just want you to consider you might not feel as stuck as you think you might, if you stay. And I think I will switch to coffee with you. It's been a long week and I'm plenty tired already."

He seriously hoped she'd ask him in, but the night was nice enough with a near-constant breeze that sitting on the porch was comfortable, and she didn't make even half a move to get him inside. It was closing in on eleven pretty darn quick, so he'd have to go shortly.

Draining his coffee, he got up and leaned a hand against the railing, admiring Theo and Justin's work. "What stain color are you using on these? I can pick it up for them."

"I'm painting them white."

"Yeah? You sure?"

"It goes with the beach cottage feel."

"Guess it does. Having them do that tomorrow?"

"Tomorrow's Saturday. Don't they have other plans?" She came over and nudged up under his arm, with a hand on his chest.

A nice feeling. He kissed her head... "Oh. Hell. Nearly forgot. Yeah, tomorrow's Lake Fest. We always go. Would you like to join us?"

"Maybe. I can meet you there at some point if I decide to go."

Not quite good enough. He wanted better confirmation. "Or just come along with us. I can pick you up."

"You can't get six in that truck. Not legally."

"Theo can drive, too. It'll give him an excuse." He dropped his arm over her shoulder. "Come with me, Fran."

Looking up into his face, her chest rose with a deep, slow breath, and she let it out just as slowly.

"You're asking me out on a very public date? With your kids? Are you sure?"

"Positive." Setting his free hand over top of hers, on his chest, he leaned closer. "I'd love for you to come with us."

"Okay, then. What time?"

George felt his whole body relax at her okay. "Justin's in the 5K, so we'll be heading out at 7:30, but we'll come back afterward so he can get cleaned up. Say eleven? We always grab lunch there."

"He's a runner?"

"Yep. Third year in the event. Kid's good at track and soccer, not so good at football, but he does it because his brother does."

"And because you did."

"Maybe. I don't push him into it. I want them to follow their own interests."

"Girls are more into football stars than track stars."

He chuckled. "Yeah, that's probably it. Gonna have to watch that one. He's too much like me."

She slid her arms up around his shoulders. "Not a bad thing." Pressing her lips in against his, Fran meshed into his body as much as possible while they were dressed. A car went by and blew its horn, likely a catcall intent, but she paid no attention, so he ignored it, as well. She kissed him so long and so deep, his knees damned near gave out.

"Mm." He planted a soft kiss in front of her ear while he caught his breath. "Lady, you're about to get us into trouble."

"Am I?" She kissed his neck.

"Except I can't stay." He hated to say it and hated the question on her face when she pulled back. "The boys will be home soon. Curfew's eleven. I've gotta be there to see that they are and to ask how things went and all of that."

"Just as well." She stroked fingers softly along his neck. "If I'm going to be ready by seven-thirty, I'll have to push my bedtime up a bit."

"You don't have to..."

"You don't want me there for the race?"

"Oh. Hell, if you want, absolutely. But..."

"I'll be ready by seven." She met his mouth, reclaiming him.

Damn he wanted to stay. Not that she meant for him to stay, but he would have liked to find out if she did. With a groan to let her know he absolutely did not want to leave, he told her good night, forced himself off her porch, and walked backward a few paces before making himself turn to walk right.

Halfway to his truck, he looked back. "What did you say earlier? When I said I trusted you?"

"I said that might not be such a good idea." She leaned against the pole he'd been leaning against.

Not a good idea? He went back to her, standing on the step below so her face was slightly above his. "Yeah? Well, you know what? Too damned late." Wrapping his arms around her waist, he claimed her mouth, and her body to the extent he could, while still on her front porch with the yellow light on and the occasional car driving past.

Her arms went around his shoulders, and one wrapped up around his head, cradling him as she allowed his claim. Unable to resist, he moved a hand up her waist, to her side, teasing the roundness he could reach with his thumb. She released his mouth, set her forehead against his, her chest rising and falling rapidly.

"Damn, I wish I could stay." It was a near whisper as he let his thumb wander further, bringing the other hand to her other side.

"So do I, G.F. But you better go now. You'll miss curfew."

He laughed. He could imagine if they *had* dated back when he had his own curfew, he might have missed it a few times, being as hard as it was to pull away from her.

"Gute nacht. Ich freue mich auf morgen."

"Good night. Okay, I'm going. Is that what you said?"

"I look forward to tomorrow." Pulling back, she gave him a soft smile, and turned to grab the coffee mugs. She was inside with the door closed before he got to his truck.

On the way home, he had to wonder what exactly she'd meant by *So do I*. She meant she wished he could stay all night, or at least longer? Or that she wished she could stay? Hard to tell. She wasn't going to be all that easy to get to know as deeply as he wanted to know her.

Especially if she didn't stay and he had to make do with phone calls and occasional trips to visit her, if she'd allow.

Seventeen

Too many people came over to talk to them, to George, really, but more to be nosy and check out their relationship while she walked around with not only George and his kids, but also with his parents who had come to cheer Justin on. He didn't push anything, didn't slip an arm around her to show possession or act like any more than a friend.

Fran appreciated the space and the way he brushed off questions about them as just catching up with an old classmate. Of course, they asked in front of his children, which was tacky, and it annoyed Frank. The boy apparently was not sold on the idea of his father dating again, or he didn't care for her even if he did like one of her music choices. It was hard to tell.

His parents were pleasant and made her feel welcome, although they didn't talk to her a lot. They didn't talk to George all that much, either. They were entirely wrapped up in the kids. It was sweet, really, but it made Fran regret that she'd never let her parents become grandparents. Her father would have loved it, for as long as he was present enough to have known who they were, anyway. Really, it was just as well that didn't happen. It was hard enough on her. If she had children who got to know him and loved him and he forgot who they were...

"Let's do the bike ride, Dad. Come on." Frank pulled at George's arm.

"You can go if you talk your brother into going with you."

"But... he just ran five miles..."

"Kilometers, not miles. Therefore, the 5K. And I meant the other one. You do still have two brothers." George asked Theo if he was interested.

"Hey, I'm good for a bike ride." Justin shrugged as though the 5K run was nothing, although most of his shirt front was soaked with sweat. Theo agreed to go with them.

"Go ahead, then. One of you stay with Frankie instead of racing each other and forgetting about him."

"No, all of us." Frank tugged on his father again. "The whole family. Lexi is old enough now. Grams and Gramps can come, too."

His grandmother laughed and set an arm around his shoulder. "Sweet one, we appreciate the vote of confidence, but we're past the days of riding bicycles twelve miles around the lake."

"Speak for yourself. I could do it." Her husband pulled his shoulders back and puffed out his chest.

Fran nearly laughed. She could easily see George doing the same in another fifteen years. It struck her that within fifteen years, he could have a handful of grandchildren, also. If Theo was no more careful than he'd been, he could be a grandpa within the next five years.

The thought shook her. Twenty years she'd wasted staying away. "What do you think?"

She realized he was talking to her. "I'm sorry. What?"

"Up for a bike ride?"

"Oh. I don't know. I'm not dressed for that."

George skimmed her loose, long split skirt and shrugged. "Just hike it up enough it won't tangle in the wheels."

"I said *family*, Dad. She's not family."

"Frank, mind your manners." Mr. McKenry jumped the boy before George could.

"He's right. You should take your children on the bike ride." Fran touched his arm. "I'm not dressed for that. Go ahead."

His chest rose and fell as though he did not want to agree, but with his mother saying she and Fran would sit and have coffee and something sweet while the men took the kids to join the ride, it was settled. Lexi tried to stay with her instead, but George insisted the exercise would be good for the girl and Marvin McKenry said if he could do it at almost seventy years old, an eleven-year-old could do it. He partnered up with Lexi so the *young hot shots* could go on ahead if they were too slow.

Expecting to pick something up from a vendor and find somewhere to land until they were done, Fran couldn't quite refuse when Gwen McKenry took her to the Regatta Grille. They sat beside the window, ordered coffee and cinnamon rolls, and Gwen started with an apology for Frankie's rudeness.

"It's fine. I understand completely."

"Do you? Your parents stayed together."

"Yes, but I can't say I didn't feel the same about all of the people who needed my mother to be on this committee or that so she wasn't home much. It's not the same, of course, but I do understand. He needs his dad's attention, especially at his age."

"Yes, and since he's closer to his mother than the other children." Gwen shook her head. "I worry about him. Don't let it give you the wrong impression. Frankie's a sweet boy. He only needs time."

"He is. All of the children are sweet-natured and well-mannered. I'm not at all offended. To be honest, I'm impressed, considering..."

"Considering their mother. No need to beat around the bush. I never liked the girl. We did try to warn George, but you know young men."

"I could hardly fault him, considering my own choices."

"We all have things in our pasts we would change, or at least that we're not proud of. Se la vie." Gwen tossed a light grin. "I often heard about not doing enough within the community, and I often thought they were right. But with three boys, I felt that raising them well would matter more in the long run. I do some volunteer work by now, around my grandchildren. I believe they need and appreciate my time more than any committee or such."

"I'm sure they do. I know George does. I mean that he appreciates how you were always around for him, and still are."

A light grin graced the small face with delicate features. Gwen McKenry didn't look much like a woman who had raised three hardy boys. She had a gentle demeanor and a slight build, in shape, though. She looked healthy and younger than Fran knew she had to be. "George... You know he prefers G.F.?"

"I do know, but to me he's still George. It's hard to call him anything else. To be fair, he still calls me Frannie, which I hate. From anyone else, I do." Fran took a bite of the sweet, light roll flavored with ... vanilla and almond, she thought.

Another nod said Gwen understood more than Fran said. "George has a very kind heart. I worried about him a lot when he was young. Frankie is just like his father. Sensitive. Caring. Theo and Justin are like their uncles, all out there and not easily bothered by much of anything. The divorce was very hard on Frankie. He is very attached to his mother, although heaven knows why. She often put him down for being too much like his father..."

"She didn't." Fran had to force her jaw closed.

"That girl, from the beginning we knew what she was and what she was after. He wouldn't listen. She wanted to be pampered and spoiled and he did far too much of it until she started neglecting the children, and that was the beginning of the end. Those children are his life."

"As they should be, and it shows."

Gwen eyed her, pondering as she cut off another piece of the roll. "I'd love to ask why you don't have children, but I know it's not my place. I suppose I worry about the little ones, the youngest two, since you and George are..."

"Dating. Casually."

A light nod said she expected they were doing a lot more than that.

"He's a nice conversationalist. That's hard to find, at least for me. My interests are ... odd, I suppose, but he's fine with that."

"Odd? He says you've picked up a good bit of gardening experience from your father, and the old shed is looking wonderful. You're doing it yourself?"

"With quite a lot of help from his children. And some from George, also, but he has enough going on, so I try not to bother him with it. The boys have just rebuilt my porch and Lexi..."

"Oh, I know. They said you overpaid them. And Lexi talks of you often."

"I didn't. They earned it. I'm happier with the way it turned out than I expected. They earned every penny."

Silence lapped up between while they enjoyed their rolls and coffee and the view of Storm Lake, the boats that reminded her she hadn't finished her sailboat painting.

"George is hoping you'll stay." Gwen kept her gaze out the window, her voice soft.

"I know."

Her focus moved to Fran. Directly. "He says you plan to move as soon as you rent or sell the house."

"Yes."

"Can I ask you to be careful, then? With the children, Lexi especially. She never had a good relationship with her mother and it sounds like she's trying to substitute you for that. If she thinks... Well, it's a hard age she's heading into and she's every bit as sensitive as Frankie. But also, with George. Justine hit him hard. He's so trusting. He denied the truth for too long and then..."

"I know. I've been nothing but truthful with him, and I told him from the beginning that I wasn't staying."

"Yes, he did say as much."

"I don't want to hurt any of them. I'm trying very hard to be careful."

"Not easy, is it? When you care for him as you do." Gwen gave her a soft grin. "It shows."

Feeling her eyes water all of sudden, Fran took a good swallow of her coffee and looked out over the water. It wasn't such a bad place. Honestly, the place itself was nice. There was the lake, the path around the lake where she used to walk, or bike. The water park, part of it outdoors for warm weather and part indoors for the winter. The university provided arts and theatre. Sioux City was less than two hours away, with its big art center and event center. It was fairly laid back. Not a bad place.

"Francis." Gwen reached over and took her hand. "I know you've had a lot to deal with, and you have every right to go on and do what you need to do. You should. Whatever will make you happiest, you should do that. I only ask that you try to maintain some distance with Lexi, and George, too, until you know what it is you want. Find that out first. George will be here. He won't be rushing into some other woman's arms; I'll guarantee that. Figure out what you want and then see where things stand." She released her hand. "Now, please, let's enjoy every bad calorie of these delicious rolls and then we can go walk some of it off until they're done."

It was the third year of Lake Fest and Fran hadn't expected much, but she was pleasantly surprised. Storm Lake was flaunting all its colors as a good tourist destination.

They'd all gone home to clean up, rest, and eat some incredible barbecue in the backyard, and now they were settled on King Pointe's great lawn waiting for the Parmalee concert to begin. Fran and George and his parents relaxed on folding chairs and Lexi and Frank sat on a blanket in front of them while the sun shimmered its wane across the lake. Theo and Justin were hanging out with friends instead, which likely included Theo's girlfriend and some other girls, and Fran knew George was thinking about what they were doing. Frank pouted about having to sit through a country concert while Lexi tried to hush him and they bickered about whether pop or country was smarter and better until George told them both to hush.

Fran appeased them as well as she could by admitting she liked some of both, but Blues was her music of choice, not because she thought it was better than anything else, but only because it suited her better. That led to Frankie asking about her Maroon 5 shirt and the videos and what happened in the newest video that was really cool...

"I don't watch music videos."

Frank looked at her like she had two heads. "But you like music."

"I like music, not music videos. I have seen a few, but unless it's only the band playing the song and nothing more, I don't want to see it."

"Why?"

"I see the stories of the songs differently than the videos and it ruins the song for me when it doesn't match well enough."

The boy frowned as he considered how such a thing could be true. Luckily, the concert started and Fran sighed a small breath of relief that she wouldn't have to discuss it further. George chuckled under his breath with a knowing grin and claimed her hand. In front of his parents.

It was the most he'd done all day and he glanced over to see if it was all right with her. She squeezed his fingers and leaned in next to his ear to tell him she'd enjoyed the day, and his company. She saw his sturdy chest puff out and release again, and his mother's warning ran through her head.

She wasn't the one who should have received the warning, though. Fran had tried to keep it casual and somewhat distant. It was George pushing the whole thing. Very possibly, Gwen warned her son, also, and it worked as well as when she'd warned her son about Justine.

It was hardly the same, however.

G.F. dropped the kids off at the house, went in to be sure Theo and Justin were awake and knew their siblings were there, and drove Fran on down to her cottage. Unusual for her, she sat in his truck until he got over to open her door and gave her a hand down. "Everything okay? Did my gang wear your nerves to their edges?"

"No."

"No to which, Frannie?" He took a chance and set a hand alongside her face.

"No, they didn't wear my nerves. Not much." She slid in against him and rested her head on his shoulder. Her chest rose and fell and her fingers caressed his side. "You're a very good dad, George. In case you don't realize it, you should. They're lovely children who will be lovely adults."

His eyes clenched and he lowered his head to rest against hers. "Thank you. Not much in the world you could say matters more than that."

"I mean it. It's not a line."

"I know that, Frannie. You're not the line type. You're the blunt truth type. Glad you are. Makes what you say mean more."

"Gets me in trouble, too."

He chuckled. "Yeah, guess it would." With a soft kiss to her head, he backed away. "I should go. Thanks for spending so much time with us today. Too much to expect to see you at the band show tomorrow?"

"I'll be there. Hopefully on time." She teased his fingers with her own, making no movement away from him. "Have time to walk me to the porch?"

"I wouldn't do otherwise."

She rewarded him with a soft grin and kept hold of his fingers, taking her time, and paused at the door.

He took it as a hint and leaned down to meet her soft lips. Her soft, full, very willing lips that pressed hard against his, opening to deepen the kiss as she gripped his shirt at his waist.

"Mm." He rubbed the moisture on his lips together when she released him. "The way you kiss sure makes me wonder how it might be to ... well..."

"You're not coming in tonight."

He chuckled. "Okay. Gotta get home to the kids anyway." With a quick stroke of her hair, he headed down the steps. "See ya tomorrow, Frannie. Have good dreams. They could even be of me if you wanted."

"I wouldn't tell you if they were."

He gave her a smile and waited until she was inside to go the rest of the way to his truck, and on home.

Home was not where he wanted to go, though. He wanted to turn right back around and see if he could change her mind about going in.

Eighteen

She couldn't resist when George asked her to have lunch with him before the concert, although she was trying to get some work done. Today, Fran intended to do a beach painting for the empty spot over the claw foot bath tub since she had no plans to replace the tub with a shower.

Baths were growing on her. She'd even picked up bath salts, to which she added essential oils, often lavender for relaxation, or citrus for rejuvenation after long work days, helichrysum when her muscles ached. There was now a little table beside the tub to hold her coffee or tea cup and a book; a bath mat lay over the side while not in use, and a bath pillow was stuck to the end. She'd splurged on both even while telling herself it was unnecessary, that when she moved, she'd no longer need them. Still, it made a long day's work end nicer.

They would end even better if George could stay with her rather than running home to his kids.

Fran told herself not to think about it while she watched him up there in the band shell with his sexy lips rocking his sexy sax. A sensual man. She couldn't help but think it.

A couple of people had actually said hello to her while they enjoyed burgers at Lakeshore Café and again when they wandered Sunset Park until it was time for the concert. She felt a touch of guilt about being glad it was only George and not his whole crew for the day, especially when he said Lexi had begged to go to his concert and he couldn't give in to her because her mother said no. She only said no because George would love to have Lexi there and for no other reason. Or so he said. Fran did hope the woman wanted to spend time with her daughter, even if he couldn't tell she did.

When he left the stage, Fran slowly wandered his direction, allowing time for him to talk with his fellow musicians, give thanks for those who stopped to tell the band how wonderful the performance was, and pack his instrument in its case. While he did all of that, he kept glancing over at her. Finally, he shook his head and met her the rest of the way.

He planted a kiss aside her head. "You could have come over."

"I didn't want to be in the way."

"In the way?" His head tilted.

And his mother told her to be careful with him. "Well, or... I'm not sure how public you want this. Among your friends..."

"Meaning you're not wanting it more public than we are already?"

"No. I don't mean that. I don't care."

"Sure about that?"

"Yes."

"Well, then..." Sliding a hand along her cheek and behind her head, he kissed her. A soft, light kiss, since they were in public, but nice. A claim. In public. "So." He took her hand and started toward his truck. "How about I go change and we do a round or two of mini golf?"

Mini golf. More public togetherness. But not what she really wanted. "Or you could come hang out at my place until you have to pick up your kids."

He stopped walking. "Hang out? As in, inside?"

Fran couldn't help chuckling at his expression. "Inside. It's hot today. I do only mean hang out, G.F., in case you're wondering."

"Damn." He threw a grin. "Yeah, I'd love to come hang out with you. Alone. Even if it's just hanging out."

G.F. had every feeling in the world that if he hadn't had to go home to meet his kids when their mother dropped them off, Fran might have not insisted on keeping it only "hanging out." She'd made them a salad full of fresh things, part from her garden, part from the farm market, with seared tilapia to go with it, plus a couple of German beers, a different kind than the last, stronger, more hearty. Nice. All of it.

She told him more about South Dakota, that she lived in Vermillion and worked at the college as an adjunct professor, teaching Italian and German. During summers, they leased a place in Rapid City and while Cal worked, she traveled into the Black Hills to sightsee, alone, and even went to Sturgis once during the bike rally out of curiosity.

He had to raise his eyebrows about her doing that alone, and she skirted around her experience other than saying once was enough. It seemed to be just before Cal left, from what he could gather. Or just after. G.F. wasn't quite sure and she changed the subject.

After he left, she drove back toward Vermillion on her own, down Route 18, sight-seeing on the way: Hot Springs, Wounded Knee, Rosebud Reservation, Scotland – where she watched a rodeo, and then settled back in Vermillion in their place, but alone. Cal had paid the rent for the year, as an apology of sorts, so she stayed the year, and then just stayed because she had nowhere else in mind to go. She made several trips to the music museum, often went to games at the university only to watch the band play, and admitted to thinking about him while the boys on the field were running around trying to knock each other down.

He laughed at her description of the game and couldn't quite deny it.

"I hate that I have to leave." He ran fingers through her hair. "Two full days in a row with you is a dangerous thing."

"Hm, since we're only hanging out, you mean?" Her eyes sparkled with her teasing.

"Right." At her door, he kissed her long and deep. "Mm, hm." Pressing his lips together, he shook his head. "Hope you don't mind if I'm hoping some day it could be more than that."

"I think it doesn't matter much if I mind." She ran fingers down his chest. "Non posso dire che mi dispiace. Forse un giorno sarà più."

His chest swelled. "Alrighty, then. Now that I wish even more that I didn't have to go, gonna tell me what you just said?"

"No. But if you'd like, I'll text what I said and you can look it up."

"Woman, you're killing me."

"Thought you liked a good challenge." Without letting him respond, Fran wrapped her arms up over his shoulders and returned the kiss, her body pressing hard against his, her hips encouraging him when he couldn't keep from showing how much he wanted to stay.

"On that note..." He forced himself to pull back. "Yeah, text me and I'll try to figure out how to look it up."

"Online translator, G.F. They aren't always exact, but it should give you the general gist."

"I'll have to borrow Theo's laptop."

"You can't do it on your phone?"

He raised his eyebrows and pulled his phone from his pocket to show her the old flip phone he still carried. "Hey, it takes and sends calls. It texts. Good enough."

"Okay. Well, maybe don't look it up in front of him." She winked and released his fingers she'd been gently gripping. "See you tomorrow?"

"Yeah. Um. We're working farther away now, so lunch isn't going to work. I hate that it won't. Come for dinner. Six-thirty?"

"I'll let you know." She went out to the porch with him and grasped his hand when he said good night and started away. "I said I don't mind what you're hoping, and ... maybe it will. But G.F., I'm still planning to move away. Maybe not too far, but still, I don't want to lead you on or..."

He kissed her fast and quick. "Got it. And you know, I don't mind driving. So if you think I won't come visit, you might rethink. Night, Fran. Please come for dinner tomorrow." He didn't give her time to answer before striding to his truck and giving her a wave as he backed out.

Nineteen

She'd given in to have dinner with them Monday, but only when he agreed to do it at the diner as her treat, as a thank you for the boys hauling the extra garbage out of her greenhouse and to the recycling center, but she had yet to accept an invitation to G.F.'s house. Lexi had come to hang out at her place much of the week. Sometimes they gardened. Sometimes they cooked. Either way, Lexi always had something to take home to her family when her dad stopped after work to pick her up.

Wednesday night, he accepted dinner at her place. Tuesday and Thursday, he'd stayed to eat with his kids and then came to see Fran for coffee. Thursday it rained, a soft rain, and they sat on the porch until the mosquitoes got too bad and she took him inside. He'd commented on how beautiful her hydrangeas were getting. They were coming out in both blue and pink with some a cross of the two that she just loved.

By now, the weekend was upon her again and he would have more time. Friday. He'd invited her for dinner, but she wasn't sure she could make herself go. The hints between them were growing every night. He lingered longer every night. She found it harder every night to put off expanding their relationship.

Was she ready for that? She thought of his touch while she gardened, while she painted, and sewed, and cleaned, and... And when she was with him, she wanted more. Always, she wanted more. It was too much like the way she'd wanted Cal. Until she didn't. Until she'd only stayed because it was the choice she'd made. Fran did not want to feel that way about George. Ever.

And yet it was different than Cal since she'd hardly bothered to put him off. She gave in too fast. That was one mistake she could not repeat, not with George. It mattered more.

With a sigh, she got up from where she'd been staring at her latest canvas and went to the greenhouse. So much work to be done. At the rate she was moving, she'd have to spend a couple of years there instead of the couple of months she'd planned. Not a terrible thought these days, if George didn't lose interest, or if she didn't. She could hang out with him for a couple of years. Take herself through the turning forty stage that terrified her beyond rationality.

Just because her mother said her father had been fine and dandy until he turned forty, it didn't mean the same would happen to her. She was very much still in her right mind, or at least as right as she'd ever been, maybe more right than she'd ever been. Why else would she be attracted to someone earthy and stable and easy-going now rather than someone who made her insides smolder just from looking at him without even knowing him? She was far smarter than she used to be. More sensible. Not less. A good sign.

Even if she had gone to the grocery store three times during the week, twice on the same day because she forgot the most important thing, the thing that made her go in the first place. But she had a lot on her mind. And she was doing more different things than she ever had at one time. Even so, she balanced them well, better than before when she had fewer things to balance.

Maybe she was opposite her father and was growing into her senses instead of out of them.

With that thought in mind, Fran absently sifted through stuff on the greenhouse shelf. Why her father had put up a wood wall blocking part of the sun to hang his small tools up on when he never bothered to put them back there but instead left them wherever he last used them, she didn't know. And not just a plain wood wall up against where the glass should be, but a wall that stuck out into the room...

Why did it stick out?

Funny she'd never wondered before. It stuck out, or rather in, jutting from the glass wall made of old window panes he'd gathered over the years from people tossing them out or offering them to him. Why did it? Were there more tools..? But how would he get to them inside or behind the wall? There was no opening.

Half determined to figure him out and half afraid to try to understand his reasoning, such as it was, Fran fingered the edges of the jutted out wood wall. Nothing. Just a block of hollow wood. Was it hollow? She knocked on it. It sounded solid, not hollow. Why?

Lowering to her hands and knees, she looked under the tall wood counter to the lower part of the wall that jutted out more than the rest, sneezed at a patch of dust she disturbed, rubbed her nose until it calmed, and tilted her head at something with a bit of a shine to it under the rust. A latch. There was a latch in the corner mostly hidden by a large spider web guarded by a large spider. She wasn't bothered much by spiders, but this one she didn't recognize and she didn't relish getting bit, so she went to find a newspaper, rolled it up, and lifted the web, spider and all, away from the corner.

"Sorry, bud. I have to get in there." Taking it outside and waiting until it scurried off the paper into the corner behind where her new herbs were filling out well, she put the paper back on the stack and returned to the latch.

Stuck. Of course. Rusted.

Instead of risking her fingers, she sat on the floor and shoved the heel of her tennis shoe against it until it gave way. With plenty of trepidation as to what she might find inside, Fran hesitated, then went back for her big flashlight.

He wasn't that crazy. She told herself he wasn't actually crazy as images of dead bodies stuffed in the little space swirled through her head. But there would be a smell, wouldn't there? *Too many murder mysteries, Francis Barrett. You need to read something different for a while. Get it together. It's just a cabinet. For tools. Hoes. Shovels. Potting soil.* Just a cabinet. Maybe empty. But locked.

Unwilling to get too close until she could see inside, she grabbed a rusted long-handled spade to pull the thing open and shined the light inside. Metal? The walls looked metal. Why would he do that? Fire proof? For garden tools?

It wasn't as small a space as she expected. The whole wall opened, which explained the countertop being cut at an angle, to allow the wall to open. The space was thin at the top, with an inset in the wall door, a wood rack holding ... something, some kind of large envelopes.

A string hung down from a light bulb and she gave it a try to see if it might still work. By some miracle, a yellow light illuminated the ...

canvases below. If there was one thing Fran recognized, even wrapped in brown paper, it was canvas on frames. At least they looked like canvases wrapped in brown paper. Of course, she could be wrong.

Except there was also an easel. And a couple of palettes. Hanging on the steel wall. The envelopes in the door inset ... art folders. In different sizes.

Her heart raced as she set the flashlight out of her way and grabbed the first canvas she could get her hands on to pull out into the sunny room. She took it out of the direct sun, just in case it mattered, and carefully pulled the browned tape from the back of the wrapped package. Freed of its concealment, Fran turned it to face her.

"Oh." Her head shook. Her eyes watered. For the first time since she'd come back home, she had to fight tears. "Oh, Dad."

She had to open them all, had to see them, even if she didn't really want to see them. By the time she had them all open and laying along the gardening tables propped by empty pots so she could see them all at once, tears streamed down her face. They were gorgeous, living, breathing, vivid, *real*. Garden scenes. Town scenes. People, old and young. And she was there. As a child, dressed in white with a blue ribbon – the dress she'd hated that her mother insisted she wear. Sunrises. Rainy scenes. Magnificent life in all shades. All with his signature in the corner. She would know his signature anywhere.

She hadn't known. Fran had no idea he'd even sketched anything, much less ... this.

There were still the portfolios to look through, one a large brown leather portfolio that looked well used and rain-stained. But she couldn't do it now. She held her hand against her heart and studied her father's work. His passion. Her mother often wondered how he could spend so much time with his plants and not have a lot to show for it.

She hadn't known, either. Her mother hadn't known. Fran wasn't sure whether to be sad or angry that she didn't.

Her phone rang from within the cottage and she nearly ignored it, but it was time for George to be off work, so she rushed to grab it before it went to voicemail, used a mostly clean paper towel from her art desk to wipe her face, and tried to give him a normal greeting.

"Hey Fran, we're doing burgers and corn on the grill since it's such a great evening, finally cool enough to be outside. How about stopping whatever you're doing, cleaning up, and coming over?"

"Yeah."

Silence seeped through. "Yeah? You said yeah? Just like that?"

"Guess I should have said yes instead, since it's what you expect."

"What's wrong?"

"Oh... So very much, actually. I'd love to come for ... corn on the grill? You mean on the cob?"

"On the cob on the grill. Haven't had it that way?"

"No. Doesn't it burn?"

"Come on over. We'll teach you something new."

"What time?"

"As soon as you're ready. We'll talk after dinner. Or before if you need. See you soon. Okay? No backing out?"

"I'll be there." Hanging up, she returned to the greenhouse, carefully put all of the canvases back in the hidden room, closed the makeshift door, and went to take a bath.

So very much was wrong.

G.F. hoped that didn't mean she was getting ready to run right back out of town. Not that he'd blame her. Between the gossip from Jim on his crew and what he'd heard around town already, he couldn't imagine why she'd stay. It nearly made him ready to move with her. Except he figured it was everywhere. People who didn't keep themselves busy enough had plenty of time to gossip about those who did while they were too busy to defend themselves. And there were apparently far too many not nearly busy enough. Pretty widespread these days, he knew.

So she'd gone to the store twice in one day. People forgot things at the store. Not a big deal. Sometimes they didn't know they needed something the first time they were there and found it out later. It didn't mean she was taking after her father. Maybe he would start going to the store twice a day and see what they'd say about him. Nothing, he supposed. His parents were still active and very mentally capable; his mother was on the town council and well liked. His father was nearing seventy and still supervising a construction crew, sometimes working a project himself. It gave G.F. a natural upper hand around town he didn't have coming on his own.

The sins of the father, or vice versa. That's what it actually meant. What you do affects your kids. It was a warning, not a punishment. Some people just couldn't read between the lines, or couldn't read metaphors. His years of reading every sci fi book he could get his hands on taught him to read metaphors well enough.

He'd done enough damage to his own kids, he figured, by not being particular enough, or careful enough. But he supposed they'd come through fine. Their grandparents, his parents, were well connected to them. The other could be overlooked to an extent.

Of course he felt like a huge ass for thinking such a thing about the woman he'd married, but there was still enough bitterness about what she'd done, it was hard not to. Especially when everyone knew what she'd done to him and since it would affect his children. He'd have to watch Lexi close.

Pulling into his drive, he shoved the thought from his head for the moment and focused on getting ready for Fran to come, to spend the evening with him and the kids. No one was going out to see friends tonight. They were all staying right there and being hospitable, even if he had to threaten to take away everything they owned.

Opening her car door, Fran paused at a sound that seemed to be coming from under her car. Closing it again, she backed up. "Okay, what are you?"

Something jumped beside and around her feet and she jumped back, a hand clutching her chest. A kitten. Muddy. Dried mud. Thin. Staring up at her with wide eyes, ready to bolt.

"Well, you're either a stray or you've been dumped out here. Lovely. Hungry, I bet."

It meowed again, creeping warily closer.

"Okay, then. Come on." She walked back to her porch, turning to talk to the thing as it followed, at a distance. Going in to dig out a can of tuna, she dumped part of it into a disposable plastic bowl she'd kept for painting purposes, added water to another one, and set them on the edge of the porch. "Come on." Backing away, she held still until the little thing got daring enough to run to the food.

A yellow kitten with what looked like white feet under the dry mud.

"Here's the deal. I'm heading out. Stay or don't. Your choice." Going back in for an old fraying towel she also kept for paint and garden purposes, she curled it onto a corner of the porch for a bed if the thing wanted it. Maybe it would stick around and take care of mice and the chipmunks that kept digging in her gardens.

Either way, she wouldn't worry. It could stay if it wanted or not if it didn't want. George and his kids were holding dinner for her.

Twenty

Fighting nerves at the thought of being inside G.F.'s house, with his pack of children buzzing around, Fran took her time as she made her way from her Explorer to his front door. The place needed work, as he'd said. And it was one of those bi-level styles she didn't like. She wouldn't say as much, of course. The dark green wood siding was darker than it had been originally, from age and lack of cleaning. There were chips splintered off some of the lower pieces. Kids, probably, when they were younger. His shrubs needed some TLC, by way of pruning shears and fertilizer.

The rail wobbled when she set her hand on the paint-chipped dark green banister. The wood showing through was greenish, showing a good bit of time exposed to moisture and shade. Fran considered asking if his boys couldn't help with their own house rather than, or along with, working on other houses and yards. She wouldn't do that, either. Not at this point.

With a deep breath that gave her a good whiff of the branch cypress on both sides of the porch, she rang the bell. Hearing nothing, she waited a few seconds, and tried knocking on the screen door. Of course they wouldn't hear that, so as much as she hated to do it, she opened the screen door and knocked on the white metal door that ineptly tried to imitate a wood look.

"Hey *Dad*, you're *girlfriend's* here."

Fran heard the yell through the door and tried to hide a grin when it opened. "Justin, it's nice to see you again."

"You too, but call me J. Everyone does. Come on in."

Her nerves about being in his house were quickly trampled by the sight greeting her. There were stacks of stuff on top of bookshelves beside the door that were so disheveled she couldn't imagine trying to look for a book on them. Shoes covered the floor in front of a stuffed-full coat closet with the door open. A vacuum cleaner sat nearby, its cord spilled down around it on the floor. Clumps of dirt littered the floor around the closet. And a lone formerly white sock was draped from a plant stand. It held a sad little plant that could be an herb, she thought, or might have been before. Rosemary, a second look at it told her. It was in a too-dark spot. Herbs needed sun. She had told Lexi that often.

She stepped back as two young boys she didn't recognize ran past chasing a large dog. Justin yelled at them and followed, with a quick apology.

"Hey, Fran." G.F. came down the stairs with wet hair and clean clothes, jeans as always, and a nicely fitted navy crew neck knit shirt with three buttons, two undone, showing a touch of dark chest hair, the shirt un-tucked. "You're fast at cleaning up. Didn't expect you so soon."

"I didn't want to make you wait and you didn't set a time."

"I didn't set a time purposely so you wouldn't feel pushed. Come on in." He turned his head toward the opposite way the boys had run. "*Lexi*, come finish vacuuming and then put it away like I told you ten minutes ago." He shook his head. "Kids. You can tell them twenty times and it takes the twenty-first to make it happen. Iced tea? I have that and coffee. Water, of course. I don't keep soda here because it disappears in a heartbeat, but I can have Theo run to the store."

"Tea sounds good. Thank you." She followed to the kitchen, slightly behind him. Stuff was piled up in there, also. It was on the table, the counter, even the floor. It reminded her too much of the mess in the shack she'd just cleared away and she nearly bolted. More messes, she couldn't handle right now. She was working too hard to clean them out of her life.

G.F. sighed and rubbed a hand over his chin. "So much for cleaning up before I got home. Always tends to get worse through the week, so by Saturday, we have to dig it out again." He handed her a glass of ice cold tea and set a hand on her back to guide her to the living room. It was surprisingly uncluttered except for kids flopped around, more than four. "I wouldn't let them go out to their friends' houses so a couple of friends came by here. Par for the course. There's nearly always either less or more than four around. Have a seat wherever you like."

                          Ella M. Kaye

More or fewer, she wanted to say, but she didn't. She took a chair close to the couch instead of sitting on the couch, maintaining some space, while Frank and Theo said hello and the two that had just run through nodded a greeting and turned back to the blaring cartoon with foul-mouthed kids.

"Turn that off, like I told you." George was still on his feet.

"What can we watch?"

"Off, Frankie. You know what *off* means."

"But what are we supposed to do?"

"Talk. We have company."

The boy stared as though his father had just turned into an alien. "But, what if we let Fran choose what to watch? What do you like?"

"Hi, Fran!" Lexi jogged in and gave her a big hug. "I'm so glad you came. I made banana bread, with walnuts. Do you like walnuts? I should have asked…"

"I do, thank you. And I brought you some blueberries. They're finally getting ripe." She handed Lexi the little bag.

"You share those." George warned his daughter. "And after you finish vacuuming."

"I did."

"You did not. There's dirt still all over the floor."

"But, it was…"

"She did finish." Justin jumped in. "These two came in with dirt all over their shoes."

George apologized to his daughter and told the visiting boys to go clean it up and put the vacuum away while Frank again asked what Fran like to watch.

"I don't watch television." She felt the stares. "I don't disapprove of it; I simply don't find it entertaining enough to be worth the bother."

"What do you do, then?"

Paint. But she didn't say so. "I often have music on. If I get bored at home, I hang out at the library, or I go to movies, although I'm finding fewer all the time worth sitting in the dark for two hours, especially when so many are so obnoxious in public anymore."

The two visitor boys snickered.

One of them elbowed Justin. "Your dad's girlfriend hangs out at the library?" He laughed.

"Better than hanging out at bars." The tone in Justin's voice hushed his friend, and Fran caught George's look. Obviously, his mother was a source of embarrassment.

"What movies do you like?" Lexi inched closer, pushing the dog back farther from Fran. Frank complained about her pushing Scruff and called the mutt over to nuzzle against him instead.

"Why don't you put him outside while we have company?"

Fran looked across the room at George and wondered if he planned to stand all night. "No, it's fine. He's not bothering me." She gave Frank a grin. Last thing she needed to do was push his dog away for her sake. And she was actually impressed that the house didn't smell like dog, as she expected, from experience. "I'm not sure I should admit what kind of movies I prefer."

"Probably sappy tear-jerker movies, like my mom." The other visiting boy nudged Theo. "Why do girls like that stuff?"

"There's nothing wrong with what someone else likes just because you don't." George eyed the boy, a warning.

While she appreciated his protective instincts, Fran was more concerned about his children at the moment. It was a test to have their friends there while she was, not only for herself, but also for George. "I watch a lot of different kinds of movies. I love a good story, whatever it is, but I'm most inclined to watch a good mystery/suspense film. It's mainly what I read, as well." Fran couldn't help vindicate herself in the boys' eyes, even if George was right. "And I don't cry at movies, not even tear-jerkers."

"Not even Titanic? I saw it at Eve's the other day and I cried." Lexi looked up at her through big green eyes, her head tilted down as though unsure she should share so much of herself.

"Not even that one, but I might have at your age. There's nothing wrong with it."

To take focus off herself, she asked the kids their favorites. Frank relaxed more when he found she shared not only one of his music interests, but also an interest in mysteries. He loved mysteries. Mostly, he watched them instead of reading them, but she mentioned some books he might like to try that she read at his age.

The night went reasonably well, G.F. figured. Fran handled the kids and their chaos okay enough. He was glad they'd warmed up to her, other than Frankie, who was still thinking about it, and he figured that was just because she wasn't his mom.

Fran raved about the corn cooked in its husks on the grill after a half hour of soaking – which should have been an hour, but Theo forgot to put it in the salt water – and she didn't cut it off the cob with a knife, but picked it up like a real person, which he appreciated. She even requested a burger with buffalo sauce instead of plain or barbecue and added pepper jack cheese. She liked spicy, which amused his older sons.

By now it was late, dark, somewhere near ten, and he wanted to take her home. Would've been easier if he'd driven the half mile past his place to pick her up, but he figured he could follow to be sure she got in okay, and to give her a nice good night kiss fully out of view of his children.

Lexi jumped up to give Fran a hug before they reached the door. George had to admit he was a bit bothered by the way Fran tensed whenever the girl hugged her.

"Can I go?" Lexi peered up at him with those big eyes.

"It's a half mile down the road. No need for you to drag yourself out."

"But..."

"No buts. And you know it's rude to invite yourself."

"How about coming to help in the garden tomorrow?" Fran glanced at him and focused on the girl. "If it's okay with your father. Late morning?"

"Have to get J to practice at ten. Can we do it later?"

"Don't make me sit through his practice again. Dad, come on..."

"Girl, you're pushing my buttons tonight." G.F. hated whining maybe more than anything. His daughter darn well knew it.

"But..."

"How about you drop her off at my place before practice and come pick her up afterward?"

Between Lexi's hopeful nagging and Fran's *why not?* expression, he didn't have much choice. "Sure that's okay? She's already been there a lot this week, which is nice since I haven't been home, but..."

"It's fine. I won't mind the company."

"Yeah well, guarantee you'll tell her to hush if she drives you crazy and I'll say yes."

With both girls' agreement, G.F. again said no to Lexi riding along with him to follow Fran home. He could hardly stand the distance of being in two separate cars even for the brief time it took to pull in beside her and walk her to her door. He'd made himself maintain decent space the whole time she'd been at his place, among his family, and tried hard to not think too much about just how damned well she fit. He'd wanted to kiss her from the moment he walked down the stairs and noticed her eyeing him the way she had. The woman had flirted with her eyes all night. Carefully. Subtly. But it had nearly the same effect as though she'd been touching him.

On her porch, she moved in close and stroked fingers down his chest, sliding all the way to his stomach. "I was hoping you might stay a few minutes. You are really good with your kids, George. Thank you for inviting me..."

He met her lips suddenly, and his tongue reached into her mouth while he yanked her body next to his. He felt only a small moment's hesitation before she gripped him hard, her fingernails pressing his back. Her groan, her body giving in to his, and her matched aggression during the kiss spurred him on, made him hard as hell, and he lowered a hand down her waist, down the curve of her ass to her thigh.

She broke the kiss but didn't move away. Instead, she held his eyes.

"Go ahead."

Her fingernails skimmed his back. "Go ahead, what?"

"Tell me I'm not coming in. I know. Gotta get home to the kids, anyway. Just... Actually, I wanted to talk. To ask if you needed to talk."

"About what?"

"What you said over the phone. That *so much* was wrong. Frannie, tell me I'm not part of what you think is wrong."

She sighed and backed away slightly, turning her head to watch the lightning bugs flash like sparklers along the grass in the dark of the yard.

"What's going on? Anything I can help with?"

She grasped his shirt where it hung just past his belt and twisted it in her fingers. "Sure the kids are okay for a while?"

"Yep. Doors are locked. Neighbors are right there if they need anything immediate. And I have my phone on. What is it?"

She reached up to give him a light kiss and tugged his shirt. "Come in, George."

"Fran..."

"Please. Come in." With his slight nod, she tugged him inside. A small lamp she'd left on gave them just enough light to see a small circle around the door. As he closed it, her hands slid up around his neck.

George gave her an easy slow kiss that worked its way down her body to her toes and she held tighter. "Frannie." With a whisper beside her ear, he kissed her neck. "Stay a while. Past the summer. Let's give this some time."

"Hm." She lowered her hands to rest on his chest. "Maybe. But I don't want to talk about it tonight. Come." Switching on the overhead light, which seemed to startle him, Fran claimed his hand.

He scanned the place. "You know, you've made the place look like a real home. Never would have expected it could."

"Let me show you my newest addition." She led him to the little bathroom to show him the painting she'd finished and hung. Hers. Unsigned so far. A view of the lake at sunset, with the teals and greens highlighted by touches of coral in the sky, and the long pier with its bench at the right side.

"Gorgeous. A local artist?"

"Yes."

"Really? Who?"

"Before I answer that, come this way." She took him back to the living room.

He stopped her and peered into her eyes. "So, your bathroom looks nice and cozy by now. Also ultra feminine, more than the rest of the place, which I wouldn't have expected from you."

"I do have that side." She rubbed the back of her fingers along his waist. "I have a lot of sides, if anyone cares to look far enough."

"I'm very sure you do, Frannie. Hope you'll give me enough time to find them all, however long that takes." He ran a hand through her hair and pulled her in for a kiss.

Before she let it go where it felt to be going, she had to show him. Breaking the kiss with a caress of his warm skin, she took him to the old desk where her most current canvas lay. A detail of the iris was painted. The rest was only sketched so far. Her palette sat beside it, brushes in turpentine.

George picked it up by its sides. "This yours?"

"Still in early stages, obviously."

"And ... the bathroom?"

"Yes. That one, too." She nodded toward the first one he'd admired, the hydrangeas and lilies.

"Wow, Fran. This is beautiful. They're all beautiful. Amazing. When did you start painting?"

"Freshman year." She picked one up from the floor where those in progress lined the wall. Hydrangeas. With large blue blossoms. "This one is closer to finished."

He took it from her, heeding her warning that it was still wet. "Is this what you do for a living? You're an artist. Are they doing well?"

"I haven't showed anyone else."

He stared wide-eyed. "Why on earth not?"

"It's for me. Stress relief. Just ... art for the sake of art and nothing more. I don't want to sell them."

"Well, I guess I can understand how you couldn't, but they're good. Not that I know much about art. Still..."

"I teach piano." She waited for his surprised stare to return. "Because of you, actually. Because I've loved it since I heard you playing in the high school auditorium when you thought you were alone. And then those boys came and decided to be jackasses and as far as I knew you didn't play again. I could've throttled them and would still like to. You played so beautifully. I can't replicate what you can do with a piano, but I learned the technique and I pass it along in hopes that someone with real talent for it, like yours, will actually use it..."

George set the painting down and swept her body up close with a strong arm. "Damn, Francis, I wish I'd asked you out the right way all those years ago."

"Probably wouldn't have worked back then. I had too much I needed to learn..."

"Same here, I suppose. But now?"

"Now." With a sigh, she dropped her head to his chest. "I don't know, George. I thought I put it all behind me and now I've been forced back to tie up loose ends and all I'm finding is that everything's more unraveled than it was before. Know what I found today?"

"A falling-apart house full of kids and mess and chaos and a man who wants you to try to deal with it all."

She chuckled. "Well, that too. But that's the easier part, believe it or not." Grabbing his hand, she led him toward the greenhouse. "Sometimes you really want to feel like you have something unique, you know? Something someone can't point at and say *you got that from your father* or *you got that from your mother or your aunt you never met, oh, you should have met her, you're so like her, including the temper...*"

"Temper?" He rubbed her back as they stepped out onto the uneven floor.

"I do have one. It doesn't show a lot, but when it does, it can be scary." Fran stopped and faced him. "Want to change your mind now? Before this goes further?"

"Are you expecting it to go further?" He lowered his face toward hers and stroked a finger along her cheek.

"J'espère qu'il va plus loin, puisque je suis tomber en amour avec vous." Without letting him ask, she continued over to the jutting out wall and sat on the floor to push the lever open with her foot. Then she got up, accepting his hand as help.

"My art was that, G.F. Mine. Yes, I got my father's gardening skills and I've done some of that as a side job, as well. At one point, I had four jobs, over 70 hours a week total, just ... well, I couldn't sit still, couldn't let myself think, and then I took up my paints again after having abandoned them with my old life, and I dumped two of the jobs. I gained back the weight I'd lost while too busy to think about eating, and then some, and I didn't care. I think I still don't. But my painting was supposed to be mine."

She pried the wood slat door open and grabbed a large canvas to show him. "Gorgeous, isn't it? Far better than my work, by a long shot. Makes me look like the amateur I am."

"It doesn't, actually, but it's nice. Whose is it?"

"Look." She pointed at the bottom right corner inscribed *V. Barrett 2001.*

"Your father?"

"Please tell me you had no idea."

"I had no idea." George took it to look closer. "It's incredible."

"It is. They all are. There are a bunch of them in there. Just what am I supposed to do with a bunch of apparently never seen canvases that I have to guess he didn't want to show any more than I want mine shown? What do I do with this? I'm already fighting how much I'm like him, how people always said I was, how I feel more like it's true every day I get older and close to forty. That's when he started losing it, you know. So Mom said. She wrote me letters giving me every detail of his growing 'memory problems' as she called them, and she called every time he disappeared so I had to worry until she called back to say he was found and of course I felt guilty enough for not being there that I came back for some time to help and saw it myself."

"You came back when?"

"A few years ago. After Cal decided he could do without me but turned around and warned off the guy I'd started to see. Five years after he left me for the woman he really wanted. Apparently I was supposed to pine over him forever."

"He was a huge asshole, Fran. Even if I shouldn't say it. Or maybe I should have said it, back when he came to town. I should have. Maybe it wouldn't have done any good, but I should have tried." He set the painting down on the dusty table. "Why didn't I see you when you came back?"

"No one did. I stayed in the house, or I put on one of Aunt

Connie's wigs to go search for him, and I stayed away from everyone. I saw you a couple of times. Part of why I stayed hidden. Couldn't deal with it right then on top of everything."

"A few years ago I was still married."

"Yes. And I heard from Aunt Connie how great Justine was looking and how her children were just gorgeous. Another guilt trip, of course, seeing as how I didn't have any and that I'd gained weight by then..." She stopped, looked away, and took a deep breath. It was in the past. Justine may have looked great and had beautiful children but she was also a bitchy cheater who didn't spend any real time with her kids. A few extra pounds were nothing compared to that.

"Anyway, it scares the hell out of me, because I see so many similarities between my father and me and this is just one more..."

He took her face in his hands. "Frannie. Stop there. You are not your father. Yes, there are similarities and I like in you what I liked in him. But that doesn't mean..."

"It might. And the big thing I keep thinking is: who the hell will be willing to take care of me the way Mom and I took care of him? Until I left again because I couldn't deal with seeing him that way. Who would do the same for me if I need it? Who wouldn't walk away when it got too hard? I thought it would be Cal until ... well, you're right and he was a huge mistake and no one I've dated in the past nine years came anywhere close to being someone who wouldn't walk away. Bad sentence, I know, but I'm frazzled and I never talk this much and my grammar is horrendous when I'm frazzled. Wouldn't some of those I've corrected through the years have a field day with that?"

His mouth closed on hers, silenced her. Weakened her knees. Strengthened her fingers as she gripped his shirt.

When he barely released her, she couldn't help continue. "Now you'll think I'm only agreeing to see you because I'm desperate, and I'm not. I don't expect anything of you. I have it worked out. I found a decent home health care service and I've notified my aunt who I've seen exactly once since I've been back home that she's to call them if I show too many signs and I'm too out of it to do it myself. I'll just have to hope she doesn't jump too fast so she can get the house she thinks should be hers…"

"Frannie. Stop a minute." It was a husky whisper beside her ear and he kissed his way back to her mouth, teasing her lips as he spoke. "I don't give a flying fuck why you agreed to see me or why you let me in your life this far. I'm just glad you did. And no matter what happens, you have do someone, other than that aunt who has never done a lick of good for anyone in the world, including her own sister who needed her when your dad was at his worst and she turned away. Forget her. You don't need her. You have me." He pulled her body against his. "If this works or if it doesn't. Okay? I'll still look after you as long as you're around. And if you're not around and I hear you're in need, I'll come find you."

She felt her head shake in disbelief. "Why would you?"

"Because I have always cared about you and I never bothered to show you. Whatever else happens, I want to correct that."

"You don't owe me…"

He hushed her with a kiss, with his tongue prodding to allow entrance, with his fingers pressing into her backside as he pulled her close. "Nope. I don't owe you. I owe it to myself. And you owe it to yourself to allow what you want despite anything else, anyone else."

To himself. Because he wanted… this. He wanted this, even knowing everything.

Gripping the bottom hem of his shirt, Fran tugged it up, away from his stomach. He caught her eyes only a second before he had her pinned against the wall, his mouth trailing from her lips down her neck, down to the gauzy neckline of her blouse.

Fran couldn't tell who was more insistent, but she led him out of the dirty greenhouse, to the circle garden, the stone bench in the center.

He looked around at the place as much as possible with only the glow from the greenhouse coming through the windows guiding their steps. "Did you do this?"

"Only some of the replanting. The rest was here. I had no idea it was. It still needs work. A lot of work. It's going to take time, more than I expected." She shoved his shirt up over his stomach and he took it the rest of the way off.

"Can I help you do it?" He nuzzled into her neck while he released her blouse buttons.

"Another double entendre?"

"What?"

"Never mind. Sorry." Fran kissed his chest, a nice hairy but not overly hairy chest, strong and sturdy, tanned enough to show he went without his shirt often...

"What's a double entendre?"

"You care about that now?"

"Turns me on." He kissed her shoulder, pulling the material away from it.

Fran stepped back. "You're making fun of me."

"Absolutely not. Come back here." He gripped her hands and pulled her against him. "Tell me."

She still wasn't sure he wasn't, and if this was some giant hoax... So what if it was? She'd turn it back on him if needed. She was plenty smart enough to do so and she had far more courage now than she'd had back then. "Double meaning. Saying one thing to mean two different things."

"Ah. Then I guess it was. Unintentionally. And I can't stay long. Should we uh ... schedule a night when I can stay longer and hold on to this thought?"

"No. Stop talking and it won't take so long."

He chuckled from deep in his chest. "A girl after my heart."

"Or after something of yours, anyway." She grinned when he paused to look at her. "Okay, maybe I want your heart, too. At least some of it."

"You've already got it, or I wouldn't be here now."

"George ... stop talking."

"I sound too corny and I'm turning you off."

"No." She hooked her fingers into his jeans and added just enough space between their bodies to watch her hands tease the soft skin underneath his belt where it curved in to form that ultra sexy V. She loved the way his jeans sat just low enough to see the top of it. A huge tease. And an even bigger turn on. Her body tensed in response to her touch of him, and her thoughts. "You can't stay long. We can talk another time."

As though she'd plugged him into a socket, G.F. – usually she preferred to think of him as, and call him, George, but at the moment, G.F. felt more appropriate – swept her blouse off her shoulders, plunged his tongue deeply into her mouth, and fumbled with her bra only a few seconds before her naked breasts pressed against his naked chest. Still, he kissed her, a bare arm around her back holding her up close and tight, the other hand sifting through her hair, undoing the scarf she'd had in to make it look almost neat, then wrapping into the depths of her hair to hold her skull in his large hand.

It was nearly frightening, the way he possessed her so suddenly, held her so close. Cal had never ... never been that great at sex, to be honest. Her want of him was the companionship, much of her interest the mystery of how his brain worked she had trouble figuring out. She'd thought mental companionship was what she'd most wanted, and he was bright, ultra bright. She'd loved that.

But this...

She let herself, for the first time, be absolutely carried away by not only the physical passion, the touch, the caress, the urgency, but also by who he was, by the way he looked at her, by the respect she had for him that made it mean far, far more than it had with Calvin. And she met his urgency at least equally, if not more.

Fran was glad he didn't say anything stupid like calling her beautiful. She'd always thought it was a ridiculous thing for a man to say when a woman was naked in front of him, as though she didn't realize it was carnal lust of the publicly taboo parts of her body exposed to him that he found beautiful. Nipples were nipples. They all turned men on, whatever they looked like. It was the opening to him, the giving in to him, that a man should find beautiful more than anything. She could never believe otherwise.

Maybe she overanalyzed sex, just like everything else.

Even so, so far, this was going much better than she'd expected.

"This thing is cold on my ass, you should know." He kissed her stomach as he sat on the round concrete table/bench and cradled her thighs.

"You'll warm up." She slid her hands through his thick blondish brownish reddish hair and closed her eyes while his lips teased her skin.

"What is this thing?"

"What?"

"Table of some sort? Will it hold us?"

"I can't say what it was meant to be, but yes, it's plenty sturdy." She caressed his shoulders, his football player sized shoulders that were even bigger now that he'd finished growing into a man.

"Interesting to have it in the middle..."

"George." She dug her fingers into his upper arms. "Stop talking."

"Frannie." G.F. tried to catch his breath as she planted kisses over his chest and neck. "How about we try this again inside?"

"You can't stay."

"You're kicking me out? Was it that bad?"

She set her hands aside his face and kissed him. Sweetly. "Your kids are expecting you."

"Oh. Yeah, I guess..."

"Forget about them?"

"Well, I kinda forgot everything, to be honest." He stroked the sides of her full breasts. They weren't saggy as some women his age. They still looked as young as he imagined they had when they were in school together. But then, she hadn't had kids. Could be the difference, he supposed. "I'd like to forget everything again, too. I'd just as soon you didn't tell them that, but..."

She clasped her mouth over his. Another sign to shut up, he supposed. It was something Justine hated; he talked way too much during sex. Always had.

"When can you arrange to stay the night?" Fran teased his lips as she spoke. "All night. Will you?"

"Tomorrow. I'll take them over to their mom's. She can keep them overnight this once. After the running is done."

"As early as possible. Yes?"

He groaned and ran his hands to the curve of her waist. "Guess it wasn't too awful bad, short and all."

"If you're fishing for a compliment, I don't do that. If you can't tell how I feel about it, it doesn't matter."

"You are an odd woman, Frannie Barrett."

"Yes, but you already knew that. Early dinner tomorrow? I'll cook."

"I'll do my best to come just as early as possible. And I definitely don't mean that as a double entendre."

She plunged her tongue deeply into his mouth, then suddenly pulled out of him, gave him a brief kiss, and got dressed.

Fran sat in her nearly overfull claw foot tub and lay her head against the inflated coral bath pillow – coral to help bring out the color of the sky in her painting – her eyes closed, her body luxuriating in the hot bath-salted rose-scented water. A man worth sticking around for, G.F. McKenry was. At least while it was working. George F. McKenry. What did the F stand for? She couldn't believe she had no idea and hadn't wondered. She had wondered why whoever had changed the name from McHenry to McKenry had done so. That had bothered her more than once. McHenry made sense. It meant *of Henry* which meant *a son of* or such. Fran had never heard of an Irishman or Scotsman named Kenry, though. Someone got it wrong somewhere along the line and it was left that way. At one point during high school, she'd convinced herself she couldn't marry anyone with such an incorrect surname, so it was just as well he wouldn't talk to her.

But things changed. Her edges had dulled. She even caught herself saying things like *yeah* and *gotta* and *don't wanna*. She sometimes cringed when she did, but less often did it bother her. Fran wasn't sure that was at all an improvement on her part.

Of course her own name bugged her just as much – and *bugged* was another phrase she never would have said before; the word was *annoyed*. Francis was how you spelled the masculine, not the feminine. She was feminine, at least enough her mother should have spelled it Frances if they had to name her that at all. Her father's idea, her mother said when she complained. Her father wouldn't say why.

She hated her name. It was old fashioned. Ancient. It set her apart too much in a world of Karens, Julies, Pams, Cathys ... and Justines.

She'd often been absolutely positive her parents had not wanted her and took their revenge on naming her not even Frances, but Francis, like the Saint. She sure hoped that wasn't the point of it.

If it was, perhaps her father had started to lose it long before he turned forty. In a way, that thought was comforting. She held onto it while she climbed into bed, closed her eyes and tried to coax herself to quit thinking of George, of their possibilities, and let herself sleep.

G.F. showered quick and plopped into bed with a huge smile on his face and his hands entwined under his head atop the pillow. Fran wanted him back the next night, early. Justine had never been quite that interested even on their honeymoon, or before their honeymoon, before she was pregnant. Of course they'd had to be careful to hide their activities, so there was that, but he figured that had been part of her interest, the hiding of it from their parents.

Would Fran want to keep it hidden? She didn't look at all like she wanted to hide their relationship, the way she'd come to his concerts, held his hand, kissed him at the lake, came to his place for dinner.

No, not hiding it at all. At least not the relationship part.

Of course for her it could be opposite, he supposed. Showing the town she was not only back, but doing one of the football players, and a still popular one at that...

Hell, he didn't give one bit of damn if that was her intent. He was enjoying every minute of it. And the morning would crawl way too slow for his taste as he waited until it was time to drop Lexi off to hang out with Fran and then waited again until he could take the kids to Justine's and go back to Fran. Inside, this time. And not rushed.

Twenty-one

By Wednesday, G.F. was frustrated as he left the cottage. Justine had refused to keep the kids Saturday night because she had *a prior engagement*, which he didn't believe for a minute. So dinner plans turned into pizza at his house and then he dropped Fran off at her door, looking forward to the next day he'd have to spend with her. And then his wife was suddenly *sick*, likely meaning hung over, and couldn't take them. He knew it was intentional. Frankie mentioned his dinner plans with Fran as a reason for wanting to leave them overnight, so the woman screwed him on purpose. Again.

Lexi was glad to be able to go to the band concert, and he was glad she was glad, but for a change, he'd looked forward to his Sunday without obligations other than the concert.

He'd taken three long lunch hours during the week so far. Of course there were comments, but he'd earned the right by almost always taking less than his hour allotment. And he wanted to see her. Alone.

Their first time hadn't been his best effort, outside on a cold concrete table with a time constraint. His lunch hour trysts weren't quite doing it for him, either. They were. He looked forward to lunch now far more than he ever had, and food had always been important to him, but there was still the time constraint and she'd yet to take him to her bed. The couch was okay. The throw rug on the floor was fine. Even standing against the refrigerator, which was cold on her ass instead of his was nice enough.

Still, it felt like an introductory course, that class you had to take to get to those you really wanted, even if you already knew the material.

She was catching up for too much alone time, maybe. Okay with him. He was glad to help her catch up. And he'd be the laughing stock of the crew if he ever said yeah, the great sex was nice but not exactly what he wanted, not ... emotionally connecting enough. He was a guy, a divorced guy; he wasn't supposed to even think about emotions or *connecting* when he was with a woman. He did, though. He had thoughts that he was more the female of the relationship, the one who'd done the chasing, the clingier one, the one willing to do it however it worked for her, the one who wanted more than a lunch time romp.

Yeah well, he was the man where it counted. Seemed she was happy enough with that part of the whole thing.

And she'd agreed to celebrate the Fourth of July with them on Friday. A big step, as far as he was concerned, particularly since it would include his parents and siblings and their families, a big picnic lunch and then fireworks.

Kissing her goodbye at her door, G.F. told her to have a good afternoon.

"What's Lexi doing today?"

"Home sulking, I would suppose, since her twin is on vacation for a couple of weeks. The friend she's always with when she's not with you."

"Mind if I ask her to go to Sioux City with me?"

"Today? That's a couple of hours..."

"Barely over an hour, only to the edge of the city, not down in the heart of it. There's a home store and..."

"A two plus hour drive just to go shopping?"

"You can say no, you realize. I'll go myself."

He scratched his chin. He never let the kids go that far without him. Still, Fran would be cautious. And the edge of the city wasn't downtown. "She's not big on long drives, but she might be willing to shop with you. I'll call her as soon as I get back to work and let you know what she said. That okay?"

"You can't call now?"

"From here? During lunch?"

"It's a phone, George, not a video camera. She can't see where you are. And if I'm going, I want to go and get back by dinner time."

"Right, but ... yeah." With some reservation, he dialed his home number from his cell and hoped the service would hold. It was better in the middle of town where they were working. Theo answered and he asked for Lexi, waited far too long, and pulled the phone from his ear when she asked if he *really* meant it. "Get ready quick and she'll pick you up in a few minutes."

"She's at work with you?"

The question he didn't want. "Nope, I stopped by her place real quick over lunch, but I'm headed back now." He saw Fran's raised eyebrows at the *real quick* part, but she stayed quiet. "Just be ready. Don't want you to keep her waiting."

Getting excited agreement, he hung up and wrapped his arm around Fran's waist. "I love what you're doing, but just a warning: let her get too hooked to you and it'll crush her when you leave. She's been crushed enough. Be careful, if you would."

"If you'd rather I didn't spend extra time with her..."

"No. I love that you're spending time with her. And it's probably far too late to worry about it. Just maybe..."

"I've warned her I'm here temporarily."

"Yeah, well. Doesn't mean she's not hoping you'll change your mind. And she's not the only one." He brushed her lips. "But I'm a big boy. I'll deal with it. She's young and already disappointed by her mother."

"A lot of us were. We get through it. But I guess I should let you know..." She slipped her arms over his shoulders. "I've changed my time frame. A lot needs to be done around here. It may take me at least through next summer, depending on how distracted I am. And I'm getting somewhat fond of this little shack and its privacy."

"You realize that makes me want to keep distracting you as much as I possibly can."

She grinned, gave him a kiss, and play-shoved him as she told him to get back to work.

Glad to finally be off for the day so he could ask his daughter about her shopping trip, G.F. stepped out of his work boots and into the house, nearly got slammed by the dog, yelled at Frankie for playing fetch inside, and called up to Lexi.

"Not home." Frankie gripped Scruff's collar and told him to stop pulling.

"Still out with Fran?"

The boy shrugged.

"Put him outside until he calms down. And you, too. Go." He watched to be sure the boy was heading that direction and searched for the phone, then gave up and used his cell. No answer. Fran would have her phone on while out, he was sure. Maybe she didn't answer while driving. A good idea. He left a message for her to call him back and went to run through the shower.

With no return message and still no answer by the time he was dried and dressed, he went down to see if Lexi might be home and paced when he didn't find her. She would have left a message if she planned to be late, as she had before. So she hadn't planned to be late.

Yelling out the back door that he was headed to Fran's to see if they were there, he nearly held his breath the whole drive. The siren he heard somewhere in the distance didn't help things, and neither did not finding Fran's car.

Cursing, he tried to call again, got a "not in service" message, and sat wondering whether to head toward the city to try to find them. A stupid thought. He'd too easily pass her on the road and not know it, or she could be in town and they'd take different routes.

He turned off the truck and paced through her yard and partway down the road toward his place and back again, his nerves fraying, his phone clenched in his hand in between trying to call every few minutes.

He should go back home. Fran would likely drop her off there. But if he did, Frankie would let them know where he was and she would come on down to her place. If he went home and she took the girl to her own place instead, he'd have to wait longer.

"*Hell.*" He tried dialing again and left another message. After hanging up, he decided his message had been too rude and called back to apologize for being rude. Then he got angry with himself for apologizing. He *was* worried. He had a right to be. Why didn't she *answer* her damned phone? What good was a cell phone if you never turned the damned thing *on*? If she could. If it was out of reach, or...

In an attempt to calm himself, he took a deep breath to fill his lungs just as much as physically possible, let it out slowly, and paced more. Back to his truck. They would go there first. To his place. Or he would get a call there if something happened. Maybe he would. Or they wouldn't. Lexi didn't have ID. Fran ... there was no legal connection to him, no reason authorities would call him unless they knew him personally. Tom would call him. The police chief knew him well, knew he was dating her. He would hear, wouldn't he?

Deciding it would be better to be at home near the house phone, he turned the engine over but she pulled in beside him so he turned it back off to jump out. "Where in the hell have you been?"

Fran's shoulders straightened and Lexi stopped her approach.

"Shopping. As you knew." Fran looked him straight in the eye.

"Didn't expect you to be this late. Is there a reason you didn't answer your phone?"

"It died. I left you a message to tell you it was about to die and said we'd be about an hour..."

"I didn't get a message." He walked up to her. "You don't have a car charger for the thing?"

"No, actually. Do you want to calm down before you continue talking to me?" She grabbed bags out of the back seat.

Fuming about how calm she was, G.F. told his daughter to get her things and wait in the truck.

"But, Dad..."

"No buts. I'm not in the mood. Go." He made sure she listened and followed Fran into her little shack.

"If you followed me to bitch, George, turn right back around." Fran set a couple of bags on her couch and headed to the kitchen.

"Next time I'm out, I'm picking up a car charger for your phone. What kind is it?"

"No, you won't." She turned back, hands on her hips. "I'm not one of your children, George McKenry. Don't talk to me like I am."

"It's only an offer..."

"It was not an offer. And I'm not that stuck to my phone just because you apparently are. I lived happily without one for a lot of years. I don't need it stuck to my hip now."

"You had *my* daughter..."

"I left a message on your phone. And I didn't kidnap her. You gave me permission to take her."

"Yes, but you said you wanted to get there and back before dinner. It's damned near seven. I never expected you to be this *late*. Know how it feels to get home and ask where your eleven-year-old is and no one has a fucking idea and you wouldn't answer your phone and you weren't home? I thought you were in a fucking *ditch* somewhere and I might have lost both of you..."

"Lower your voice and stop cursing at me. I left you a message..."

"I didn't fucking *get* it."

Fran raised her chin and stiffened her back. "Just go. I don't have to be talked to this way. Leave, George. And don't worry, I won't take her outside town boundaries again."

"Look, I'm not cussing at you..."

"Yes, you are."

"I'm cussing at the situation. It scared the hell out of me."

"I'm sorry, but I'm not at fault here. Curse at your phone for not letting it through if you wish, but do it at your own place. In the shower. In the backyard. Somewhere not in my house."

"I *did curse my phone*. And *your* phone, too. Didn't help."

"Still not my fault."

"*Fault?* That's all you can think about? Of course you don't know how it feels. You don't *have* kids. You don't know the worry, the every fucking day worry when you *have* to be *away* from them to work and you can't rely on them reaching their worthless mother, never mind *I pay* for her fucking phone so they *can* reach her..."

"Lower your voice and go home to calm down."

He clenched his jaw and paced around her cottage.

"Go home, G.F."

He turned back. "I'm supposed to be picking you up for dinner."

"I'm not coming."

"We have it planned and ready..."

"I'm not coming." Fran held his stare. No, she didn't have kids, and she didn't need it rubbed in. She'd done nothing wrong and no longer would she let anyone yell at her for something she hadn't done. She'd dealt with that bullshit enough. No more. He could take his ass right back home and she'd think about whether she'd allow him to return.

"Fine. If you change your mind, you know where we are." He half slammed the door as he left.

Fran heard the truck door slam and took a deep breath.

She didn't usually like to shop, but it had been a wonderful shopping day. The girl was a pleasure to be around. Lexi even enjoyed picking out summer annuals for the circle garden. Pickings were rather slim since it was late in the season and all those anxious for spring to come so they could beautify their yards had grabbed first choice. Usually Fran would have started her own from seed so she could have full flats at little expense. But she'd moved too late in the year for that and hadn't planned to stay so long.

Obnoxious man. Where did he think Lexi would be if she wasn't at home? Did he think Fran would have dumped her off alone at the mall or something even more ridiculous? She wasn't a parent, but she did have brains and common sense.

In a ditch somewhere. Both of you.

Sipping chamomile tea with a sprig of fresh peppermint, Fran calmed enough to remember what he'd said and took another deep breath. What made him think she didn't understand? She understood fine. She'd had to force herself to assume all was well until she heard otherwise through first the years of Cal always being away for "work," so he said, when she wouldn't hear from him for days, and then through her mother calling every time her father wandered off until he got picked up by the local police or a kind neighbor who took him home. She'd had to learn to not worry about not knowing exactly where someone was, for her own mental health.

But he was right: she didn't have kids. Fran imagined that wouldn't be as easy to make yourself not worry about.

A worry she would like to have had the chance to know.

"Dad, it was *my* fault. *I* said it was okay. You shouldn't have yelled at her. I *like* her, she's *great* to shop with, and now she won't take me anymore because you *ruined* it."

"Lexi, I understand you're upset, but mind your manners,

anyway."

"Why? You didn't."

"I'm your father..."

"And she's your *girlfriend*. You *shouldn't* yell at her. It's not okay. She won't let me go with her again now."

He sighed. "You're right. I shouldn't have yelled at her. I'll apologize. Now calm down and remember who you're talking to, if you don't mind."

The girl gave him a big pouty frown and leaned over to hug him. "I'm sorry we scared you, but we had fun, and she's a careful driver like you are, not like Mom, and she likes chocolate like I do, like she's *in love with* chocolate like I am and she bought a bunch of those little round balls in foil, the really good ones, and we sat and had coffee and talked and ate chocolate like I was a real person to her, not just a kid..."

"You had coffee?"

"Yes." She shrugged. "Kind of. It was mostly milk with some coffee in it for flavor since she wouldn't let me have a real coffee without your permission..."

"You like her a lot." He almost dreaded hearing it.

"Yes." It was a near whisper. "It's okay, right? She's your friend and she can be my friend, too, right?"

"If I haven't chased her off as I'd deserve." He caught her frown again. "Even if I have, I imagine she'll still be your friend. Don't worry, Lexi. She's too mature to take it out on you if she's mad at me. One of the benefits of age, at least for those of us who actually decide to grow up." With a kiss to his daughter's head, he urged her out of the truck so they could relax and get cleaned up for dinner.

Twenty-two

Fran wished she had the exact measurements, but she'd have to make do. A simple pattern. Fast to put together. And the waist was elastic so it didn't have to be perfect. She figured she could eyeball the girl's size well enough.

She shouldn't have kicked him out. But he'd hit a sore spot. A couple of sore spots. And Lexi probably heard it all. Poor baby. After the nice day they had, Fran felt awful that the girl had to end it feeling guilty.

She wanted to paint tonight in order to unwind, but the skirt came first. They'd found material similar to the one she had been wearing when she met Lexi, the one she'd loved so much. Even if G.F. decided to call things off, Fran wanted Lexi to have it.

Her stomach growled and twisted, but she ignored it while cutting out and sewing the long blue skirt with red- and white-vined flowers. She couldn't tell what the flowers were supposed to be since the petals didn't match the leaf shape. The artist was obviously not green-thumbed. But Lexi liked it.

By seven thirty – the man had fully exaggerated how late it was since she'd been working on the skirt for an hour – Fran had it put together and ready to wear.

Deciding to walk the half mile to his place in order to work off the remaining steam from being so angry and holding it in, she grabbed her big flashlight, although she supposed it would still be plenty light on her walk back since she didn't plan to stay more than two minutes. Rolling the skirt loosely so it wouldn't wrinkle in the bag, she made sure her door was locked.

G.F. told the kids to go on and finish cleaning up from dinner and he answered the door himself. They too often used it as an excuse to get out of work and he wasn't in the mood tonight. He wasn't in the mood for a salesman, either, or...

"Frannie." He got a hold of himself fast by remembering she hadn't cared how worried he'd been. "You missed dinner, if that's what you came for. And don't bother telling me you can't end a sentence in a propositional phrase."

"G.F., I imagine you could end almost anything in a *propo*sitional phrase, but you meant *pre*positional phrase, and I'm here to see Lexi."

Damn. He knew better. She just made him so damn tongue-tied...

"Can I see her a minute? I'll wait here if you'd rather."

"Might as well come in since we were expecting you, anyway."

She eyed him as she slid through the space he barely left for her to come in. "I don't know why you were expecting me. I told you I wasn't coming."

"Yet you're here."

"For Lexi. I thought she might like to have this tonight since our nice day ended so badly. I hope she's not upset."

He propped himself against the closet door. "She yelled at me all the way home for *ruining everything,* meaning she doesn't understand any better than you do how scared I was..."

"You know what?" Fran shoved the bag at him. "Give this to her for me, if you would." When he took it, she hurried right back out the door.

"Hell." He dropped the bag on the bookcase and started after her. The woman could move fast when she wanted. Talk about a double entendre if there ever was one. "*Fran.*"

She ignored him and kept walking. She'd walked. Her car wasn't in the drive. An excuse to let him take her home? If so, he'd blown it.

"Hey, wait up." She didn't, but his legs were longer and he caught up easily. She jerked her arm from his hand and he moved in front of her, walking backward. "You obviously planned to stay a while since you brought a flashlight. For the walk home? Didn't think I'd take you?"

"I wanted to walk. Don't read anything into it."

"And that big light?"

"Precaution. I believe in precautions. If needed, it would swing easily. No, I didn't intend to stay long, but a lot has happened I didn't intend to happen."

He nodded. Definitely a double entendre. "So an old golf putter by the door and a flashlight for walking. That's your big self-protection kit?"

"Stuff I already had."

"A sturdier lock on your door and pepper spray would be a might more effective. And maybe a hand gun."

"What would I do with that when I move back to the city?"

"My guess is you'd need it more in the city, all things considered. And I thought you were thinking about staying."

"I'm not sure there's any point in it."

A huge breath filled his lungs and released. "Okay, I'm sorry I yelled. I am. It was uncalled-for. But don't make it a bigger deal than it was. You don't understand what it's like to worry about your kids..."

"Say that to me one more time and I'll punch you dead in the face."

At least she'd stopped walking. And he kept himself from laughing. It wasn't hard not to laugh after the first couple of surprised seconds. She was dead-on serious and looked angry enough to do it. Maybe even with that easy-to-swing flashlight. "Fine. I shouldn't have yelled. And I'll leave it at that. Will you come back to the house so we can talk?"

"So you can take me home tonight for make-up sex, you mean?"

He rubbed his chin. "Is that an option?"

She veered around him and he caught her hand, refusing to let go this time, catching her waist with his other arm. "It was a joke. And you brought it up."

"Isn't that what you want?"

Again, she was dead-on serious. "You think that's why I was chasing you? For sex? I can get that easy enough..."

"Easily enough."

"Okay, that too." He tugged her closer. "Don't want to sleep with me? Don't. Fine with me. But come on back to the house. We still have dessert. Lexi must know you better than I do already since she insisted you would come and we had to wait for dessert. She wanted to wait for dinner, but I was starving..."

"She says you're always starving when you come home. And often irritable about it."

"Yeah, she has me pegged, too. Either way, I'd like to have you around, sex or no sex…" At a gasp beside his neighbor's door, he looked over at another old classmate of theirs. The woman was married to the only boy she'd ever dated, and never failed to bring up the fact she was still married to that one boy because of mutual trust and respect, an obvious dig at his divorce. Never mind it wasn't George who hadn't been trustworthy and never mind the woman barely spoke to her spouse any longer and the guy was always talking about her behind her back. "If you don't mind, we're talking."

"In *public*, in front of *my* house. What if my kids had heard what you're doing over there? *That word* doesn't belong in public."

"Your kids are probably more informed about *that word* than we are, if you want my opinion. Now do you mind?"

Her jaw dropped, only for a second. "I've a mind to call child services. This is why children should be with their mother instead…"

Fran squeezed his hand. "If you do, I'll be sure to let them know you only called them as payback for your dear husband propositioning me a few days ago, in front of his daughter, and in front of G.F.'s daughter."

The woman blanched. "That's not true."

"Ask him. Or ask your daughter. She at least had the decency to be embarrassed."

Before G.F. could sort his thoughts enough to react, Fran headed back toward the house, his house.

"He what?"

"Don't worry. I took care of it. And I told Lexi to stay far away from him. That kid was always shady. He's even worse as an adult." She stopped in front of his porch steps. Her chest heaved. "What are we doing with this, George? I didn't think it mattered much, and if not for your children, maybe it wouldn't, but…"

He leaned down and kissed her. "Come in for dessert. Give Lex whatever you brought for her and I'll take you home so we can talk."

"Or we can talk here so we'll actually talk."

"Or that. Either way is fine by me." He skimmed fingers along her face. "I am sorry I yelled."

"I'm sorry you were worried."

"All I wanted to hear." His thumb ran across her lips. "Let's go in before someone else accuses us of public indecency."

Lexi loved the long skirt as well as the scarf Fran had secretly bought to go with the skirt fabric. She gave her a huge hug and permission for her to "keep" her dad if she wanted him. G.F. fussed at the girl for her impertinence, and then had to define *impertinent*, but Fran found it adorable. Frank frowned and left the room. With an apology, G.F. went after him, leaving her with the rest of the kids who didn't seem to know what to say next.

Which abruptly ended when the large, very furry dog covered in dirt at one end and dripping slobber from the other came to her at a dead run and landed in her lap.

"*Scruff! No!*" Lexi yelled and the boys jumped in to pull the dog off, but it started to bark, and in the scuffle Justin got knocked on his rear and Fran tried to get up off the couch to prevent another jump, which only excited the dog more...

"*What* is going on?"

"*Dad!* Get him *out* of here!"

Fran could only sit beneath the dog's paws and turn her head away from his awful breath until George yelled loud enough the dog jumped away and ran to a corner under a table, or at least tried to go under it but managed to knock it over and spill papers and books and a glass of something blue and icy all over the throw rug and Lexi's new skirt.

"*Theo!* Drag that mutt out of here *now!* And tomorrow you find him a new home where he has running space."

"*No!* He's *mine!* You *can't!*" Frank threw himself over the dog as Lexi cried about her new skirt being ruined and Theo tried to get his younger brother off the top of the dog to get him outside.

"Lexi, stop that now. It'll wash. Frankie, go outside with him if you insist, but get him *out* of here."

The boy argued more and Fran went to Lexi, assured her they could get the stain out, and took her to the kitchen to find a wet towel. The girl sobbed as she hugged Fran and said she was sorry and she hoped she was okay…

"Shh, honey. It's all right. Like your dad said, it'll wash fine. Come on now. Go change and bring it back and we'll get it cleaned right up again." She stroked her girl's hair, nearly the exact color of her father's hair, and thick, almost as thick as her own. "It's been a long day, hasn't it?"

"Don't leave us, Fran. Please. I don't have a mom, not really, 'cause her boyfriend is more important than me and I don't like him and she gets mad at me because I don't like him and you can't leave us, too."

"Honey, I'm not leaving." She saw George watching from the door as she heard herself say it. Ignoring him for the moment, she lowered onto a chair and pulled the girl into her arms. "I'm sure you're far more important to your mom than any boyfriend could be. People just get a little odd for a time when they start a new relationship. It'll adjust again, I'm sure. You should tell her how you feel and talk about it."

"She won't talk to me like you do. I don't understand anything, she says. But I do."

"Of course you do." She smoothed the tears from the sweet face. "Of course you do, Lexi. You're very smart for your age. I think you understand quite a lot, more than people might give you credit for. Right?" The little head nodded. "I know how you feel and it'll be okay. You'll grow up into that smart head of yours and things will be better."

She sniffled and wiped at her eyes. "If I promise Dad I'll be home on time, can we go out again?"

Fran looked over at George. It wasn't her place to answer.

"Of course." He answered from the doorway and came to them. "You can go out with Fran whenever she's willing. Don't beg her to go. Let her ask you. But as long as it doesn't interfere with anything, yes." He set a hand on his daughter's head. "I'm sorry about today, but we're fine. Okay? Fran's welcome any time she'd like to be here."

"I didn't ruin anything?"

George's face melted Fran's heart as he swept Lexi into his arms. "Baby, of course not. But you remember that I love you like crazy and you and your brothers matter before anything else. Okay? Go on up and change now and we'll get that beautiful skirt washed up and ready to wear again." When she started away with a light nod, he caught her little hand. "Hey."

"Hey, what?" Her eyes showed a bit of a spark.

"Hay might be for horses but I love you more than a horse."

Lexi imitated a whinny, smiled, and ran off.

Fran stood up next to him. "That made absolutely no sense."

"No. It didn't when she made it up when she was about seven, either, but it's become our private joke. Glad so far it's still funny to her."

"You are a really good dad."

He raised his eyebrows. "And again, you sound surprised by that."

"I am." She slid her hands up his stomach to his chest. "No offense."

"You're a good mom, too, even if you aren't. And I'm not even a touch surprised."

With a nod just so she didn't ignore it completely, she backed away.

"Hey." He caught her hand and moved close again.

"I'm not playing that game."

A chuckle rumbled through his chest. "Don't worry. Just wanted to know if you were going to let me drive you home."

"I think you better."

"I better?"

"Your dog messed up my skirt far more than Lexi's." She held up a long tear in the side. "This won't wash out. Do you have a safety pin?"

"Damn. Frannie, I'm sorry. I'll replace it…"

"No need. I can fix it. Just thought I'd take advantage of you feeling bad about it tonight." She spoke quietly beside his ear in case of little ones around and backed away again. "You promised dessert."

"Another double entendre?"

She returned his grin and walked away.

Twenty-three

The McKenrys had a yearly tradition of spending the first part of Fourth of July at King's Pointe outdoor water park, the mid-afternoon at the Star Spangled Spectacular where the boys participated in the cardboard boat races, then a family picnic, and fireworks. George said they also did an indoor water park day in early February to chase away the winter blues.

Fran wasn't sure she'd go for the winter family day. If she was still around. Once might have been enough.

She'd refused the offer to spend Saturday with them after all day Friday the Fourth, and not only George and his kids but his loud and rambunctious but generally friendly older brothers and their families, as well. She needed the work time, she'd insisted. Actually, she needed the quiet time. By now it was Sunday morning and she had done more resting than working. A half day of waterslides, which meant climbing a ridiculous amount of stairs but also the gorgeous view of Storm Lake from the top, until she gave up and floated along lazy river in her inner tube, then walking along the lake to watch the races, and playing badminton during the picnic exhausted her body. The nerves about being with his extended family exhausted her brain. It would take a couple of days to catch up, she supposed.

In the meantime, she planned to keep to herself in her cottage and do some painting. The restoration work would wait another day.

Except she needed to get a job soon. Rent from the house was paying her bills fine, but her mother drummed it into her head to always keep saving for a rainy day. *Don't rest on your laurels. Keep moving forward. You'll get stuck in a quagmire if you don't keep moving forward, no matter where you are or what you've already accomplished.*

Two days of rest, though, wouldn't get her too stuck, Francis supposed.

She'd tried to refuse to barge in on their holiday, especially since his ex was supposed to be there. When George said Justine had other plans and *couldn't* make it, and Lexi nearly begged Fran to come, she gave in.

It was going fine until his ex showed up. To be honest, Fran hadn't moved from the waterslides to the lazy river because of exhaustion. She was used to moving right on through exhaustion and thought nothing of it anymore. But the scene when Justine showed up with her live-in sugar daddy, as G.F. called him, and yet threw a fit about Fran being there with *her* children was more than she wanted to deal with. So she bowed out and told Lexi to stay with her dad instead when she tried to go with Fran.

It didn't keep Justine from accusing her of trying to steal her kids away. Fran calmly said no one could steal a child's affection from her mother if the affection was as strong as it should be.

She shouldn't have said it. She said it where the kids couldn't hear her, but she shouldn't have said it at all. One of G.F.'s brother's snickered. The woman screeched. Poor Lexi and Frank were mortified. Theo told their mother to stop yelling and pulled her off somewhere. Fran walked away.

G.F. found her later and sat with her on the lounge chairs, their backs to the lake, while Lexi and Frank played in the pool and Theo and Justin went to race each other on the dual speed slides. He apologized for his ex. But he kept some distance as they watched the fireworks and then dropped Fran off at her door and took them home to settle in. Fair enough, she figured.

His parents had been friendly but not overtly friendly. Of course she knew it could have been her own distance that kept them from being too friendly since she still heard Gwen McKenry's warning in her head to be careful with him. She'd kept wondering just how much they knew, as though she and George were still teens in need of permission to go out.

She brushed that thought away with a long deep breath. Fran loved Sunday mornings by herself. Leaving her phone off and inside, she lazed with a book on the porch where the sun streamed in and stretched her legs out into it to absorb the vitamin D and hopefully add to her very pale legs G.F.'s brothers had teased about, considering how tanned her arms were. She always gardened in jeans, socks, and sturdy tennis shoes. She wasn't afraid of dirt or critters, but she didn't particularly want to be bit, either.

Her hydrangeas, actually her father's hydrangeas, were full of blooms now, big, hand-sized blooms, some fading into a soft lavender with blue tinges. Wherever she moved, she would plant more, as many as possible without overcrowding. Maybe she should go ahead and get starts of the ones her father had planted so many years ago and take part of him with her that way. They took some years to get going when started from a cutting, but it would be nice to have them.

When the two kittens came up to her, the yellow one she first met and its black and white more skittish brother that appeared the next day — at least she expected they were brothers since they looked the same age with the same long tail and the same white feet and neck — Fran thought about overcrowding and G.F.'s small backyard and the dog he gave in to let Frank keep even if there wasn't enough space for George, the 4 half-grown or more kids, their friends, and the large dog. They all needed more space. Of course, the two oldest could very well move out in a few years. Still, yard space was an issue. It was barely big enough for a barbecue with the few friends of the kids.

He'd said he would buy her parents' house if he could afford it. Maybe she'd offer it at a price he couldn't resist. The yard was huge. The house was big. It would be taken care of, so she wouldn't have to worry about that. If her spinet was still there, maybe he'd even play it. Maybe she could walk over and listen to him play.

Looking forward to the quiet day of painting with the windows and door open to let the beautiful summer breeze in, Fran stroked the kittens' heads, sighed luxuriously, and thought she might not paint, either. Maybe she would simply sit right there and read. At least until she got restless. Which she would. Then she would paint until time for his concert.

"When I track Lexi down, I'll *bring* the kids over to you. You *know* how she wanders. And don't yell at me again for not watching well enough when she did it to *you* three times as much as she does it to *me*. And she was *younger* then." G.F. tried hard not to yell at his ex, but he was already frustrated that the girl took off again and Fran didn't answer her phone when he called to see if she'd walked down there.

Eve was still on vacation, so Lexi wasn't there. He'd already called the three other nearby friends to see if she'd stopped by, which he hated to do because it made it too obvious he couldn't keep the girl from wandering off without letting someone know.

He'd done it plenty often as a kid and his mother still harassed him about it whenever he complained about Lexi, but things weren't the same as when he was young. Every kid did it when he was young. No one thought anything of it. They all played outside after dark and went home when the mosquitoes annoyed them too much and their parents just said to go get a bath and wash the dirt off.

It was different these days. And Lexi was a beautiful young girl, not a stocky boy used to fending for himself and for others. It was different.

If Fran wouldn't answer, he'd have to run down there. Letting Justin know where he was headed with instructions to call if Lexi decided to wander back home, he stormed out to the truck and shortly pulled into her gravel excuse for a driveway.

She didn't even get up. She sat on the porch watching him as he called from beside the truck. "Lexi here?" Her eyebrows raised but she didn't answer so he went up to her. "You didn't answer your phone."

"It's Sunday morning. I don't have it on."

"Great, Fran, but it makes it hard to reach you."

"Apparently not too hard. Want coffee? It's fresh."

"No, I'm looking for my daughter. Thought she might have wandered this way since you two are thick as thieves by now."

"I thought she was with her mom today."

"Supposed to be. Can't find her to take her."

"She doesn't want to go. I heard her say it Friday. I know you heard her say it."

"Yeah well, she doesn't have that option. Court said she doesn't. Not my doing. Is she here?"

"No, I haven't seen her. Did you try her friends?"

"Of *course* I tried her friends. This isn't my *first* rodeo with this kid."

"Don't yell at me."

He rolled his shoulders and made himself calm down, just enough. "I'm not yelling at you. I'm just yelling. The girl infuriates the hell out of me when she does this. You've no idea where she is?"

"I have no idea, but I'm sure she's fine. It's just her way of protesting the *court order*. Maybe they should rethink that."

"Yeah, you tell them. Either way, it's my ass in a sling if I don't get the kid over to her mom and she's not above making a stink about it. I can't afford that."

"Didn't she voluntarily give you custody?"

"Yeah, and I don't want to lose it."

"If she doesn't want it, why would you lose it?"

"She'd do it just to piss me off. Okay? Look, we can discuss this some other time. Right now, I need to find my daughter."

Fran rose and came to him with a hand on his chest. "Calm down, George. We'll find her. I'll go back with you and we'll take a walk around town. Someone's had to have seen her."

"I can't go walking around town. It'll look like I'm flaunting the order and just don't give a damn..."

"Fine. Go home. I'll take a walk around town. She'll come to me if she sees me, I'm sure, and I'll call you. Okay? Relax. She's fine."

"*How* in the hell do I *know* she is? None of her friends have seen her. She doesn't have that many." He shoved a hand through his hair.

"You haven't heard otherwise. Assume she is. It'll be easier on you and you'll be less angry when you find her."

"Easy for you to say when you..." He stopped. He couldn't make that mistake again.

"When I don't have kids. Fine. But I do have experience you don't know about, so don't write me off like an idiot, if you wouldn't mind."

"You're not... I'm sorry. I'm just so pissed off. Does she not *want* to stay with me? Is she trying to get them to take her away again and force her back to her mother where she *doesn't* want to be? What *sense* does this make?"

"She's not thinking like that. She's eleven. She just didn't want to go. Nothing more." Fran hugged him. "It's okay. I'll help you find her.”

G.F. figured her hug and words should calm him, but they didn't. He had to go back home and he'd call the whole damned neighborhood if needed. At least they'd know he gave a damn about where the girl was and was trying to get her to where she was supposed to be.

The last person Fran wanted to run into while walking around town in the guise of window shopping as she looked for Lexi was Tana White Berger.

"*Frannie*. Well *hello!* I heard you were still in town, but I haven't seen you for months. Are you hiding from me?"

"Not even two months, actually. And I've been out and about a lot. Storm Lake isn't as small as it used to be."

"No. Crazy, isn't it? So I hear you have been *out*. With G.F. quite a lot, from what I hear. Jim says he actually takes a full lunch break these days and sometimes a long lunch break. Interesting that it started after you came home. Something going on with you two?"

"Yes. And I imagine you know that already. We've been seeing each other, and I've been getting to know his children. Speaking of, have you seen Lexi this morning?"

"Lexi. That girl is going to get herself in trouble. Too like her mother, I'm afraid. That Haden girl was never good enough for G.F. and I tried to warn him. I tell Jim all the time Lexi is taking after Justine far too much and she's going..."

"I'll take that as a no, and Lexi is a beautiful young lady who does not deserve for you to talk this way about her, so please don't. And I don't mean only to me; I mean to anyone. It's not right and it's high time someone told you what you do is not right." Fran stared her down for a second before walking away from the old gossip who had no call talking about someone else not being good enough. Even if Fran agreed.

She felt her hands shake and made up for her nerves about the confrontation by walking faster. She hated confrontations. If the rumors had been about herself, again, she would have ignored it. She would not ignore it about Lexi, or about any of G.F.'s children. She absolutely would not.

Stopping in her tracks, she realized she sounded like their mother, or what she supposed a mother would, or should, feel when someone attacked their young in any way. It was too soon to feel that way about it. She'd only known his kids for a couple of months.

But Lexi was a sweet girl, a real young lady. Fran admired what she saw in her, what she knew Lexi would become. The girl was someone she could be real friends with as she got older, and it was unusual for Fran to feel so strongly that a friendship could work.

Hoping the girl was home by now, she called George at the house, got Frank, and asked.

"No, and Dad is really freaking out. He's out looking for her. No one's seen her. He's scared to death. Do you think she's okay? She's never done this."

"Sweetie, calm down. I'm sure she's fine." Maybe she shouldn't have said as much, but the fear in the boy's voice made her kick in to ... to motherly mode. Where was their mother now? "Do you want me to pick you up so we can walk around together to look?"

"Yes, but Dad won't let us out of the house. Except Theo. He's out looking, too. So are Grams and Gramps. Dad's really freaking out. Lexi doesn't do this. She's always with one of her friends and we always find her right away."

"Okay, sweetie. Help me out this way, then: what does she do when she's upset?"

"Huh?"

"When she needs comfort, who does she go to or where does she go? To her room alone? To a favorite place?"

"I dunno. She doesn't get upset too much."

Fran figured she did a hell of a lot more than she showed. "Okay, but when she is..."

"We used to have a play house and she sometimes went and sat in there when Mom was yelling too much, but that was at the other house before Mom moved into the condo."

"Where was that? Where did you live with your mom?"

Trying to understand his directions since he didn't know the address, Fran told Frank again to stay calm. She went back to her car and hoped to find the green house with dark red shutters that sounded like a dreadful combination.

"Quit fucking bitching at me and go out there and try to *find* your daughter if you're so *worried.* Bitching at me helps *nothing* and ties up my phone." G.F. hung up on Justine. He was mad enough. Worried enough. The last thing he needed was his ex yelling at him while he retraced steps he'd already traced and called the house twenty thousand times to ask Justin if she'd come home yet.

He'd let the police know to watch for her, but with her history of wandering without permission, they weren't real concerned. He had a good crew of his own out looking for her – friends and neighbors who apparently gave more of a shit than her mother did. He hadn't seen or talked to Fran, but Frankie said she'd called and was still looking around town.

Three in the afternoon. He hadn't seen her since before eight a.m. She never disappeared that long, even at her maddest. He was sick to his stomach and his head throbbed and hazed enough he had trouble thinking what to do next. His buddy Paul had taken over directions for the search group and kept up with everyone.

She would be starving by now, wouldn't she? She'd have to go somewhere to eat. Out of desperation, he stopped into all of the places she liked to eat. Some servers and owners he asked looked sympathetic. Others looked judgmental. He didn't give a shit either way. If he was overreacting and embarrassed his daughter too awful much, they'd pick up and move ... wherever Fran moved.

Except she'd be mad about that, too. Lexi needed her friends. They were too important...

His knees tried to give out and he lowered onto a concrete parking stop at the Phillips 66 where he'd pissed and then bought coffee.

"G.F. That you?"

With a grimace, he raised his head to peer across the asphalt parking area and made himself stand up.

"Find the girl yet?" Jim sucked in so much of a large slushie, he should have frozen half his brain.

"Not yet."

"Darn kids. They just don't get it, do they? Wait till they're parents. Bet you hope one of her young 'uns do this to her someday so she'll know how it feels."

It was all G.F. could do to keep from throttling him. "Why in the hell would I want that? So I could worry about my grandkid, too?"

"Well, so she would understand..."

"You're a fucking moron." He shouldn't have said it, but it came out and he wasn't sorry he said it. He walked away.

"That's gotta be that *woman's* influence." Jim called behind his back. "You ask me, you should keep yourself and your kids away from that one. She's wicked mean and she's gonna end up just like her old man..."

G.F. turned back and forced himself to keep his hands at his sides as he stood in his coworker's face. "Mean? She's *mean?* You ever actually *talk* to her?"

"Nah, but the wife did earlier. The crazy woman said horrible things to Tana."

"Like what, exactly?"

"Like she wasn't acting right and like she was saying anything about folks that aren't true."

"What in the hell is so mean about that? She's right. Your wife has always been a backstabbing gossip and she hasn't bothered to grow out of it. Don't talk that way about Fran again. You've got no room to talk. And if you're not going to help me find my daughter, stay the hell out of my way." Maybe he'd have to pay for it later, at work, but he couldn't care about that now.

Mean? Frannie? What a fucking moron that man was, and his wife, too. About time someone told them.

Taking a deep breath to try to calm himself, he tried again to think where to go next, what to do. For the life of him, his brain just wouldn't work. "Lexi, come on, baby. Call me." He got back in his truck and sat there in a daze. "Where are you, baby?" A flash of memory back to high school when he was getting ready to try again to ask Fran out and saw her talking to that guy in a Corvette just passing through scared him even more. An out-of-towner. Someone who hadn't known her all her life, didn't know her family or the rumors. She'd attached right to him and his sweet talk and his worldly manner.

Lexi wouldn't do the same, would she? Folks were jumping off Interstate 80 all the time passing through, getting gas and food before hitting Des Moines or after getting by it, and there were the young visitors in groups hitting the water park...

But Frannie had been nineteen. Lexi was eleven. She wouldn't... But she was curious, and friendly, and...

Gritting his jaw, he dialed Fran. "Please pick up. Come on..."

"Hey. Find her?"

His spirits sank at the question. "No. Frannie, where in the hell would she be?"

"I don't know. I've just come from her mom's old place and looked around. I didn't see any sign of her. Probably..."

"She wouldn't go there. She hated it there."

"Hard telling what a kid will do when you least expect it. Never thought I'd take off with a near stranger, either, but there you go."

The pit in his stomach burst into flames and he leaned out his truck just barely in time.

"George..?"

Cleaning up as well as possible, he returned to the voice in his phone. "Yeah, not what I wanted to hear."

"Oh. No. I'm sorry. She's just a kid. She didn't... Where are you?"

He managed to tell her while his head dropped to the steering wheel.

"Stay right there. I'll meet you."

Like he wanted to try to drive right now, anyway. He'd have to go in and find a bucket of water, get the mess out of the way so some kid wouldn't step in it. And before Fran got there.

Pull it together, McKenry. You've got a child to find.

He managed to look together and in control when he asked for a bucket and had to buy one and then went to the men's room to fill it. She pulled up as he was finishing and he tossed the bucket in the back of his truck.

She looked beautiful, together, strong ... and worried although she looked to be trying to hide her worry. "How are you doing?"

"I'm glad you're here."

With a light nod, she set a hand on his face for just a second. "Okay, what we're going to do next is go back to my place so I can make you eat something because I'm guessing you haven't..."

"Not until I find her."

"George, she's probably just found a little hiding space to wait out the day until it's past time to be at her mom's and then she'll come home. No one's seen or found her. That's a good thing."

"How in the hell is that a good thing?"

"It just is. Follow me home."

"Fran..."

"Not asking. Or should we leave your truck and come back for it? I'll go tell them..."

"No. I'm going to go..." He stopped. Where? He'd been everywhere already.

Her look said she was thinking the same. "Maybe she'll come by my place. I haven't been there. She could be..."

"Your place. She would go to your place."

"I left her a note that if she did, she was to get right back home and call you, but I haven't checked recently..."

"Let's go."

They didn't see any sign of her when they pulled up or went in, but Fran managed to get him to sit and started fresh coffee. She set out a plate of crackers and cut up some fresh cheese. He stared at it until she picked some up and handed it to him.

"It's after four. Eight hours. She wouldn't do this on purpose. I can't believe she'd do this to me on purpose. Something's happened."

With no words that would help, she hugged him standing behind his chair, leaning down over him.

"You can't even argue anymore." He tilted his head to see her.

"I still have to think she's hiding out."

"Because you *want* to think that, not because your head tells you it's the truth."

"Yes, I want to think that." Her voice was low. She had to be the calm one, had to help him, whatever happened.

"You're nearly as scared as I am. Don't try to deny it." His eyes pierced hers, dared her.

"Yes." She shifted and lowered onto the chair next to him, grasping his hands. "Okay, I am scared for her. And for you. It's impossible not to be, but I have to think ... have to tell myself... Like I did whenever my father wandered off. I had to tell myself he was fine so I wouldn't go crazy with worry every time. I've had practice at this."

"It's not the same..."

"How do you know?" She bit back her sudden anger. "Okay, I'm sure it's not, but that doesn't mean I don't understand. I love her, too, George. Scoff if you want, but she's become important to me..."

He gripped her hard, pressed her in against him, buried his face against her neck. "She's my baby, Frannie."

"I know." She stroked his hair. "Come on. Eat something and we'll go back out."

"To do what? Look where?"

"Anywhere. Because it'll make you feel better."

Twenty-four

When George hung up from the most recent call and slumped onto Fran's couch, she sat next to him and rubbed his shoulder. "What is it?"

He scrubbed his face with his hands, held his breath, let it out, and dropped his head against the back. "Do you know why I quit playing piano?"

"Because of those boys..."

"Yes. Partly. And because they found out my middle name."

"Your middle name? I don't even know what it is. Is it that bad?"

"Frederick. George Frederick McKenry, after George Frideric Handel. My mother pushed me to take lessons. I threw a tantrum about it more than once, although to be honest, I loved it. But try being the youngest of three boys, the others rough and tumble, and taking piano lessons so you're supposed to turn out like a great composer, and then have the whole Freshman class find that out because your brother got mad at you and spilled the beans."

"Not the whole class, obviously, since I didn't know."

"Well, most of the class. Anyone..."

"The popular kids, the ones that mattered. You can say it. I know I wasn't. But you were a football star, one of the popular kids."

"Later. Only because I quit music and used the anger productively, as my father always taught us. Be angry, but use it wisely. I liked football, so it worked okay, but..." He slumped forward to rest his elbows on his knees. "Lexi wants to take piano lessons. I keep stalling. Mom's taught her some basics. Or she did some time ago. She may have given up by now."

"What does this have to do with her being..?"

"Missing? I know she is. You can say it." Throwing her words back at her, he stood and returned to his near constant pacing. "She went to a slumber party Friday night after fireworks and moped around all day yesterday. I figured she didn't bother to sleep since they generally don't ,and I didn't ask what was wrong, just told her to knock off the grouchiness. Well, one of the girls finally admitted to her mother that the whole group made fun of Lexi, not only because a couple of them saw Justine throw her hissy fit at the water park, but also for her new skirt. They said it was weird and made her look like an upside-down umbrella and laughed harder when she tripped on it going up the stairs."

"Oh no."

"There's more. The little Stonestreet brat I've always tried to keep her away from mentioned…" He turned to look at her, to watch her reaction. "Us. Apparently it's a big deal among her friends, and probably their parents, that we're together."

"Only small people have nothing better to talk about."

"That may be so and I wouldn't give a rat's ass for myself, but my kids…" He lowered onto a chair and shoved a hand through his hair. "Fran…"

"George, don't let them do this." She went to him and touched his face, raised it to hers.

"Where is this going? Anywhere? Until you leave? You know what that'll do to my kids?"

"That was your choice. You chased me, remember?"

"Did I?" He bolted up, across the room. "I'm starting to wonder."

"Let's not do this now. Wait until she's back and you're not upset, and then we'll talk."

"About what, exactly? Yeah, you said you weren't staying but you know damned well I expected to change your mind and yet other than to extend it a couple of months or so and getting close to my daughter…"

"Don't do this. You need to stop now."

"Why? Is this a game to you and you're afraid I'm figuring it out? Figured you'd come back to town and do the guy who embarrassed you in front of a couple of other football players and pay him back and then run? Might be fair to me, but it's not fair to my kids. To Lexi."

Fran walked out of the house and slammed the door. A game? He hit on her. He chased her. What right did he have to blame her for anything when she was honest with him, when it was his choice to pursue her after she told him... *Damn* men. What *right* did they have to think a woman would just change her mind and give in after they had sex? To change things to fit what *they* wanted just because they wanted it? It was only sex, after all. She didn't have a kid with him. She didn't even have a marriage contract. She'd promised him nothing.

It was raining softly after threatening all day, but she didn't care. She went out to pull a few new weeds littering her garden beside the fully blooming deep red iris. It was incredibly beautiful in front of the pink and dark blue hydrangea blooms.

"You're getting wet." He stood on the porch and stared at her, leaned against the pole as he had that day...

"Go home, George. If I see or hear from her, I'll call you."

"Frannie, come back in here."

"Don't give me orders. Just go home. Your boys are worried, too. They need you there." The rain got heavier, a cold rain, and she shivered as her lightweight ivory blouse stuck to her back, but she didn't want to hear one more thing that man had to say.

Instead of leaving, he came to her and tried to pull her up from the grass that started to puddle in the low places. She shrugged him off. "Go home. Go back to your kids. Don't embarrass them any longer by being here."

"I didn't say..."

"Yes, you did. Just go." She shoved his arm away when he tried again. "*Go.*" Fran hoped like hell that Lexi was inside somewhere, not out in the cold rain, in the growing dusk.

He walked away.

She watched him, his backside, his slumped shoulders, the rain hitting his shoulders as he went to his truck and got in without another word, without another glance at her.

But he just sat there, his head dropped against the head rest.

Fine. Let him sit there. Fran went into her cottage and shivered again. She had to get dry. Going to the little chest of drawers she kept beside what used to be a storage or linen closet just outside the tiny bathroom and was now her wardrobe, she pulled out old sweats and a thick loose T-shirt.

A thump caught her attention as she pulled the wet cold blouse over her head. Had he come in? Carrying her shirt, she went to look. The front door was still closed. No one there. Another thump. In the greenhouse. An animal? Too loud for that. Maybe. Unless it knocked something over.

Fran pulled the shirt on and grabbed the old putter G.F. had told her to replace with a better weapon and tried to decide whether to go out and see if he was still there and let him investigate the noise, or to steel herself and go check. An animal, probably. In which case, she'd call for animal control to capture and release the thing where it belonged.

Her heart pounded as she stood on one side of the door that led to the greenhouse, set a hand on the old knob, and turned slowly. A face peered back at hers and she jumped about a mile. Had she screeched? Damn, she hoped she hadn't...

"It's just me." The young face stared in fear at the raised putter that Fran didn't remember raising.

"Lexi." She exhaled the words as she started to breathe again. "What are you doing here?"

"I fell asleep. It's late, isn't it? I was only... I didn't mean to fall asleep. I was working in the garden. I'd been walking around town, along the lake, but there were too many people and I wanted to think. Somewhere alone. So I came here. The door was locked, but I climbed up over the garden wall... I'm sorry I scared you."

Fran dropped the putter and hugged the girl hard. "Oh honey, the whole town has been looking for you all day. Your father..." Her father. "Come on." She dragged the girl by the hand, hoping George hadn't left, through the cottage and out the front door. The rain had softened but it wouldn't have mattered if it was still torrential.

He was still there. Sitting in his truck. His eyes closed, head against the headrest. Fran dragged Lexi over and knocked on the window. When he wearily looked over, she put the girl in front of her.

George nearly knocked them both over when he pushed his door and jumped out and grabbed Lexi up in his arms, holding her tight against his body. "Where in the *hell* have you been?" He released her to grab her face between his hands. "Are you okay? You're not hurt?" He scanned her and stared into her face again. "Tell me. You're not hurt?"

"I'm fine, Dad. I'm sorry..."

He pulled her back in, tight enough Fran wasn't sure the girl would be able to breathe, especially with the large hand holding her head against his chest as he kissed her head over and over.

"Dad." Lexi wriggled, trying to get space. "I'm fine. I'm sorry..."

"*Where* have you been? I should ground you for the next *thirty years.*"

The girl repeated what she'd told Fran and more, said she couldn't sleep at all the night before and couldn't deal with her mom because she'd been so embarrassing at the water park and she came to talk to Fran about it, but she wasn't there, so she decided to work on the garden until she came home, but she rested her head on the patch of grass and next she knew, it was raining on her. She apologized about twenty times in between for scaring him, that she didn't mean to and gave him hugs and begged him not to send her back to live with her mom instead.

The rain grew heavier again. Fran looked up at it, let it run over her face. An excuse to hide her own emotions. Then she gathered herself and took a deep breath. "Come inside." Dirt streaked Lexi's face and her clothes were wet and muddy.

"We're going home." George started to push the girl toward the open truck door. "We have to let your mother know. And your brothers. They're worried sick."

Fran touched his arm. He was shaking. "Come inside and call them. You need to relax a few minutes before you drive." She had to coax him by tugging his arm, with Lexi's help saying she was too dirty to get in his truck. Not that George cared at that point, but he gave in and hugged his daughter again as soon as they were inside.

Fran went to find her long thick robe and took it to Lexi. "Here, baby. Go take a warm bath and drop your clothes outside the door so I can get them dry for you." An excuse. She wanted to give George a minute away from his daughter to calm down.

"I have to call..." His hand shook against his phone.

"Let me. I'll call your boys. They can call their mother. You don't need to talk to her right now." She used her own phone, got Theo, told him Lexi was there and safe and they'd be home soon.

"Let me have this." She gripped the hem of his shirt and started to pull it.

"I have to get home."

"She's in the tub getting warm and clean. You're staying until she's done, so let me get this dry for you."

"Frannie, I…"

"Later. Okay? Let me have this."

His arms blocked her, heavy against his side, and he sank onto the floor, against the wall. His chest heaved. His hands pressed hard against his face.

She lowered beside him and pulled his hands away. They were soaked from his tears and he tried to pull back from her, but she wouldn't allow it. "George, it's alright. She's fine. You don't have to hide from me. It's okay."

"All the stuff I was thinking…" His breath was heavy between his words.

"I know." She forced his head to where she could cradle him. "Okay. George, it's okay."

Suddenly, he took her face in his hands and kissed her hard. "Forgive me. I'm sorry. It's been a hell of a hard few years and I'm taking it out on you when it's the last thing I want to do…"

"We'll talk later. Let me have this."

Allowing her to pull the wet shirt over his head, he gripped her again, leaned in, ran his hands along her side, up to her breast…

She pulled back. "Not with your daughter in the house." Escaping, she took his clothes and Lexi's to the washer, added her own as she stepped out of them, and went to find something dry. He followed, caressing her stomach, teasing her neck with his lips, apologizing, asking her again to please forgive him…

And he startled at a knock on the door.

"Go check that." She turned to touch his face. "But give me a minute to dress before you let anyone in."

Twenty-five

The last people she expected were G.F.'s parents. In between asking him twenty questions about Lexi, they stopped to look over at Fran as though surprised she would be in her own house.

"Francis, dear." Gwen McKenry came to her where she'd stopped a distance away from George, who was shirtless with mussed wet hair. "You've done wonders with this place. Constance talked of tearing it down, it was such a wreck, but what a nice little … getaway you've made of it. I love the colors."

"Thank you, but my aunt has no right to do anything with it since it belongs to me."

"Of course, and she was told as much when she tried."

"She tried?"

Gwen glanced at George but his father filled in the details. Her aunt Connie had gone to Marvin McKenry within days of her father's passing to ask if he did demolition or knew who would. Marvin asked first if she owned the building, to which she skirted around the answer and finally said she didn't yet but would soon. Marvin had put the word out around his fellow construction companies to be sure she had ownership before doing any work for her. Made her mad as a wet hen, so he said, when she ran into the same wall every time she tried.

"Thank you for stopping her. She has no idea what she would have destroyed that way. Let me go check on Lexi." She touched George's eyes and walked away, back to knock on the bathroom door. "Are you okay in there?"

The soft *yes* that came through the old wood that needed stripped and re-varnished and sealed wasn't convincing and Fran stood a minute wondering if she should ask again.

The door opened and the girl looked too much like a frightened nearly drowned little mouse with her long thin face and big eyes sticking out from Fran's big fluffy robe. "Can I stay here tonight?" She looked up with her head tilted down, too waif-like.

Fran set fingers under her chin and raised the girl's head. "Look up into someone's face when you speak to them. It makes you look more confident, as you should be."

"I can't."

"Yes, you can. And no, you can't stay with me tonight. Your father will need you home with him after worrying all day."

"I'll have to go to Mom's."

"I doubt that. But Lexi, if you ever need to talk to someone, you can talk to me. Okay? Girl to girl."

"Dad's mad at you, too. I heard him."

Heard how much? "Well, I think he's not too awfully mad. Come on out here. Your grandparents are here checking on you..."

"Grams is here?" At that, Lexi swirled away, dragging the length of the robe on the floor behind her.

Fran stood back as the girl lunged into her grandma's arms and said again she was sorry and something more that muffled under the tight hug. George skimmed a hand through his hair, his chest flexing, his face hiding emotion she didn't want to see anymore right now, so she went to check the laundry and waited the couple of minutes for the spin to stop.

"We'll get out of your way for the night if Alexis can borrow that robe she's wearing. I'll make her keep it pulled up out of the mud."

She turned to him, alone, half bare, fatigue setting about his whole body, so it seemed. "Or you can stay for about fifteen minutes. I'll throw a dry towel in with your things and they should be dry by then. It's a little machine, but highly effective."

"Like someone I know." He wandered closer and touched her face. "Can we come back tomorrow? I'll take the day off. They'll understand. I mean Lexi and I both. There are things maybe we should talk about as far as..."

"As not letting her go so attached to me? You're going to suggest she keep her distance as you're trying to do?"

"What do you expect?"

She ran the backs of her fingers up his hard stomach, up to his chest, between the firm pecs, over the curly brown hair, turning her hand to caress her palm with his soft sleek hardness.

"Stay, Frannie. Not for a few months or a couple of years." He leaned in and kissed her, a hand cupping her backside to bring her closer, the other cupping her head. "Don't plan to move. Just stay."

"I haven't embarrassed you and your children enough?"

He pulled back to catch her eyes. "I ... I was distraught..."

"Which is generally when people most mean what they say. I can't talk anymore tonight and I don't want you to come tomorrow."

"Fran..."

"It's fine. I understand. But know one thing, George McKenry. I absolutely did not come here with any kind of vengeance in mind or any idea of doing one thing more than getting this place ready to sell so I could move on with my life. If you don't believe one other thing in the world, believe that. I don't use people. If I did, I sure as hell would never use you or your children, especially not your children."

G.F. couldn't even answer. The day had been too long, too taxing, and he'd regretted accusing her as soon as it came out. He did it too often. It was one of the problems in his marriage, and he knew it, tried to fix it, but Justine wouldn't listen. Didn't want it fixed, maybe. Fran was more reasonable. Maybe he could get her to understand. Another day. When he was less tired, less vulnerable.

He wanted to be home with Lexi and his boys, and his parents if they would stay a while. "I'll at least come back for the clothes tomorrow. You can kick me out after that, if you want."

She followed him at a distance, stopped somewhere, and caught up to hand him a shirt. "It's a man's shirt. Should fit enough to keep you warm."

He started to argue. No way in hell he was wearing Calvin's shirt she still had in her damn dresser...

"It was my father's. One of the few things of his I've kept. It makes a good house shirt, and it was big on him, like his gardening shirts always were, so it should work well enough."

Her father's. Maybe that he could do. And his parents and daughter were watching the exchange. He couldn't make it a big deal. Pulling it over his shoulders, he felt the snugness – he was far bigger than Virgil Barrett had been – but it smelled... He brought his arm up to his nose. "Smells like you."

Did she actually flush? He supposed he shouldn't have said it, judging by the way his parents shuffled around and pulled Lexi farther away.

"As I said, it makes a good house shirt since it's loose on me. You can bring it back tomorrow when you pick up your things." Dismissing him, she went to Lexi and gave her a hug. "Unwind tonight so you can sleep well, baby. You don't want to get too tired after getting soaked in the rain."

Lexi nodded and scratched at her arm. Again.

G.F. went over and pulled up the sleeve of the robe. Four red bite marks were surrounded by a red rash.

Fran took the girl's arm to study it. "You just got those?"

"Mosquito bites. She always reacts like this. Have more?"

Lexi nodded and scratched at her leg.

"Okay, time to go find your cream. Fran…"

"Here. Hold on." She hurried to her kitchen and came back with a plastic container of an oily paste-like substance. "Try this."

G.F. stopped her. "What is that?"

"Just coconut oil with a drop of peppermint. It should soothe and heal it. It might tingle a bit, but that's okay."

"Tingling would be tons better than this itch." Lexi trusted Fran; it showed, maybe too much. She stuck her arm toward her.

To her credit, Fran did look to him for permission, and of course he gave it.

"That's better already. You're amazing. Thank you!" Lexi hugged her with her unscathed arm and accepted the container to go put it on other spots that needed it. His mother asked if it was something Fran learned from her father and she replied she'd done her own natural research and almost always now used natural relief methods instead of chemicals. His father gave him the raised eyebrows look. Again. He'd have to deal with them later.

And he knew it sounded ridiculous not to wait the ten minutes or so for their clothes to be done, but he did wait for Lexi to borrow actual clothes and change into them before he nearly pushed her out the cottage door. He thought he heard the beep of the dryer finishing as they left the front porch, but he acted like he didn't.

It gave him an excuse to return the next day after she'd said she didn't want him there. She wouldn't hold his clothes hostage, he supposed. She'd let him in at least that long.

Twenty-six

If George McKenry thought he was fooling her or anyone else, he was sadly mistaken. Fran knew darn well why he'd refused to wait for his clothes. She'd told him not to come tomorrow. Maybe she wouldn't open the door when he came. Maybe she just wouldn't be home. He could come Tuesday instead. During lunch.

Stop thinking of his body, Francis Barrett, and get your head together. The man insulted you. Don't just take it because he's … he's…

She dropped onto her couch. He was an imperfect man, but a good one. Naturally good. *Real* good. Not fake good, like Cal. George's faults annoyed her, but they were far better than Cal's … than his anything.

Including his body.

With a sigh, she went to put music on her small stereo. Which did she want? With a nod to her quirky sense of humor, she grabbed one she hadn't played in some time. Maroon 5. Their first. Cal had hated the concert, except for all of the girls, young girls, surrounding them, girls as skinny as the band's lead singer and some of them nearly as tattooed. Just after the concert, he talked of her getting a tattoo. On her breast. Stupid man. As if she didn't know why that was suddenly a turn on? That young girl showing most of what she had and her big lips tattoo of which only the top half showed over her tight white tank top had his attention all night. She'd nearly left him there to find her after the show.

She should have.

Either way, the show was good and she finally ignored him and focused fully on the music, the lyrics – the lyrics were what she loved, not the music itself and not the lead singer since he was far too skinny for her personal taste – and let herself truly enjoy the night, with Cal, a near stranger to her even after four years together, enjoying himself differently at her side.

She could just as well have gone alone. And she should have.

Letting herself absorb back into the memory of being part of the crowd, she turned off the big light to leave only a glow from a small lamp, closed her eyes, and swayed to *This Love*.

Appropriate for thoughts of Calvin. She stopped the CD and changed it to a mix of Blues artists, one she'd put together herself so they were only her favorite songs.

Time for a real love instead. She'd always known Cal would be temporary, not real. It drew her toward him when that's what she thought she wanted. The infuriatingly annoying man she had now, though ... was what she wanted. He infuriated her mainly because he couldn't tell how much she wanted him. Fair, maybe, considering he knew how fast she'd picked up and run with Cal, as did the whole freaking town, of course, which was why she'd stayed away, why she hadn't been there for her father's funeral and more importantly for her father when he still needed her. She'd consoled herself about not being at the funeral because she figured he didn't need her anymore, anyway. And she didn't give a rat's ass if her aunt had needed help. Obviously, she didn't, since she'd planned everything so fast Fran couldn't get there in time.

G.F.'s phrase. *Rat's ass* wasn't something she'd ever said. Or thought. She was thinking, not talking, so the correct way to say it, or think it, was...

Just stop. Not everything was about how you said something. It was about what you said, or more importantly, what you meant. About the intent. It was all about the intent.

Which was why she couldn't be as angry at George as she wanted to be, or thought she should be. He hadn't meant it the way it came out. He meant he was unsure of her. He meant he wanted her to stay. It came out ... in the form of a distressed man, which was fair, she supposed.

Turning the stereo louder, Fran wandered into the greenhouse. She hadn't looked at her father's paintings again since that night, the day she'd found them, the night George first stayed with her. Not *stay* stay, since he'd had to go back home, but stayed *with* her. And he'd truly been with her at that moment, the whole time. Every part of him screamed he was only right there in the moment, not thinking of a business deal or how long it would take for her to be done enough or what would come next or anything at all under the sun except that he was there with her, inside her, and loving every second of it.

With a sigh, she kicked the secret door back open and pulled the paintings out. Nature. Flowers. Details in large scale and landscapes in nearly blurred views. They showed far more about the artist than about the subject matter. He was a romantic. A dreamer. Of course she'd known that. Her mother had yelled about it often enough. But there was more. She saw part of him in his art she'd never known existed, but she couldn't quite finger what it was.

There was still the big portfolio she hadn't touched. It could be empty, she supposed. Or it could be more of the same, those he'd taken off the wood frames to reuse the frames.

Time to find out.

George knew he should not go back to her that night, but he knew he wouldn't talk himself out of it, either. Lexi, for some reason, did not want to stay at home and would not go to her mother's place, so he let her and Frankie go with his parents for the night. He stayed home until they called to say they were in and safe and Lexi again told him she loved him and to not be mad at Fran...

Mad at Fran. He assured her he was not. He had to assure himself she wasn't mad at him, although she had the right to be. Theo and Justin assured him they would be just fine on their own, they were *nearly legal,* at which he rolled his eyes and told them to just stay in because he couldn't handle one more kid he couldn't track down that particular weekend and that he'd have his phone on.

"Call me if you need anything. I'm just a half mile away..."

"Dad, we're not children. We're fine. And we know where you'll be." Theo threw him a sly grin. "Have a good night with your girlfriend. Maybe she can help you relax."

"Don't be fresh."

"Hey, we're only saying we don't care. In case you wanted to know. Frankie does, but we don't." Theo shrugged.

"This isn't the same as..." He stopped himself.

"As Mom's friends? Yeah, we didn't figure it was. We like Fran

okay. She's pretty cool. Night, Dad. Don't do anything we wouldn't …
at least when we get your age."

"Don't have girls over here."

"Then can we go out?" Justin smirked.

"No. Hell. I should take you to your grandparents', also."

"He's kidding." Theo shoved his brother. "No girls. No going
out. I'm going to raid his castle and steal all of his food and see if he
can figure a way out of it. Survival skills, you know."

G.F. rolled his eyes again as they harassed each other on the way
to their room about that game they always played. He figured they'd
be far too into it within about two minutes to bother thinking about
girls, but he yelled after them that he could be right back at any time.

And he probably would be.

Fran spread the intricately detailed paintings out across the
greenhouse tables. She shouldn't have opened the portfolio. This was
a side of her father she'd never wanted to know.

Body parts mingled with every kind of flower she could imagine.
Naked body parts. Mostly women. No faces, fortunately, at least none
recognizable as anyone in particular. Profiles of faces blended with
hydrangea blooms, their colors bleeding together, or sheltered by lilies
to hide their identity. Iris. There were a lot of iris, bending gracefully
in imitation with or in contrast to the bend and curve of the bodies.
Rose buds hid nothing but instead complemented the highlights,
shadows, curves, rising proudly or dipping in a bow from their stems.

She never would believe her father had done this if he hadn't
scrawled his name across the bottom. It was his writing, his signature.

At least he'd never shown the things. As far as she knew. There
would be major talk about that if he had, so he hadn't. At least not
locally. Had he done anything with them?

A harsher thought slapped across her brain: were these women
local? Did he have them there, in the garden shack, posing for him?

She shouldn't have looked tonight. A very long day. Topped by
this.

"Who were you?" Fran whispered up into the dusty greenhouse
air. And she walked away from them, from the sprawled out

nakedness of flesh and passion and beauty, out to the garden where Lexi had hidden, had fallen asleep. "Why am I still here? Why don't I just pick up and go again? It's not that hard. The hard thing is staying." Still a whisper, this time to fresh, cool, rain-washed air scented by flowers and herbs now blooming pretty and pert, thriving from her attention. And from Lexi's.

Fran had thought the hardest thing she'd ever have to do in her life was to come back, to clear out the shack, her father's shack, to deal with her regrets, with her memories of the last time they really talked, with the ghost of his garden remnants.

It was nothing compared to the thought of staying.

G.F. was an idiot for thinking she'd plotted to embarrass him, to use him. She'd hoped not to even see him. Now she spent every day hoping to see him and hoping not to see him. She spent every night wondering how it might have been if she'd stayed, if she'd said yes that day he asked her out.

Maybe they would be divorced now and hating each other for who they were that they used to love or thought they'd loved. How did you change your mind so drastically? She'd barely changed her mind about Cal. He was never more than companionship and escape and so she had few hard feelings for him, no more than she had for herself for knowing deep inside what he was, for being told what he was, and figuring she wouldn't get better than him, anyway.

G.F. was far more dangerous.

He meant too much. He was bringing out too much inside she'd had locked away that was now budging against the inner bounds of the tightly tied ropes binding it. Like her father, apparently. The quiet polite self-contained man who only started to show himself, figuratively and literally, once his mind started to go.

Fran hoped to hell none of those body parts in the paintings were his own. Or her mother's. A shiver shook her whole body and she wrapped her arms around herself.

G.F. tested the door when she didn't answer. Unlocked. Free for anyone to just walk in. Determined to show her just why she needed to keep it locked, and to get a better lock, he turned the knob slowly and stepped in quietly. At the current moment, he hoped to hell she didn't heed his advice and get a better weapon than the putter. And he watched for any sign she was ready to use the putter. It'd be damn hard to work with a broken knee cap or shoulder or wherever the woman decided to whack him.

Music filled the place, loud enough it wasn't surprising she didn't hear him knock. Stevie Ray Vaughan. *Texas Flood.* More a long guitar solo than a song, so he'd heard it described. He never would have imagined Fran listening to Blues. He barely did, at rare times, enough to know this particular tune.

Dim light guided his path through her ... well, it wasn't quite a living room, but he didn't know what else to call the small main space of the cottage. His eyes turned up to her bed in the loft. He saw no movement behind the sheer teal and white layered drapes hanging from the center of the opening and pulled out to the edges of the bed. Too feminine for his taste, but it was her place and he had to admit he liked that part of her more than he would have expected.

Noticing the door to the greenhouse cracked open, he made his way over, again quietly, again watching for her putter. She wasn't there, either. The place was much cleaner than the last time he'd been in it, their first night together. No dirt littered the tables. Containers were cleaned and stacked together.

Paintings caught his attention as he moved toward the side door, and he stopped there first. Nude paintings. By her father. He had to chuckle as he perused them. Nice work. Interesting concept. He picked one up to study it closer and shook his head in amusement. The old man had a more interesting side to him than he expected. Although he wasn't too awful surprised. What man didn't like nudity, if he was honest? It was tasteful, anyway. Romanticized instead of too awfully realistic, and artistic instead of crude.

Of course Fran might not be as understanding, or as appreciative.

He caught a glimpse of her when she moved out in the shadows of her father's garden. Her arms were crossed tight in front of her breasts. Her head was dipped. She ambled about slowly. Not appreciative of them at all, he figured.

As he got to the door, a song he recognized began. *Fever.*

Appropriate. A deep male voice sang it; he didn't know who it was, but it was a nice version. He called her name softly from the door, speaking barely over the music. The last thing either of them needed tonight was more of a fright, but she jumped as she turned to him.

"Hey."

"Why are you here?"

He wandered closer. "Seems you have a penchant for that question."

She was silent until he got up close. "I guess it's the biggest question I have these days. Or one of them. Might be hard to say, with as many as I have."

"Well." He ran his fingers up through her mussed hair. "Maybe I should clarify it for you, then." He dipped his face close to hers, teased her lips, let it turn into a full blown kiss ... except her arms remained wrapped tight around her front. Keeping distance.

"That clarifies nothing." Her eyes were nearly fierce in their glare, under the hazy moon and mist.

"That's not what I meant. That was only a precursor." Holding her beautiful wary face between his large hands, G.F. kissed her nose. "I'm here, Frannie, because I'm in love with you, because I want your company, because I want to make up for time we could have had if I hadn't been so dense and so hormone-driven back in my younger days..."

"You're not hormone-driven now?"

"Hard not to be around you, but not the same. Did you hear the rest of that?"

"Yes."

He nodded, waiting.

"George..." She stepped back and took his hand, led him back into the greenhouse, to the paintings. "My father's, apparently. I just found them."

"Nice work."

She turned a surprised stare to him. "That's all you can say?"

"What more's there to say? A shame he never showed his artistic talent. Have to wonder why."

"Why don't you?"

He was more taken aback at the question than he should have been.

Fran turned to him, turning him with her grip, and slid her hands under his shirt, set them flat against his stomach. "It scares me to be so like my father, to find all the time I'm so much more like him than I ever thought."

"You do porn paintings, too? That, I'd really love to see."

"They aren't porn. They're... and no. I don't. I have. I mean... sketches..." She pulled back and her cheeks reddened.

"I find that highly adorable, you should know."

"That you've made me admit something I never have and embarrassed myself?"

"No. And don't be embarrassed. That you've done porn sketches."

"Not porn. Art. Studying the body, the technique. It's about the technique, the..."

"Right. Technique matters."

"Now you're making fun of me."

"Absolutely not." He shrugged. "Okay, maybe. But only because I do find the thought of it so adorable." Before she could gather herself enough to answer, he ran his fingers softly over the images on the closest canvas. "Almost thought I'd be able to feel the texture. Of the flower, not the canvas."

"Of the flower or the woman?"

"Well, both, to be honest. Look." He took her hand, shaped it so her first two fingers stuck out, and ran them along a beautifully detailed flower petal. "Do you feel it? Or think you should be able?" Then he ran them along the thigh of a curvy young woman. "You can feel her warmth, right? Or is it me? Am I a pervert enough to think I can?"

"You're certainly pervert enough to run your girlfriend's fingers over a naked woman in a painting."

He laughed. Then he released her and shifted to stare directly into those incredible round eyes. "You called yourself my girlfriend."

"Aren't I? Your kids think I am."

"After today, I wasn't sure. I was such an ass, Frannie. I am sorry...”

"You said that already.”

"But I’m not sure you’ve forgiven me.”

"And you still want me to be your girlfriend.”

"Absolutely. Are you?”

"Your parents don’t approve.”

This time, he laughed out loud and grabbed her in a hug. "You have to understand. I’m their baby boy. The older two are ... well, Mom and Dad were just as glad when they moved out and got out from under their roof where they destroyed half of what mattered most with their wrestling and fighting and such. I was the peacemaker and the least trouble. And the baby. I think Mom hoped I’d avoid girls altogether, except she adores the grandkids, but...”

"No one will be good enough for you?”

"Right. Well, that’s the idea. Not true, of course.”

"Justine wasn’t good enough for you. Not by a long shot. Do you know how often I wanted to tell you that? Do you know how badly I cringed to see you pay attention to her?”

"Wish you had told me.”

"You wouldn’t have listened.”

"No?” He ran his hands down along her thighs.

"No.”

He kissed just above her ear and spoke into it gently. "You’re wrong. I would have listened to you.”

"George...”

He slid his hands up under the back of her shirt. "I would have. And I will now. Who’s singing this?”

"Buddy Guy. And I’ve heard a lot of lines in my day, G.F. McKenry...”

"Not a line. Try me. And can we start it over again?”

"Start ... what? Us or the song?”

"The song.” He nuzzled into her neck. "I feel no need to start us over again. Going pretty well, isn’t it? Not perfect, but all things considered, not too shabby, either.”

"We can start the song over. It’s one of my favorites.”

"Mine, too. At least now it is.”

She slipped one hand up on his chest and gripped his hand with the other. "Dancing is healthy, you know. Do you like to dance?"

"Yes. And I know it is."

"I mean ... there are studies. It supposedly..." She paused as he teased her lips and swayed her with the music. "I'm glad you do. Like to dance."

"Hm. Studies about?"

"Never mind."

"No, go ahead. There's a reason you brought it up now."

"It supposedly helps dementia, also. Helps fight it off."

"Stop worrying about that, Fran. The worry is going to hurt you more than whatever you might have inherited." He pressed his lips against hers.

She pulled back to lay her head against his shoulder. "You should be home with Lexi."

"She and Frank are at their grandparents'. She's fine."

"Good. Stay tonight, George. All night. Stay with me."

"If I do, will you? And you know what I mean."

"As long as I can."

Checkmate. Exactly what he'd been waiting for. His move.

Forcing himself to release her enough to grab his phone, he dialed his parents, glad to get his father since there would be fewer questions, and asked him to go pick up the boys and take them home.

Fran questioned him silently.

He shrugged as he hung up. "I'm all yours tonight. All night. Think I'd back out and let you off the hook?"

"I hoped you wouldn't. One question, though."

"Shoot." He gripped the bottom of her tee and raised it.

"Doesn't it scare you?"

"I don't scare easily. Does what scare me?" He pulled one of her arms out of the sleeve.

"How much I'm like my father. What if I..?"

"You won't."

"You don't know that."

"I do know that, and I'm not scared."

"I am."

He freed the other arm. "Don't be."

"But I, if I…"

"Shh." He raised it over her head.

"I don't want to be a burden to you, if we're together that long…"

"I have every intention of us being together that long. And stop worrying."

"George…"

He set his hands aside her face. "Frannie, don't worry. You won't. And if you do, I won't leave you. I won't desert you like your mom did your dad, and yes, I know she did for the most part. I know she hired help so she wouldn't have to do it herself, and I know she rarely saw him at all the last couple of years. I wouldn't abandon you that way. If it came to that. But it won't come to that. I've known… I knew your dad for a lot of years. You're not the same."

"But if I do, I want to go away somewhere they'll take care of me, strangers who are trained for that, not you…"

"No chance in hell. We do this, we do it all the way." He kissed her neck and her shoulder, let his hands find the soft pale flesh on the undersides of her breasts. "Up until now has just been the prelude, playing with the idea. After today, the hell of today, when you stood with me… Frannie…" He met her eyes, trying to find the words.

"Anch'io sono innamorato di te, e non ho idea di cosa dovrei fare con te."

"Hm. That's terribly sexy, but I only caught *idea* and *with me*." He kissed her neck. "What is it you're thinking about doing with me?"

"I don't know. That's the problem. It's scary, George. I mean, after all these years…"

"Yeah. Might agree with you there. But we're toughened and wizened old birds by now, right? We can do this as we should have years ago."

"I think we shouldn't have years ago." She unbuttoned the shirt she'd let him borrow and slid it off his shoulders. "But I think we damned well should now, scary or not." Dropping it over top of hers, over her father's paintings, she caressed fingers down from his chest to his stomach. "I said I'm in love with you, too, and I'm not sure what I should do with you."

"No? I have a pretty good idea."

Fran wasn't sure who dragged whom back into the house but when he headed to the couch, she shook her head and took him to the ladder-stairs.

He glanced upward. "Sure we won't fall out?"

"It's guarded. Afraid of heights?"

"Not likely. But I'm not much of a ... well, one position man."

"This isn't our first go-round together." She unbuckled his belt.

"Go on up, Frannie. I'll be right behind you. And enjoying the view." He patted her on the rear. "Go."

"Careful, G.F. I'm not a woman who takes orders." She curled his chest hair firmly between her fingers, as a warning.

He glanced down at them with a grin. "That'll just turn me on. And I bet you will. At least now and then. When you decide."

"Which is the operative phrase. When I decide."

"Of course." He teased the underside of her breasts with his thumbs.

"Which makes it not an order, but only a suggestion."

"If you wish."

"Nothing to do with what I wish. Grammatical logic. If I only listen when I decide, it's not an order, no matter how you make it sound."

"Frannie." He tasted her lips. "Stop talking."

"Turning you off?"

"Not at all. I wanna be able to get up that ladder behind your beautiful ass without falling because I'm too awful distracted."

"Awfully."

"Hm. Okay. Just go."

"I still do it, you know. You're liable to get tired of it."

"Yeah, probably will. Don't care. Go."

"You don't care now because of... well..." She looked down at herself, half naked in his exploring hands.

"Stop talking, woman, and get up those steps before I carry you up."

"Excuse me? You can't..."

"Like hell I can't. We're not that damned old yet." Without warning, he hiked her up to one side, part over his shoulder, his arm under her buttocks.

"Okay. Stop." She pushed herself off, when he allowed her to push herself off, since his grip was incredibly strong, and turned to head up the steps herself. "You won't be much good to me if you fall off and knock us both into unconsciousness." Fran heard his chuckle and purposely took her time climbing.

His look as he came up the opening beside her, ducking so he wouldn't hit the ceiling, said he was very much too awfully full of himself. But she kind of liked him that way, she had to admit.

Despite his bossy insistence down the ladder, now that he was in her bedroom, George kissed her gently, taking her into his arms just as gently, caressing her skin as though he'd never touched it before. He finished undressing her as slowly as she'd climbed the ladder, with kisses to her stomach and her hip, her outer thigh. He got no more intimate until he was just as naked, still ducking from the ceiling, and lowered them both to her mattress.

Far more slowly and gently than ever before, he caressed her with fingers and eyes, with his lips, and his tongue. Unwilling to allow her to do the same for him, he muttered a *lie still* under his breath beside her ear. And he entered her just as gently, his gaze locked on hers, adoring, moist, soft...

A true *in love* gaze if she'd ever seen one. And so far she'd only seen it in the movies, by actors who weren't. He wasn't acting. She'd never believed that look on screen was real. This was real.

Fran pulled his head down to hers and kissed him in a way he couldn't mistake for anything except the same thing. An *in love with you* kiss. An *I don't want you to ever leave my side* kiss. She held him in it until her body released its longing, for him, for this, for the past twenty years of not knowing this kind of need and want mixed so fully together she couldn't tell one from the other. She felt him quake in return. And he relaxed, first on top of her and as he started to get heavier, at her side, holding her in against him tight, so tight.

Twenty-seven

Fran wiped paint from her fingers onto her old shirt and stepped back to look at her canvas from a distance. It wasn't quite right. She'd been working on it the past two hours while waiting for George to get up, and it wasn't right. Worse, she had no idea how to make it right.

She needed her music. But the man was exhausted from the past weekend when Lexi scared him so much he took the next day off for a family day, and then from spending every lunch hour at her place, often only talking, and coming back after dinner while the kids were doing their homework and chores before returning to be sure they got in bed on time. She didn't want to wake him at eight o'clock Saturday morning after he'd made arrangements for the kids to stay at friends or his parents' again the night before.

Nothing much was getting done on her end. Too much time was spent on daydreaming as she fiddled in the garden and made more skirts for Lexi since the girl had decided to laugh with her friends about her umbrella look and make the most of it. One of them said she dressed like a "loony artist." Lexi took it as a compliment, bless her little soul, and now wanted to keep fueling that image. She was a smart little thing, smarter than Fran had been way back then. She was paving her own personality path instead of hiding it away. Very smart little girl. Fran was as proud as if Lexi were her daughter.

"The hell with it." She dropped her brushes into the thinner and went to work in the garden.

Except she didn't want to work in the garden.

Finding herself in the greenhouse where tiny shoots of herbs and marigolds were coming up through the potting mix, she stood in the middle where the morning sun streamed gently through the old greenish glass ceiling and considered what to do with it. The thing was larger than the cottage, with more livable space, more open and light and ... and it should become an extension of the cottage, to turn it more into a house. She'd have a far easier time selling it that way.

Her yard was secluded enough, the glass walls wouldn't matter, but she could add soft draperies most of the way down the wall for a more private look and leave the far end as greenhouse space. Dividers would section it off easily enough without destroying the ability to turn it all back into greenhouse area if needed.

Her eyes turned to the ceiling. It would have to be more substantial, in case of storms. There were no big trees close enough to fall on it, but still, when it stormed she wouldn't go out there. She never had. Whoever bought it, or considered buying it, would likely feel the same.

She cringed at the thought of selling. No. She didn't want to sell it. She'd told George she would stay as long as she could. She could keep it. Live there. At least until she decided what to do next and how long *as long as she could* turned into.

G.F. stretched his hands back and instead of hitting them against his headboard, he reached the floor with his fingertips. Fran's floor, beneath her mattress. Her too-small mattress. He liked room to move. Having her right there close all night, though, he could deal with. She hadn't tossed and turned and punched him in the face or stomach or balls the way Justine had. He hadn't always been sure the woman didn't do it on purpose. Even after he bought the king mattress.

He turned toward Fran, but she wasn't there. The cottage was quiet. The hardy aroma of strong coffee hit him and he rolled his large body to the edge of the mattress that could be a nice one on top of springs instead of on the wood floor. Edging into the bottom half of his clothes while half sitting on the mattress and half crouching under the V of the loft's too-low ceiling, he shook his head. A cute place, but far too small for a full-size man. Fran's father hadn't been all that small, either, but he hadn't slept in the loft. He'd done the wise thing and left his mattress on the main floor, on box springs.

He might have to suggest they stay at his place instead.

Waiting until he had room to roll his shoulders and stretch the kink in his back better, he made his way down the ladder steps and surveyed the space. Still no Fran. The greenhouse door was open. G.F. helped himself to a mug of coffee and wandered that direction, but he was stopped by the canvas on her desk. In progress. Technique as beautiful as her father's. But harsher. The colors more vivid. The lines more sharp. The woman had an intensity Virgil never had. From her mother, he supposed.

Scratching his chin and wishing he'd brought his razor and deodorant over, he headed into the greenhouse and grinned. She was sitting on one of the tables, her legs crossed like a teenager, staring up at the glass panels that shone light down around her. Only half willing to bother her meditative state – was she actually meditating? – G.F. ambled over slowly, sipping the strong coffee. He was directly in front of her and she didn't acknowledge he was there. Maybe she was...

"How sturdy do you think that still is?" Her focus didn't shift as she asked.

"Good morning to you, too."

Finally, she looked at him, at his hair, his bare chest, his jeans and bare feet. "You look good in the morning. A modern-day renaissance working man model if I ever saw one." She shoved a hand through her hair. "And I'm a mess."

He set his mug down to slide his hands beneath her barely buttoned shirt – his shirt – over stretchy short pants and leaned in to kiss her nose. "You are a mess. But that works for me." Reclaiming his coffee, he studied the mostly glass ceiling. "Looks pretty sturdy, I would say. I'm not the expert, though."

"You said you've done construction."

"I have, but kind of pro-am, not pro. I know an actual pro quite well if you want a better opinion."

"I can't ask your father..."

"Why can't you?"

"Well, because..."

"Worried about taking advantage of me?"

"No."

"No?"

She broke from her pose to stroke one finger down his chest. "No. I figure you're getting as much out of this as I am, or at least I hope you feel like you are, so there's no point in worrying about that petty stuff. It is what it is and I'm fine with that. Aren't you?"

G.F. had to stop and think about that one a minute. Petty stuff. Like taking advantage? How was that petty? That would be a pretty big deal, the way he figured it, if she was. He'd been there. Had that. It was a damn big deal.

"George? Are you not getting as much out of this?"

"Oh, yeah. At least."

"Then why the sudden silence? Don't say yes if you don't mean it."

"I don't say what I don't mean. Guess I'm wondering how you can think taking advantage of someone is a petty thing."

"That's not what I meant."

He thought of her words again but couldn't figure how else she could mean it.

"And I meant I couldn't ask your father because, well honestly, because they don't approve. Not that it matters a great deal to me whether or not they do, but I won't impose on someone who doesn't want to be here."

"Well." He scratched his beard. "To be honest in return, I don't see how you could know whether or not they approve since I don't even know. Haven't bothered to ask. And I'm old enough they know it's my own business, so they haven't commented."

"It was in their expressions."

"Was it now?" He eyed her while taking a swallow of coffee. "Sure it wasn't in your own mind? We tend to see things the way we think of them or the way we expect to see them more than the way they are."

"Anais Nin." Fran eyed him in return.

"Yeah, I guess she said it, too. I think plenty of smart folks have realized that, though. I always hesitate to attribute any one thing to any one person."

"Even if you read it in something they wrote?"

He shrugged. "Maybe, but who says they didn't hear it elsewhere and just repeat it in their work? If I remember, William Blake said about the same thing."

"You paid more attention in English class than you pretended."

"Maybe." He set his mug down again and raised his hands aside her head, sweeping his fingers back into her unbrushed hair. "And maybe it was you I was paying more attention to than I pretended." With a light tease of her lips, he slid his fingers down to her shoulders, down her arms, to grip her hands. "Frannie, you have to know by now that I'm in love with you and I want you at my side. Every night, not only when I can arrange sitters, and well, my thought is you feel the same, or at least it looks to me like you feel the same about it."

"How do you know you're not seeing that only because you want to see it?"

"Touché, mon amour. Mais certaines choses sont trop certain de ne pas voir."

Finally, she graced him with a smile. "You've learned French. I'm impressed. And yes, some things may be too certain not to see, but how can you be certain it's not only what you want to see that makes you so certain?"

"Okay. You got me there. But how was the accent?"

"Bad. But very cute. Und könnten sie recht haben."

"German?" He scratched his beard again, wishing again he'd brought his razor. "You'll have to translate that one."

"Maybe I will. One of these days." She pushed him from her enough to get down from the table, then grasped his arm at his elbow. "Let me make you breakfast before you have to get back to your kids."

"How about spending the day with us?" G.F. caught her hand as she started away. "If you're not sick of us. And I guess I wouldn't blame you by now. We could go to the lake. Should be plenty warm enough to swim."

"Spend the day with you publicly? It won't embarrass your kids?"

He sighed. "Okay, I deserved that. You're still mad."

"No. I just think maybe you're right. Maybe it's unfair to them."

"Fran, I was upset. Don't take that as more than it was."

"I'm not. I'm taking it for exactly what it was, and I'm admitting you're right. So what are we going to do about it?"

"Make it official." It just came out. As soon as it did, G.F. knew it was the wrong thing to say. "And I mean ... make it more public.

Keep showing our faces together, all of us. Gossiping about us won't be fun if we go out and show it doesn't bother us, that we're saying publicly, *Yeah, we're together, what do you have to say about it to our faces? Right?*"

"And the kids?"

"They see we're not ashamed of it, they have no need to be, either."

"Oh, George. Life's not that simple."

"It is to me." He moved in close, touched her face, stroked a thumb down her cheek. "Won't be long till they have someone else to jump on for doing something imbecilic, since that happens most every other day, and then they'll forget us. This isn't that worth talking about."

"Isn't it?"

"Nope. Just a couple of old friends who decided to be more now that life is less in the way. Happens all the time. Not a big story."

"Except there's more to it than that. I'm Virgil Barrett's daughter. You're..."

He leaned in fast to kiss her hard, and eased up as she gave in to him. "I'm a man who has always been intrigued by you, charmed by you, and now I'm a man in love with you. I don't care about the rest. Spend the day with us, Frannie. Let me show you."

She *was* as nuts as her father. She had to be.

Fran sighed as they pulled in front of the McKenry place. How did he talk her into dinner with his parents? It had been a nice enough day. She got more red than she liked out on the lake, and there were more stares directed at them than she appreciated. George, though, greeted everyone around as though showing off, as popular as he always was. Nicer, though, now that the teenage boy edges had been worn off some. He played beach volleyball with his older boys and Lexi and kept up with them well. Frank chose to build a sand castle instead and did a good job of it while his big brothers teased about being girly, until their father heard them and told them in no uncertain terms to knock it off. They had to bite their tongues when Frank's sand castle turned out so well a couple of girls came over to *ooh* and *ahh* over it and spent the rest of their time talking with him.

Lexi kept up with her older brothers well. A spirited girl. She wore a loose tee and old shorts over her bathing suit and couldn't be talked out of taking them off for anything. Fran appreciated her modesty. G.F. worried about her self-esteem and her obsession with her looks.

"Better for her to be too shy than too showy." Fran took a rare occasion to touch him, since they were alone a moment. "I'd be more worried if she was like one of those girls." She'd nodded toward young girls in bikinis leaning forward while talking to boys passing by.

"I'd ground her for three years if she did that." G.F. had stiffened like a board about to swing by itself.

"Then just be glad for who she is. You're doing a good job. It shows."

He'd leaned in for a quick kiss. "You sure know the way to a guy's heart, Frannie. Compliment his kids. Can't think of anything that would work better."

"No? Not even the way I'm trying so hard not to admire you in how little you're wearing?"

"Little? I'm covered decent." He looked down at his long swim trunks.

"Decently. Yes. But your sexiest part is still showing well." She'd traced a finger down his chest.

"Think I should be offended if you think that's my sexiest part."

"Well. Other than this, of course." She'd raised her hand to his head and swept her fingers back through his hair.

"My hair?"

"Your head, George. I like how you use your head."

"Getting out?" He drew her back to where they were by holding her door open with an amused grin. At his parents' house. For dinner.

"I think I'll wait here."

"You'll do no such thing." He claimed her hand and leaned in close so the kids wouldn't hear. "Let's get this over with so I can take you back home and send them off to crash in their rooms. Looking forward to getting you alone and..."

"Careful about assuming, George."

"Not assuming. Hoping. Big difference." With a charming grin, he stepped back to nudge her out of the truck.

Fran didn't think she'd been so uncomfortable since high school. The McKenry house was, as always, perfectly groomed with a large variety of colorful annuals backed by taller perennials in front of the dusty-red brick two-story colonial style house. There wasn't a weed to be found among the natural brownish gray mulch. Gwen McKenry always spent a lot of time in her flower beds. In the evenings, anyone who passed by the house would find her donned in loose pants and a long-sleeved white blouse, completed with a wide-brimmed white hat as she pulled weeds or planted something new or yanked out faded blooms.

Fran's mother always said the McKenry woman could have used that time more productively by working for the community. A snotty comment. Fran had always admired Gwen. She was at nearly every football game watching her sons, volunteered to chaperone trips for her sons' classes, worked part time in a legal office, helped her husband's business, and maintained her yard on her own, and it was pretty, not plain or boring.

Fran's father had often talked about how intelligent his beautiful wife was and how much she'd given up for him, but all Fran knew was that she used to work in a school somewhere. Not a teacher. Not a secretary. Her mother wouldn't talk about it. It was in the past, she'd said. It didn't matter. From the time Fran remembered, Gloria Barrett ran around with her community groups, took care of the house with some paid help, and her one child, and made comments about the neighbors. At least she only made them to Fran and her father, never publicly.

G.F.'s kids ignored the sidewalk and sprinted or ambled through the lush grass to the front door. Fran stayed on the sidewalk, which amused George. As a way to stall, she crouched to look more closely at a lupine's yellowing leaves.

"I can't figure out what's wrong with them." Gwen McKenry's voice came from the porch. "My first year planting lupines and I'm not having much luck."

"Aphids." Fran accepted G.F.'s hand to rise to her feet. "They love lupines. And they'll spread to your other plants soon."

"So I need to get spray. I try to avoid that." The white in her hair shimmered as she came out into the sun.

"You can use dish soap in water, but you have to do it every morning for a while and then rinse it off again about an hour later."

"I don't see myself doing that, to be honest."

"It is a hassle. I use ladybugs instead." Fran glanced at George to see if he was going to smirk at the ladybugs reference. To his credit, he didn't. "You can also put up a hummingbird feeder or two. They eat aphids."

"If ladybugs do the job, we shouldn't have an issue, with the way they congregate around the door. It's horrible."

"The orange ones?"

"Yes. I don't see many of the red variety anymore. We used to have them."

"Asian Beetles, the orange ones, are pests. They aren't supposed to be here. They will eat aphids, though. You could try putting a few solar lights in your garden to attract them there instead of to the door."

"I will try that." Gwen McKenry tilted her head slightly. "George says you've picked up quite a lot of knowledge from your father. You might consider sharing that experience. We have a garden club. They invite me constantly, because of my yard, I suppose. I haven't much interest in clubs and groups, though, I must confess, other than my work on the town council. Maybe you don't, either."

"Not too much. But thank you for thinking of it."

"Fran, look." Lexi tugged her hand. "This is *my* garden." She pulled Fran over to a corner of the porch, to a large wide decorative pot where seedlings were sprouting. "Grams helped me set it up, but I take care of it. Look. The mint is flowing over the pot already!"

"You're doing a great job." And mint was easy to grow. Fran had started the girl with a couple of pinches of her own mint plant and told her not to put it where she didn't want it to spread. They were working up to the harder-to-please herbs.

She relaxed somewhat while Lexi talked with her father and grandmother about what she was learning from Fran until Mr.

McKenry stepped out the door and asked his wife if she planned to let them in the house. All in all, Fran would just as soon have stayed outside to talk, even if she used to wonder about George's home way back when. It wasn't his now.

It was the antithesis of his own. Stark was the first word to come to mind. Modern. Minimal. Fran never would have expected as much based on the glorious colors outside the house. Slipping her shoes off since the rest of them did, she felt every bit of the ceramic tile under her feet. George's hand on her back was almost comforting and his expression said it was meant to be. Her tension showed. She would have to force herself to be less tense.

The piano did it. A baby grand. Black. Shiny. Its top closed.

"That's George's baby. I can hardly make him play for me anymore though, the stubborn boy." Gwen nearly whispered as though she was telling a secret, although her son was right there and heard her fine.

"Fran plays. If you ask her nicely, maybe she will."

She threw a fast glare. "No. I don't..."

"You said..."

"Lessons. Not the same. I'd love to hear you play again."

"Again?" Gwen moved her gaze from one to the other. "I didn't realize the two of you knew each other that well back during your school days. Or do you mean he's played for you recently? If he has..."

"No. And we weren't. I mean, we didn't. I..." Fran was as nervous as she always used to be. A dreadful feeling she didn't want again.

George explained. And he took Fran farther into the house, away from the piano, to a hard sofa where he sat next to her as he reminded Frankie not to run inside.

G.F. couldn't quite say no to Fran after she'd been so patient with his mother's twenty questions, and then some, through dinner and dessert, with Lexi hanging on her and Frankie avoiding her. Through it all, she stayed calm and polite, elegant. So opposite Justine. Gwen McKenry wasn't an easy woman to impress, but she was impressed with Fran. His mother even got her to speak a bit of Italian. She had a beautiful accent.

Getting her alone just enough, he said he'd play the piano for her if she'd talk more Italian to him later. In private. He took her very slight nod and grin as agreement.

He was rusty and felt it and so warmed up with a simple tune he'd played so often as a child, he could never forget it. *You Are My Sunshine.* A favorite of his mother's. She had sung it to him whenever he was down for any reason, but she made up new words to fit better.

His mom kissed his head as a thank you and then told him to really play something. Thinking a moment, he started one he used to do way back when. He grimaced at the hack job and stopped three quarters of the way through. "Been too long."

Fran sat next to him on the little piano bench. "It was beautiful. I've missed that." Her eyes were moist. "What was it?"

"Jimmie Vaughan. Stevie's big brother. A lot of people have no idea he's also a blues guitarist and still out there playing."

"Yes, but ... guitar, not piano."

"My own version of *Slow Dance Blues.* His is far better, of course, especially since it's been so long..."

She kissed him. A quick kiss. Then she looked embarrassed, likely because his parents were right there listening. When she started to get up, G.F. grasped her hand and asked her to stay, he'd try to remember more.

He had no idea how much time passed while he retrained himself as she sat at his side. She wouldn't play no matter how often he asked, so he stopped asking and indulged her, and his kids who asked for a song now and then. Lexi sang with a couple of them. The girl had a nice voice for her age. Justin had a nice voice, but it was hard to get him to show it and he wouldn't in front of everyone.

"Okay, enough showing off my lack of talent for one day." He got up and stretched his shoulders, then offered Fran a hand. "You guys about ready to get home?"

At the cacophony of groans, arguments, and one 'if you want' from his eldest, G.F. said he'd just leave them all there and enjoy the peace and quiet.

"Yes, you should leave them with us." His mother jumped all

over it without a second's hesitation. "We'll get them home in the morning, early enough to change clothes to go to their mom's. How does that sound?" She was asking the kids, not him. "I'll have Grandpa light up the fire pit and we'll roast marshmallows for S'mores..."

Nothing G.F. said would matter at that point, so he threw up his hands, kissed them all on the head, even Theo who groaned a protest, and then thanked his parents for dinner. Before anyone could change their mind, he dragged Fran out the door and to the truck and helped her in, then went around to jump in beside her. "Well, that was easy."

"Your plan?"

"Nope. Wish I could say it was. Mom must like you." A second thought hit him. "Or she's worried that Lexi will take off again so she can skip out on her mom's tomorrow. Didn't think of that. Guess she won't do it from here. Long walk to town. Should I..."

"She won't do it again."

"Sure?"

"Absolutely. We had a long talk this week while she was helping me garden. And I um ... gave her a couple of pointers."

George put the truck right back into park and looked her in the eye. "Pointers for what?"

"She's a little worried about your wife's boyfriend."

"Ex wife, if you don't mind. That's hard enough to have to admit... Wait. Why? Worried about what?"

"She says he's sleazy."

His heart jumped. "*What* in the hell did he *do*?"

"Nothing. And she's always with one of her brothers, if not all of them. She just doesn't like him. To make her feel better, I gave her a couple of self defense tips, not that she'll need them, but it's good for a girl to know, anyway."

George turned the truck off and jumped back out. Fran caught up before he got to the door and begged him not to say anything; it was a private conversation and she didn't want to lose Lexi's trust. So he calmed himself, went back in the house, straight to his daughter, and told her if she was uncomfortable at any time for any reason when she was anywhere at all, she should call him right away and he'd be there.

"It's okay, Daddy. I won't hide again." She gave him a long hug and raised to her tip-toes to tell him how much she loved hearing him play piano and maybe he could teach her.

"I'll try." He glanced at Fran. "I'm not good at teaching though, so maybe we can get help with that."

A warm smile graced his girlfriend's face. He took it as a yes.

Twenty-eight

He woke to a noise. The door. The front door. Fran squeezed him tighter when he moved and he gripped her hand. "Kids are home."

She sat up, pulling the thin blanket with her.

"Stay here. I'll be back." With a kiss on her nose, then a quick one on her lips, he got up, pulled into his jeans and a T-shirt, combed his fingers through his hair, and went down to meet them.

Theo and Justin snickered but hushed at his look.

"Can I be sick today?" Lexi attached to his side. "I don't want to go to Mom's."

"Sorry, baby. You'll get me in hot water again. You don't want your dear dad boiled and peeled, I would hope."

"That's gross."

"Yeah, it would be." He scuffed her hair. "I'll see if I can pick you up early. Get changed and I'll take you. Be quick about it."

"Grams is here. She's taking us." Theo gave him a sly smile. "So you can ... uh, have the day off."

"She's not coming in?"

"Nope. Thought it best not to, she said. So we'd hurry more."

Fran heard the rustling about in the house and muffled voices. She got up and dressed as soon as George left the room, just in case, and stood staring out his small bedroom window out to the backyard. It was a small yard bordered by a vertical wood privacy fence. The grass was patchy and there were holes dug by the dog, a dog George told her he hadn't exactly wanted but was kind of fond of when he was behaving well enough. When Frankie found him wandering, dirty, skinny, with stickers matted in his fur, George didn't have the heart to turn him away. Instead, he cleaned him up, combed every sticker out of his fur, and took him to the vet to have him checked out.

A big heart, that man had. She loved his big heart. And his big hands, his big shoulders and chest. She loved ... pretty much everything, if she was honest with herself. His temper could use some work, but she could even understand that, given his situation. Anyone who had been faithfully married to Justine Haden for nearly sixteen years would have to have an outlet.

Don't be bitchy, Fran. She is the mother of his children. His beautiful children. His beautiful Lexi.

Fran did want to claim her.

Shoving the thought aside, she hoped the girl would have a decent day with her mother.

"Hey."

She jumped at his voice.

George was in the doorway, door wide open, a hand on his hip. "You're dressed. Why are you dressed?"

"Your kids came home."

"And they're out again. Mom's taking them over for me. Bless her heart. She hates to go there. I swear it's harder for her to see Justine than it is for me, and that's saying something."

"You're her baby. Of course it is. If anyone did to one of your kids what she's done to you..." Fran made herself stop. It wasn't her place.

"I wouldn't be half as nice as my parents have been to whatever asshole would treat my children that way. Of course I know they only stay decent to her for the kids' sake." He joined her at the window and shook his head about the dog digging yet another hole.

Sliding her hand up his chest and neck to the side of his face, she felt her body tense and relax all at once and her eyes tried to water. She fought that back, but held his eyes.

"What are you thinking?"

"I'm thinking ... that I'd much rather put up with all of the snide comments and the looks from everyone who knew my father than ... than to ever leave here. To leave you. I don't think I can do it. You would have been a good man to have children with, George McKenry. I wish I'd stayed around and... And I've never in my life before wished I had."

"Damn, Frannie." It was a hoarse whisper and he caught her up in his strong arms, holding against his body, his strong, sturdy body that had been naked against hers all night. "I wish you had, too. Doesn't matter anymore; just stay now."

She felt herself nod against his chest. Holding him in the silence of his house, his messy chaotic usually noisy very warm home, Fran wanted to disappear into him.

"Why did you never have children?" His voice was still soft, less hoarse.

"Cal didn't want them."

"Okay. But after Cal?"

"After Cal, it was too late. I made sure he wouldn't have to be a father because he wouldn't do it and ... and I was stupid. So it's just as well you have enough of them." Fran was trying to be funny, but it got to her all of a sudden, the thought that she maybe could have had at least one beautiful child with George if she hadn't been stupid, if she hadn't left, if she'd told him way back when...

So many ifs that made no difference now.

George pulled back enough to raise her face to his. "You're staying with me."

"Is that a question or a demand? I don't do well with demands."

"If you did, I wouldn't be interested. I mean ... from what you've said, you sound pretty intent on..."

Enough. She needed breathing time before going further. So she pulled from him and headed toward the door. "I think I'll make us breakfast before we pick up the kids."

G.F. hated to have to come back for the band concert. Almost hated it. Fran enjoyed listening, so there was that. But he hadn't let her make breakfast. He'd whisked her to Des Moines to his favorite breakfast spot and then took her to the Art Center where she stared for some time at Georgia O'Keeffe's version of a lake, and longer at Van Gogh's etching of Dr. Gachet. His only etching, Fran said, done a short time before his death that she didn't quite believe was by his own hand. She was a Van Gogh fanatic and shared some of what she knew of him and his work while they wandered the Sculpture Park, where she alternately held his arm and rubbed his back. Both too full from breakfast to want a full lunch, they stopped at a coffee shop and had pastries to hold them until dinner.

And she remained by his side when he pulled his sax from the back of the truck and went to join the band. Generally, she'd stayed out on the lawn, joining him only after he was done and had split from the group. G.F. took it as a good sign that she held her claim in public, finally.

Three flutists whispering together looked over at her and then away. G.F. shrugged it off. Rumors always happened about new relationships in a small town. When a couple of French Horn players did the same, he felt his eyes roll and went right up to them. "Curtis. Trent. Problem?"

They glanced at her and said there wasn't.

"We are both single adults. Whatever issue anyone has with our seeing each other needs to stop right here." He felt Fran squeeze his arm, to hush him, maybe, but he'd never put up with that innuendo bullshit well and he wouldn't now.

"No issue with you seeing each other, G.F. It's the accusation everyone's wondering about."

"Accusation of what?"

"What she said to Carly. Your neighbor. About her husband. The woman is mad as a wet hen and making that known, which ole Bill isn't any too happy about, as you can imagine."

"Guess he shouldn't have hit on her if he didn't want it known he did. His own fault. And the man best stay clear of her from now on."

"Could be it wasn't ... quite what it sounded like?" Trent glanced again at Fran.

"It was exactly what it sounded like." She raised her chin. "The man hit on me. In front of the children. If she chooses to look the other way, she's a fool and everyone will know she is."

"Is that a threat?"

"No. It's fact."

"Carly threatened me, for the record." G.F. was pissed all over again thinking about it. "Said she'd call child services. Fran was sticking up for me. That's the truth of the matter. How about we drop it now?"

"Child services?" This time it was their tuba player. "Those kids adore you. What on earth was her reasoning?"

"I said the 'S' word on the sidewalk in front of her house where she was eavesdropping."

"S word? Shit?"

"Sex. Wasn't doing it, just said it."

The men laughed and shook their heads.

"Speaking of your kids..."

G.F. followed Fran's gaze across the yard. Not only his kids, but his kids with his ex. He stifled a groan, left his sax beside the bandstand, and told Fran he'd be back in a minute, unless she wanted to come with. He wasn't at all surprised she didn't.

"Thought I was picking them up afterward."

"Your daughter was throwing a huge fit..." Justine gave Lexi a shove toward him. "*Had* to be here, she said. Just *had* to be."

"It'll be done soon and I've only been to one this year." Lexi's shoulders were ducked in. "I hope it's okay."

He wrapped his arms around her and kissed her head. "Of course it's okay, baby. I'm glad you want to be here."

"You know it's only for that woman. It's not for you. All I hear from her anymore is Fran this and Fran that and those ridiculous skirts she's wearing are just..."

"Stop there, Justine. Lexi, Fran's over there if you want to say hello." He told the boys they could wander but to stay close and waited until they were all out of hearing distance. "Don't degrade her for her clothes again. I mean my daughter, by the way. Fran doesn't give a rat's ass what you think of her and neither do I."

"*Our* daughter. Have you forgotten I'm the one who gave birth to her?"

"Yeah, but that's about all you've done for her, the way I see it. And if I see you shove her like that again, I'm going right back to court to keep her from having to spend *any* time with you. The whole town knows by now that she hid to keep from having to go to your place with your boy toy she doesn't like. He makes her uneasy. Won't be hard to convince a judge she shouldn't have to be around him. So either treat her like the daughter you love or stay the hell away from her.”

"He doesn't make her uneasy. He's just not *you*. You have her so spoiled, no one else is good enough.”

"Have you *asked* her what she thinks of him?”

"No need. I know my daughter.”

"Sure about that?”

"Fine; that girl is more like you every day and I had enough of that the sixteen years we were married. If she doesn't want to come, she doesn't have to. The boys still come, though.”

"We'll see. I have them. You can go on with your day.” As he turned from her, he did his best not to look as angry as he was, for his daughter's sake.

"By the way, *he's* not the boy toy, G.F. *You* were. I just got stuck more than I intended.” Tossing her hair, she threw an evil smirk and stalked away.

He was the boy toy? The woman was insane. *He* was the one who got stuck. She tried hard to get him to forgive her for cheating and let her stay. Whatever. She could think what she wanted. He was going to do his best to get out of having to take any of the kids over there unless they chose to go.

When he returned to the side of the band shell where musicians and instruments cluttered the ground waiting for two o'clock to come, Lexi looked up at him from her tilted down head, her shoulders still hunched. He raised the beautiful little chin with two fingers. "You don't have to go back to your mom's again. You can, but you don't have to. Okay?”

"Really? You won't get in trouble?”

"I won't get in trouble. It's up to you.”

She hugged him tight.

"Alright, Lex. Keep Fran company while I'm busy, then we'll all go home and I'll make your favorite dinner. How's that?”

As they walked away together, he saw Fran gently straighten Lexi's shoulders and say something into her ear. It was about damned time the girl had a real mom. G.F. meant to keep it that way.

To appease Frankie after having to leave his mom's early, George let him pick the music. When they cooked together on Sunday nights, whenever they were home early enough for Sunday dinner, they put a CD on to make it go faster. Frankie chose Maroon 5 and Fran had to wonder if it was a test for her, so she talked with him about it. And when she said she liked *Moves Like Jagger*, George went over to restart the song and danced to it while he cooked, making his boys roll their eyes and Lexi smile and dance with him.

Fran enjoyed the time with the kids and Frankie loosened up with her throughout the evening. G.F. said Justin had been talking to him, smoothing the road for her, he called it. And the petty part of him wanted to tell his ex that her favorite son was standing up for Fran, but he wouldn't. No sense stirring the flames, he said.

Glad to get him alone in the quiet of her cottage after the hectic weekend, Fran wanted him to stay. She wouldn't ask. His kids needed him home and she couldn't be selfish enough to ask for three nights in a row away from them.

He sank onto the couch, reached out to her, and pulled her in close, a hand on her waist, the other mixing into her hair. His mouth closed over hers in a long, sensual, soft kiss, and she dropped her head against his shoulder, nuzzling her face against his stubbled neck.

"I can't stay tonight."

She stroked fingers down his chest. "I know."

"Can I come for lunch tomorrow?"

"Double entendre?"

"Hm. Maybe. Not intended."

"I know. Yes."

"Frannie..."

She looked up at him when he stopped. "What is it?"

"Justine... today..."

"I saw her shove Lexi, if that's what you're trying to decide whether to admit or not."

"No. I jumped her ass for that. It's why she doesn't have to go back. She knows I'll use it in court if I need."

"Good. Was there more going on? She hasn't been violent toward her, has she?"

"No, I asked Lex. She was just as shocked by it as I was."

A large sigh of relief overtook her body.

"The woman said I was her boy toy. This new guy is... I guess the real thing to her and I was just... She said she never meant to get stuck with me."

"That's a lie, George." Fran touched his face. "It's a lie. You were all she ever talked about in the locker room. It was all set up. She wanted her parents off her back and they liked you and she figured that would..."

"Her parents."

"That's what she said. I didn't believe her at the time and I still don't. She wanted you. Some of them didn't think you were cool enough, even if you were a football star, because you were too clean cut, too much a hometown boy. So she used them as an excuse, but that was a lie. You were all she ever saw."

"Yeah? Why in the hell would she cheat on me after she had me, then?"

"Because you finally grew up and saw who she was. She would have to see the disappointment..."

"Only because she wasn't a good mother. Other than that, we were fine."

"That's a pretty big thing. And it's damned hard to accept that the one person you truly care about, as far as their opinion, is disappointed in you. For whatever reason. She ran from it instead of trying to fix it."

"So it was my fault for complaining about the way she treated my children?"

"No. You had to do right by them first. You did. She should have fixed it. She was never strong enough for you, George. I could always see it."

His chest heaved in a sigh. "I loved her."

"I know you did."

"I'm sorry it ended the way it has." He caught her eyes. "But I'm not sorry anymore that it ended."

"You need something different now than you did then."

"Yes. I'm too damned old to be some boy toy. I need to be..."

"The whole package."

He nodded. "Am I by now?"

"You are for me, George Frederick McKenry. But then you always were to me." She claimed his mouth and pulled him back to her, wishing again he could stay, just to be there.

"I gotta go." He kissed her neck.

"I know."

"I don't wanna go."

"I know that, too." She released him and stood. "See you tomorrow."

"You bet." He slid the backs of his fingers along her face and she walked him to the door, watched him sway along to his truck, and closed and latched her door. Tomorrow she'd agree to let him fix the lock.

Twenty-nine

Fran jumped at a noise. It was dark in the cottage. She'd been deeply asleep. A dream, maybe. Her dreams had always been vivid enough she had to stop and wonder if they were real once she woke.

She could just see the glow of the moon through the little window above her bed, plus the glow of the night light from below. She heard nothing. A dream.

With a deep breath, she closed her eyes. Another bump and she opened them, listening.

"*Sh.* Be quiet, you idiot."

A male voice. Someone was in the cottage. The bump had to have been the pathetic excuse for a lock, as George called it, giving way. Her heart thudded as she tried to remember what she had up in the loft that could be used as a weapon. Her old putter was by the door. She should have at least thought to take it to bed with her. What would they want from the cottage? She didn't have valuables. She had only basic furniture. Not even a television. What would anyone want enough to be worth a break in?

Fran forced herself to breathe as she heard them moving about, at least two of them, and listened to where they were. Where had she left her phone? On her desk, she supposed. It was always... Except George had asked her to keep it on at night. At hand. So it was...

The shuffling came close to the ladder that led up to her loft and she groped around the floor beside her mattress, finally found it, and tried to hide the light of the thing when she hit George's number. She wouldn't dare talk unless they started up the ladder, but he would know something was wrong. He'd come check.

"*Stay here. I'm going up.*"

Her breath caught. She knew the voice, even in a whisper. The one that had hit on her. Carly's husband. Lurch, they'd called him. She couldn't think of his real name. The kid she'd never trusted. In her cottage.

In a near panic at the creak of the ladder that led up to her loft, she heard George answer and whispered back at him. "In the house. He's coming up the ladder."

"What was that?" The other one whispered loud.

"Shut the hell up." Lurch was halfway up the stairs.

She heard George ask ... something, but she froze. Until she saw the top of the intruder's head and sat up, backing away, gripping her phone hard enough it hurt. Figuring he'd think it was the police, Fran gave her address loudly into the phone and dropped it behind her.

Lurch looked up over the loft's floor. She could just make out a wicked sneer on his face from the glow of the moon through her window.

"I just called the cops." The thump of her heart made her voice shake.

He snickered. "Figured you might, but they'll be busy about now. Car fire in the middle of town. That'll keep 'em wondering too long to worry about a prank call. Been a rash of 'em lately." He crawled up onto the loft's floor, at the base of her mattress. "Got everything covered. And here you thought you was the smart one all these years."

George would be there. *George would be there.* Any minute. She kept the thought in her head and forced herself to stay calm. She hadn't warned him about the second guy. She'd said he, not them. What if one of them had a weapon? What if she'd drawn him into a trap? His kids needed him. She should have...

Lurch held his smiling sneer as he crept forward. "Had to go and tell my wife about our little conversation, did you? And all those band geeks, too? Made me look bad. Now you get to pay for that before you skedaddle right back out of town again, which you're gonna do if you care anything about those McKenry brats. Play nice with me tonight and then shut up and leave and all goes back to how it should be."

Did the man honestly think she would be that easy to manipulate? So many years with Cal at least taught her a thing or…

His *kids.* She'd called him over and his children would be alone. What had she done? Was there someone over there, too? Waiting till he left? Panic tried to take over between the thought of his beautiful babies in danger and with as close as Lurch was getting. "You know if anything happens to those children, G.F. will come after you."

"Yeah, we'll just see about that. He's always been a pain in my backside, starting with taking Justine from me. Turn about's fair play. Ain't that how it goes? Now be a good girl and come on back over this way." Looking below, he yelled down to whoever else was there. "Turn on the lights so I can see what I'm doing up here."

Her heart and head both pounded when the light switched on. She had nothing but a book and her phone in the loft, and a little lamp. The lamp. Old. Ceramic. She inched toward it and found the cord, yanking it from the outlet as he came closer. He saw what she was doing and reached for it, exposing himself just enough to allow her to draw her foot up and shove it hard into his groin.

A satisfying yell made the guy below ask what was wrong. In between holding himself and groaning, Lurch grabbed her ankle and yanked her closer. He was a hell of a lot stronger than his tall, wiry frame looked, even part incapacitated.

The second guy started to stomp up the ladder while Lurch pushed her down and dropped over top of her, but she managed to grab the lamp. Finagling it into a good grip, she smashed the base over his head with all the force she could muster. Fran only half hoped she hadn't killed him when he slumped on top of her.

"What the fuck..." The second head popped up over the ladder. "You *killed* him?"

She didn't recognize the kid, but he was young with a stupid look on his face. "And you're next if you don't get out *now*."

He looked like he believed her bluff at least for a few seconds, which was all she needed to get out from under the unmoving body enough to grab a big shard of the lamp. "*Go*."

He stared. First at her, then at Lurch, who started to groan again. "He ain't dead."

"Not yet. Should I fix that?" Fran posed the shard against the small of the man's back. Of course it wouldn't work, but she hoped Mr. Accomplice wasn't smart enough to know it wouldn't.

"*Frannie.*"

George. She almost collapsed in relief at his voice but forced herself to call down to him. "Up here. Two of them." She heard his heavy fast steps tread across the floor while he threatened the guy on the ladder. The young thug gave Lurch another glance, then looked down at George, and started down slowly.

"Whoever else is up there better get your ass down here *now* before I *blow* you down from there."

"He ain't kidding, Lurch. He's got a gun."

A gun. George was safe. She swallowed hard and took a deep breath. "They still call you Lurch?" Fran saw her fingers shake as she pulled back. He did nothing but groan. "G.F., this one is ... not feeling well. You might have to help him down."

"You okay?"

"Yes. Left the putter downstairs, but the lamp worked."

"Good. Hang tight. I'm coming up as soon as this one's secure. Go for his throat if he makes a move."

His throat. The shard wouldn't do much to his back, but it would do a good bit of damage to his throat if needed. She heard scuffling and scooted back as close to the wall as far away from Lurch as possible. The shard was still clenched in her hand and she felt it cut into her skin, but she wasn't letting go until he was farther away. He was still moving too much while he groaned.

"Frannie." George's head popped up over the ladder at about the same time she heard sirens. "Thank God you're okay." He glanced at Lurch with a scowl, put the gun somewhere behind his back, and came over to her, shoving the intruder out of his way. "Tell me you're not hurt." He smoothed fingers along her cheek and cupped her head.

"No. Clobbered him with this." Her hand shook when she showed him the shard. "Well, with the lamp. This is what's left."

"Good for you. Let go now. I got it." Gently prying her fingers open, he tossed the thing aside and pulled her into his arms. "Thank God you're okay." He kissed her head. "Still think you could use a better weapon, though."

"My foot worked, too." In his arms, she calmed enough to realize he was only half dressed. She was holding bare skin...

At another groan, he looked over at Lurch holding himself and chuckled. "That'll give him something to remember for a while."

"G.F?" A man's voice came from below and she tightened her hold.

"Up here, Tom. Come get this piece of shit out of here before I push him over the edge."

Relief trickled in as George talked to her, running fingers over her head, asking again if she was okay. "Your kids. George, he mentioned your kids."

"Mentioned how?"

"Threatened me... them, if I..." Her lungs gulped air. She had trouble talking.

"Alright, calm down. Just big talk. He wouldn't dare." He looked over at Lurch. "Isn't that right, Larry? Touch my kids and you're dead. Slowly and painfully. You know that, right?"

She heard what could have been an answer but sounded like a grunt. Still... "He has friends. The car fire, he did it, or someone did it for him, as a distraction."

"Okay. Take a breath. Relax."

"Your kids..."

"I woke Theo. Doors are locked."

"You shouldn't have left them. They..."

"Theo and Justin are well trained, Frannie. They're fine. Anyone walks into that house and they'll be greeted with a shotgun. The kids are fine. Relax now."

G.F. kissed her hand around where he'd bandaged it and held her in close, glad to finally have everyone out. He'd called his kids and his parents were there; Theo had called them right away. He let them know Fran was okay and to stay in the house, he'd be home soon. And he wasn't about to leave her. "You're coming home with me."

She surrendered into him and her body shook.

"I don't mean only tonight. You're staying with me. Or with my parents. I'm not leaving you out here alone anymore." He kissed her head. "You scared the hell out of me. I'm too old to do that again and I can't risk losing you again. So it's for my sake."

"Want to hear something funny?"

With his fingers, he gently raised her head to see her face.

"I was just thinking last night before I went to sleep that I'd let you fix my lock."

"Should have done it sooner, with an argument if need be." He kissed her nose. "Doesn't mean they can't still get in. Until things settle..."

"I'm not letting them chase me out. I have work to finish."

"Frannie..."

"George, I..."

He felt her shake. "We'll talk about it later. For tonight, what's left of it, you're coming home with me."

"You forgot your shirt." She stroked fingers over his bare shoulder.

"Barely took time to pull my jeans on, to be honest. Glad the belt was still in them. Worked well as a make-shift rope."

"I'm glad you convinced me to keep my phone on and handy. It would have been on the desk, and..."

Swallowing hard, G.F. told himself not to think about the what ifs. She was shaken, but unharmed, and he was shaken enough himself to know she had to stay with him. "Don't think of it. Let's get you a few things to take to my place and get out of here."

It only took a few minutes for her to change out of her pajamas and to pack a few things, but he stayed with her partly because she asked him to and partly because he would have, anyway. On the way out, she stopped to look at her desk. "I don't want to leave them here. Not that they're... And my father's paintings..."

"Those two are not getting out of Tom's grasp tonight."

"But if they have friends..."

He ran fingers through her hair. "Tom's checking into it. If there are others involved, they'll lie low or leave town. But, I'll go put your paintings in the safe with your dad's and lock it up good. Okay? No one knows it's there. He protected them well. And Tom will have someone buzzing around watching your place. Sit tight. I'll be right back."

She nodded and he grabbed what he could from her desk and the floor around it without smearing paint, listening to her warn him about which were still wet and assuring her he wouldn't mess up her work.

"Don't..." She grabbed his arm when he headed to the greenhouse. Her face showed fear.

"Come on with me."

She was jittery about noises, but otherwise calm while they got everything she wanted in the steel-lined art safe, locked the temporary house lock Tom provided, and got out to his truck. She grasped his arm, holding it until he got her to his place.

Lexi nearly jumped on her when they stepped inside.

"Why aren't you all in bed?" He asked the younger three, since he knew Theo would wait up for him.

"They insisted on being sure all was all right." His mom asked Fran if she was.

"Yes. Thank you." Fran ran a hand over Lexi's hair. "Just a bit of a scare. Everything's fine."

"Okay now, off to bed with you. She'll be in my room tonight, so come on down to the couch if you need me." G.F. saw his oldest boys glance at each other, but decided to ignore it.

With Justin, Frankie, and Lexi gone up to their rooms, he looked at Theo.

"Hey, if I'm old enough to guard the house, I'm old enough to know what really happened."

"Guess you're right on that." He rubbed Fran's back while he detailed who it was that broke in and how Fran dealt with it so well herself. "Just so you know, he did threaten her with all of you. It's just talk, but to be safe, watch your whereabouts for a while till it settles down. Your sister is not to be out on her own until I say otherwise. Alright?"

"Will do." Theo gave Fran a hug. "Glad you're okay. And don't worry. Like Dad said, he's full of big talk. That nephew of his, the one who was with him, can't stand him and he'll tell everything. We went to school together. He'll be glad to have his uncle locked away for a while. But we'll keep an eye and ear out."

Losing the composure she'd been holding, Fran wiped at her eyes.

G.F. held her in, told Theo good night with a hand on the boy's shoulder in thanks, and spoke beside Fran's ear. "You're family to them already. Might as well get used to it."

Fran cuddled underneath George's blankets and melted into his mattress with his strong arms wrapped around her. He would move to the couch soon, he said, since the kids were home, but it helped her relax to have him right there. He said again she needed to move in with him.

But she didn't want to be chased out. She didn't want to give in to the fear. He would give her a better lock. She'd keep her putter beside her bed, or get pepper spray. A taser, maybe.

"Shh, Frannie. Don't think about it anymore tonight." George whispered beside her ear. "I'm right here. You're safe. Just sleep now." He was lying on the outside of the covers and she felt them tug when he moved.

"I think I should show them."

He hesitated. "Show who what?"

"My father's paintings."

"Um, okay. Show them where?"

"At a studio. A gallery. Somewhere. They shouldn't just sit in there hidden. If they are local women who modeled for him, that was their decision, right? His work shouldn't have to be hidden..."

"I agree."

Fran expected more questions, arguments, concern. Something. "But he didn't. He hid them. Wouldn't he have done a show if he wanted them shown?"

"Not necessarily. Maybe he didn't know how to go about it. Maybe he didn't want to be there to see the reactions. Who knows? But he saved them. He'd have to know they'd be found eventually."

"Maybe."

"You should show yours, too."

She grabbed a deep breath. "Maybe."

"Why would he name you after an artist if he didn't want anyone to know art mattered to him? That's what I've been wondering. Did he think they weren't good enough?"

"After an artist?"

"Francis Barrett Faulkner. An artist. He did murals. Helped with the war effort during World War I. You didn't know?"

She sat up, staring at him. "No. Are you sure?"

"That's what he said, said he knew people thought he was nuts for giving you a boy's name or spelling it that way, but it was after the artist who he was pretty sure is an ancestor but hadn't proved it yet."

"He never told me."

"Maybe he wanted you to find your own path. He often said Mom shouldn't push the piano at me, that I should be whoever I was and not what they wanted. Maybe he didn't want it to influence you. Like I said, a smart man."

Didn't want to influence her? Except he continually taught her everything he could about gardening. It sure felt like influence, like he thought that's what she should do. "I've never heard of Francis Barrett Faulkner."

"We'll go to the library tomorrow and look him up. Or borrow Theo's laptop. Tonight..." He nudged her back down beside him and kissed her forehead, and her nose. The man had been planting soft kisses all over her face since he'd come to her rescue. "It's time to sleep."

Sleep. Except he'd go down to the couch when she went to sleep and she wanted him at her side. Always. She wanted him always at her side, at least every night. "Tell me this isn't a game for you, George. You and me."

"Not even close, Frannie. Like I said, you scared the hell out of me. Probably put tire marks on my drive pulling out of here to get to you. I don't want to lose you again. I want you to stay." He wrapped her tighter, then released her to move underneath the blanket so she could feel his hard, hot body against hers, and held her that way until she felt herself drifting to sleep.

Thirty

On Tuesday, George finally went back to work, at Fran's insistence. The day before, after they'd rested from the middle of the night activity, he'd taken them all to town where the kids wandered the library while she and George looked up Barry Faulkner. A muralist who, with a group of other artists, formed a civilian camouflage unit to help with World War I efforts, which later turned into an official military unit. She was especially interested in seeing his work at Connecticut's Bushnell Center, but although the history was there, photos weren't to be found. George suggested they might have to go out and visit it someday.

After the library, he treated them to a ridiculous amount of sweets from Kristi's Kandies, then pizza, and a stop at the farm market for fresh produce to counter the sugar and grease. His parents met them in town for dinner. George said it was an act of solidarity. She was family, as far as they were concerned, and he wanted the town to know it.

Fran figured it was far too premature for that, but it was better than sitting home thinking about it, which she also figured was George's idea.

She would not be scared off, however.

Insisting Lexi not go with her, she went home. She walked, since her car was still at her place, and no matter what she said, Theo wouldn't be talked out of walking with her, to check things out, he said. A sweet boy. He would be a good father someday. While they walked, he told her his dad had taken him and Justin to the range often to be sure they knew how to handle a weapon, and they'd both been hunting with him. Justin wasn't a big fan of it, but Theo went as often as he could. He was a good shot, he said, trying not to sound like he was bragging.

He carried his hunting rifle to her place since his dad had told him to be careful for a while. At least he gave in and went on back home to the other kids once he'd looked around. He left her the pepper spray Lexi usually carried.

Fran was more nervous than she'd ever been by herself, but she had to do it. It was her place. Her father's place. He left it to her. She would not abandon it because of two idiots who were in jail. Carly had already packed up the kids and left town. Fran couldn't blame her.

Glancing around at the front gardens, she sighed and went to the greenhouse to grab her trimming shears. The dead stalks were still sticking out around the otherwise lush and full hydrangeas and she didn't want them there. Carefully, she busied herself with cutting away every non-blooming branch she found.

Sweat rolled down her back. The sun was hot already. Nearly August. If the end of July was this hot, she had to wonder how hot it would be in the middle of August. Her herbs would need extra care.

With thirst overwhelming her, she went into the cottage and poured a glass of tepid tap water, listening to the silence. But the silence was too eerie, so she put on a CD for company, Buddy Guy and Bonnie Raitt, and let *Feels Like Rain* wash through her overheated and anxious system.

Her herbs would be nice with the leftover cucumber salad and the pork chops she planned for the night's dinner, a thank you to George and his kids for... A thank you. She wouldn't think about the why.

Turning the music louder, she realized her trimming shears were still in her hand as she headed out to the herb garden. She decided to keep hold of them along with her smaller scissors that would work better for clipping off parsley, thyme, and basil.

A noise made her jump until she realized it was a toad hiding within the coolness of her garden. Movement from beneath the shrubs made her jump again. The kittens. Coming to get a scratch on the head and a reminder to feed them. Lexi had befriended the things, so they were always around. She knew they were there and she knew they'd come up to her in the garden. She was far too jittery. Fran hated being jittery at her own place.

As soon as she had plenty of herbs for dinner and enough more to dry for later, she rinsed them under cold water and lay them on top of clean kitchen towels to dry. Then she made herself return to the front yard. Her hydrangea trimming was only half done. The long sharp clippers were still in her hand and she held them in front of her like a weapon while she scanned the area. "Stop being ridiculous. You work out here alone all the time."

Making herself tune into the soft blues she could hear through her open windows, Fran threw herself into her work, letting go of her nerves, of her fear, allowing the calm of nature and productive work to take over.

Until a vehicle pulled into her drive, and her heart pounded as she turned, clippers in hand. "George."

With a slight tilt of his head and a slight frown, he came to her, noting her defensive posture. "Why are you out here alone?"

"I'm working. And I live here."

"Fran..."

"I told you, I won't be scared off."

He took her free hand. "And yet you're shaking like a frightened rabbit."

"I'll have to get over it." She pulled away and continued cutting off dead hydrangea branches.

"Your father always left those. He said it added to their beauty."

"Yes well, I don't have to do everything the way my father did."

Running a hand down her shoulder and arm, he planted a kiss aside her head. "You're right, Frannie. You sure don't. Glad you realize it."

Turning, she saw both the sweat-matted hat-creased brownish blondish reddish hair across the top of his forehead that showed he'd come from work, with a streak of dirt alongside his face that showed he hadn't bothered to wash at all when he stopped in at home, and both concern and compassion in his expression.

"He forgot who I was." Fran dropped the clippers carefully beside her and went to sit on the porch steps. When George sat next to her, she took a deep cleansing breath. "When I came back to help, he knew me. For weeks, he knew me. Until that one day I was helping him put his sweater on because he was cold, and he pushed me away. He asked me who I was and why I was in his house. He asked *me* who

I was. I couldn't deal with it. So I left again. I don't want to do that to you. I don't want to forget you. And I don't deserve you to stay if I do get to that point. I left him. I left Mom to deal with it alone..."

"She wasn't alone with it. She had hospice care helping her on top of the girl she hired. Someone sent them over. She never knew who it was..."

"I did. When I left, I sent them. But I should have stayed."

"I figured you had. Pretty sure your mom figured you had, as well." He took her hand and kissed her fingers. "And I think you were right to leave. The whole thing has you scared enough. Probably good you didn't see more than you did."

"It was my place..."

"You did the right thing."

"How do you know? Not only about whether it was the right thing or not, but ... about hospice or what Mom knew or didn't know or guessed. How do you know?"

He sighed and rubbed a hard thumb over her fingers. "I um, I checked in on them from time to time. Like I said, I knew your dad well. I helped... Doesn't matter, but he wasn't alone. He didn't always know who I was. I went in knowing I'd have to tell him most days. Toward the end, it didn't matter what I told him. He didn't know your mother, either, kept telling her to get away. When he told us both to get away, always, not only on occasion, she called the home. Not much choice on her part. She couldn't do anything with him and he didn't know who she was or where he was. He was already gone, Frannie. Wouldn't have done you any good to stay. You did the right thing."

"Why?" She barely got the words out. "Why you?"

"I was willing." He shrugged. "I respected him. The man deserved as much dignity as he had left to remain intact. I tried to help him do that."

Her head nodded while her heart sank. "You were a son to him, like he wished he'd had. Instead of me."

George pulled back and raised his eyebrows. "Is that what you think? Because that's not at all true, Francis Margaret. Your father never wished for anyone instead of you. Trust me on that. I know he didn't. He doted on you like ... well, like I do on Lexi. On all of my kids, but my Lexi ... she reminds me of you a lot. Hard not to dote on her. Your father loved you and he was proud of you. Most of what he said toward the end was about his Frannie and how incredible you are."

Fran's chest tightened and she got up. She had to walk. To move. Not away, though. Not from her George.

She wandered to the greenhouse with him following. "Still think it's okay to ask your father to help make this sturdier?"

"It is. But Frannie..." He eyed her, concerned.

"I've been thinking." She looked up through the greenish glass and the peeling white paint from the old windows nailed together. "I like the main house. Always did. I think maybe I'd like to live in it again."

"Yeah?" His voice was a mix of optimism and caution. "Can you afford that? Without the rent... Not that I have a right to ask and I'm not trying to be nosy, but it's gotta be..."

"Yes. Once I get a job again, I can. It was paid off long ago, so it's just insurance and taxes and such. And this..." She sighed deeply. "This would make a beautiful art studio. Wouldn't it? It needs work, of course, but I can do most of it if I can get help with the structure, to make sure it's sturdy and safe. I think I'd like to open it to the elderly of the community, the ones who need more activity, socializing, something to keep their brains active. I could provide paint, charcoal, canvas, and help with technique here and there. Plus gardening. Part of it can still be a greenhouse. A mix of the two, maybe. They say art and socializing and learning new things helps prevent dementia, along with exercise for oxygen, to be sure the brain gets enough oxygen..."

"So dancing is helpful, as well."

"Yes. Dancing. Walking. Moving around more than..." She stopped to notice his grin and agreed when he offered his arms.

He moved her with the strains of the blues, and dipped her gently. "We could provide music, too. Dancing is a good thing."

"We?"

"We. I want to do this with you."

"There's a piano in the house. We could move it out here, and add a stereo. I could offer gardening workshops. The raised beds will make it easier. Not so much bending. We could add more beds..."

"Yes. We could." He kissed her neck.

"Will your father help me get this in shape enough? I'll pay him of course..."

"I'm sure he will, and I doubt he'll allow you to pay him, being you're family. He'll count it as community service. The kids and I will help, too."

"I wasn't asking for..."

"I know you weren't, and you're free to offer to pay him. Just don't be surprised if he won't take it."

"Then I shouldn't ask."

"Of course you should." He kissed in front of her ear. "Or I will."

"George..."

He twirled her and leaned her back in a larger dip. "Yes?"

"I think I'll stay."

"I think you better." Before she could argue, he covered her mouth with his. A short kiss. Deep. But short. "How about a quick rendezvous before I take you home for dinner?"

"Oh. I'd planned to cook. I forgot..."

"Lexi's doing it. She ordered me to bring you back. But we have a bit of time, so..."

"Not in the loft." The thought of going back up there made her shiver.

"Nope. We're both too dirty for that." He wiped sweat from her forehead and rubbed it off on his jeans.

"We're too dirty for the couch, too."

"Not for that bench, though. It'll be like the first time."

"It might be cold on your ass." She lowered her hands to the gentle roundness of his buttocks.

"Doubt it, in this heat. And it's gonna take a lot more than that to cool me down by now." Sweeping her up off her feet, he carried her out to the garden and gently set her on the stone circle.

Fran thought maybe she should get a large outdoor pad for the thing, with the way they tended to use it. Between unbuttoning his shirt, she stroked a finger along his face. "Sie könnten recht haben."

He gave her an amused, sultry look and unbuttoned her jeans. "Gonna interpret that?"

"Puede que tengas razón."

"Try again?" He pulled her shirt up over her arms.

"Si potrebbe essere giusto."

He kissed her neck, and her shoulder. "Very sexy. What's it all mean?"

"It's all the same thing." She smoothed her hands up to his shoulders, removing his shirt and letting it fall. "German, Spanish, Italian. It all means the same."

"Yeah? Well, until you teach me Italian…"

"You want me to teach you Italian?"

"Have to try to keep up with you somehow, Lady."

"No, you don't. But I will."

He kissed her nose. "Gotta get home for dinner soon, Frannie. You wanna talk or you wanna…"

"Vous pourriez avoir raison."

"I could be right about what?"

"Some things are too certain not to see." Fran waited until he remembered the conversation.

George nodded softly, his eyes moist. "Je te aime de tout mon coeur, mon amour. I love you with all of my heart, my love."

"I understood you the first time."

"Just wanted to say it twice. I have loved you since that first French class we took together when you corrected the teacher. Didn't know that, did you?"

"I was so impertinent back then. I can't imagine why you didn't snicker at me like everyone else did."

"Because you were standing up for what you knew was right, despite her authority. Something most of us wouldn't ever do, at least at that age."

"That teacher never liked me since then."

"Nah, but I sure did. Still do. Always have."

"I love you, too, George Frederick McKenry. Always have."

Thirty-one

Fran was ready to sit and listen to the Rude band after the day of wandering Storm Lake's Wood, Wine, & Blues festival. She and George and the kids had watched several chainsaw carvings in progress, marveled at those already completed, and stopped at several vendors. She and Lexi shared a taste in jewelry and Fran completely overindulged the girl, and herself. At times the boys wandered with them. Other times they went off with their friends, including Theo's girlfriend who stayed with him when he hung out with his family. A sweet girl. Fran liked her. George seemed to not want to like her, although the sparkle in his eyes said it was an act.

Justin's girlfriend came over with her parents to meet George. They were plenty friendly to him, not so much to Fran. Relatively new to the area, they talked mainly about their tiny town in Nebraska and having to move from there for work. The girl didn't look like she'd appreciated having to move, and she hardly said two words to them, although she had a pretty, friendly smile. Justin spent most of his time walking around with her family instead.

A couple of Lexi's friends walked with Fran and George and he told her she could hang with their families, also, if she wanted, but she wanted to stay with her dad. The girl had been staying close since the day of the break-in. Fran wasn't quite sure if it was fear for herself since her brothers had been highly protective of her since then, watching close and saying too much about it, or for George, since he'd run toward trouble and she'd mentioned he could have been hurt.

George said it was Fran that Lexi was worried about, but she disagreed. Lexi hung all over him, or at least close to him, whenever he wasn't at work. She would not go to her mother's house, and neither did Justin. Frank wanted to go, so Theo went with him at least for part of the day, driving them both and picking his brother up when he left early.

George's parents showed up in the middle of the day but didn't stay long, only long enough for Gwen McKenry to restock her wine supply, as her husband teased.

Finally, with Lexi off walking around with Eve and her parents, after a slight push from George, Frank hanging out with a group of his soccer team, and the older boys wandering the lake with their girls, she and George were alone.

It was early evening and the sun showed signs of waning. The heat of the day started to break. A perfect time to grab the blanket from the truck and lower onto the ground with a couple of plastic glasses of wine. Fran sat close, her legs curled to the other side next to George, who had one leg out in front of him and the other tented with his arm resting on it.

The wine was a touch sweeter than she liked, but it had a wonderful fruity flavor. It was the third she'd tried so far, stretched out during the day, in between plenty of water.

"Okay." He watched her reaction to it. "Find one we need to take home yet?"

"They're all good. The second one is my favorite."

"Figured it was. Should I go grab some?"

"I have their card. We can go find them another day. How about just sitting a while and listening?"

"Tired feet or enjoying the music?"

"Both. And I'm glad to have you to myself for a bit." She was also glad they were sitting far enough back from the stage to keep it easy to talk and to hear each other.

With a grin, he rubbed a hand over her back.

"This is nice. The festival. There's not much Blues music for a Blues fest, though."

"No. I hear there's a big one in Des Moines in February. We may have to go check that one out. Without the kids. What do you think?"

"Sounds good." She linked her hand around his arm. "I'm glad you like Blues."

"I'm glad you decided to stay." He set a kiss alongside her head. "Although, the living arrangements aren't quite working for me. Too much back and forth. Glad you're in the house rather than the cottage so I can stand up in your room without bumping my head. Still...”

With another swallow of wine, she leaned in close. “Well, George McKenry, if you want me to live with you, you know what to do about it. I do have some standards.”

“Yep. I have a good idea about that.” Propping his still half-full plastic glass in the grass, he pulled a small box from the jacket he’d retrieved along with the blanket and shifted to kneel in front of her. “Frannie, *this*, you and me together, is to certain not to see. Always has been. Guess we just needed enough time to clear our eyes.” He opened the box to reveal a large sparkling diamond ring with two small diamonds on each side of the large center stone. “Five diamonds because this is kind of from all of us, since we’re a package deal. You’d have to say yes to the whole gang. And before you answer, realize in a few years, there’s likely to be more of us, the way those kids are growing. What do you think? Can you deal with all of our messy chaos long term?”

“Oh, George.” She slid a hand along his thigh. “Je te aime de tout mon coeur, mon amour. I love you with all of my heart. Yes. I would love to deal with you and all of your chaos long term, as long as you’re sure you’re not afraid of my long term mental capacity.”

“Don’t worry, Lady. I have a lot of dancing left in me. And so do you.”

“Okay, then.”

“Okay, you’ll marry me?”

“Yes, I’ll marry you. But we’re moving into my house. I don’t like yours much, to be honest.”

He laughed. “Neither do I. Never have. Wasn’t my choice. And it sounds like I’m getting the better deal.”

“We’ll see.”

“She said yes.” It was a whisper to the evening dusk. Then he said it louder, to somewhere behind her. All of his children swarmed them throwing out hoops and hollers as he slid the ring onto her finger and gave her a nice sensual public-safe kiss.

“So much for them being off with friends?” Fran gave him a teasing grin.

“They wanted to be here but not in the way. They figure they’ll be in the way plenty often from now on."

"I wouldn't have it any differently."

They settled down again with his family and a few friends crowded in close, Lexi at her side talking about all of the things they could do together, Frank talking about concerts they could attend, listing names she didn't know but would let him introduce, maybe even with videos. Theo and Justin said it would be nice to have someone around to calm their dad when they were out on dates.

Until George hushed them so they could hear the music that wasn't the Blues.

Epilogue

With a shiver, Fran set the last journal on the desk, the old leather-topped desk that was her father's, now newly refinished to allow the gorgeous oak to show off its gorgeous veins. Some of George's handiwork. The man was always playing with the house and the old furniture within, showing its glory the way it deserved, he said.

Much of his reticence in taking care of his house had been because he'd never liked it. Justine insisted on having the place. He'd kept it only for the kids. None of them cared at all about moving out of it, not even Frank. He loved Fran's big stone house and especially not having to share a room anymore. He loved Scruff's dog house in the back yard that was big enough for him to play inside along with Scruff. George had put a pretty wood fence around enough of the back property for the dog to run around full speed, often chased by Frank, and added a heat lamp in his big doghouse for the winter. He sometimes joined the kids in their basement family room, but the rest of the house was off limits.

Lexi's cats had gravitated over from the cottage and by now were also sleeping in the dog house. Scruff had no issue with them. On cold days, they often snuggled up against him to sleep. George had promptly had them fixed and vaccinated "since they're going to be hanging around."

The old greenhouse had been stabilized and set up for community use, and every first and third Saturday saw Fran holding art lessons amid her growing things. Double duty, she told George: being surrounded by greenery was good for the aging body, also. In the winter, her container plants that wouldn't make it outside through an Iowa winter were moved inside the greenhouse. She'd added wicker furniture with soft cushions in a corner where she could sit and sketch or read to help her get through gray, frigid days.

Now and then, they held socials with music loud enough to enjoy but quiet enough to talk over and invited anyone who needed some conversation. During the week, she gave piano lessons on her old spinet in the cottage. Gwen McKenry insisted George take his piano to his house, now that he had room for the baby grand. Often in their alone time, George and Fran sat side-by-side at the beautiful instrument and played together. She was slowly relaxing into it enough to play with a better artistic quality, fueled by his.

Frank, who was closing in on eighteen already and quickly growing into a man's build, always went to the cottage with her for the after-school lessons. He said it was good homework time, since there was no television or computers in the cottage, but she knew full well he was simply being her guardian while his dad was at work. She didn't need one. It had been nearly four years since her fright and no one had heard anything from Lurch since then. Still, she enjoyed Frank's company. When Lexi was home, she was likely to be there, as well. Mostly, the girl was still off running with friends after school, usually within one of her extracurricular activities. And she had her driver's permit, which made George a nervous wreck, so Fran was teaching her to drive.

Restless after finishing her journey through her mother's written thoughts, Fran went to the large window in the fairly sparse entry room, as they called it since it was just to the right of the main door, and pulled the sheers back to peer out at the snow-covered lawn. The sun was starting to set already. Short days were the hardest part of winter. Cold, she was okay with, if it didn't get extreme. She didn't get cold easily, and she did enjoy the break from constant garden maintenance. But the lack of sun got to her fast. If not for George, she likely would have moved south somewhere, at least for the winter.

The landscaping was coming along well. As soon as she moved from the cottage to the main house, Fran began adding color and variety. The shrubs were growing out naturally, which so far, made them look a bit messy, the way a hairstyle did when it was in between short and where it was heading. Another couple of years and they'd be lush again. George had suggested raised bed gardens at each corner of the front of the house to make it look less square, and once they were put in, Fran turned them over to Lexi. During the summer and fall summer, sunflowers filled the beds, along with asters and pansies for color and height variation. The girl had a natural artistic touch. She also worked at the piano every day. She played like her father, a natural.

With a sigh, she let the sheers fall back into place, blocking out the snow. She'd had enough of a garden break by now. It was February. They were at the end of winter. She was always antsy to get back to the dirt, other than her greenhouse plants, by February.

At least the sunset meant George would be home any time.

He came home energetic these days, his hands chilled from the nearly zero degree air, but clean. He was always clean and hug-ready when he came in the door now. She almost missed his road crew smell, but only almost. He was okay enough with the desk job, and on days like this, he was glad not to be out on the roads in a plow throwing salt. Except for days he filled in, which happened somewhat often during flu season and when unexpected minor squalls turned not so minor.

A flash of bright light made its way through the clouds and trees and hit her in the eyes, and she turned the vertical blinds to an angle the sun wouldn't hit the desk. It was nearly an insult to be hit with sun when it had hidden all day and was about to fade into dark. Or she was only moody from being cooped up inside for so long.

With a sigh, she went back to the desk, smoothed her fingers over the plain black hardcover journal, embellished with no more than a red pen marking the dates written on the spine, in the white area left for that purpose, and put it back in the box to go take care of dinner.

Except she ended up standing next to the kitchen counter staring out the window where trees cast long shadows across the otherwise sparkling red-orange sun-highlighted snow, studying the colors of the bare trunks, the bends and curves of their branches, and the design they made against the part navy part gray sky. "Okay, it is pretty. I'll admit it."

"Talking to yourself again?"

Fran turned to Lexi's smile. "Convincing myself I'm fine with this weather."

"Is it working?"

"Not yet."

With another smile, the girl came over and gave her a hug. Now fifteen, she was slightly taller than Fran, and she was good at hugging. "I'm making dinner. Dad says you need time to unwind tonight."

"Honey, that's okay. How about your homework?"

"Done. Did you find anything interesting in your mom's journals?"

A sigh enveloped her involuntarily. "Yes."

"Can you tell me?"

"Someday."

"You want to talk to Dad about it first, right?"

Fran kissed her forehead. "You have me pegged." Giving in to Lexi's insistence that she would cook and hearing her happy humming as she pulled stuff out of the pantry, Fran returned to the library next to the front door that she'd turned into an entry room by removing the beige carpet and putting in an easy-to-clean linoleum tile in a brown swirl pattern to anchor the teal and cream décor. George was always glad to have her in the entry room when he got home, the one room in which she didn't ask them to take their shoes off.

She barely sat again, this time on the love seat next to the fireplace, before she heard the door open and his voice.

"Frannie?"

"In here, love." She remained seated and let him come to her. "How was your day?"

"Same ole same ole, but I've been wondering about yours."

"I finished the last one only a few moments ago."

With a glance at the box of journals, still sitting beside the desk where he'd put them for her after he found them in the attic while he and the boys cleaned it up to start preparations for a greenhouse getaway room, George sat next to her and grasped her fingers. "Need to talk about them?"

"You smell nice."

He lowered his nose toward his chest and sniffed loudly. "Smells like air to me. Or am I missing something?"

"It does smell like air, mixed with you." She kissed his cheek and felt the roughness of his whiskers growing back.

"I missed you, too. But you're avoiding the question." His eyes teased with a sparkle. "So, what did you find out about your mom?"

Setting her head on his strong shoulder, she held onto his arm for the physical support to go along with the emotional support he always gave her. "She used to work with special needs kids. That's what she did at the school Dad mentioned. In Fort Dodge. He met her at the art museum. Branden. The first one in Iowa. She took her kids there, and to the library, to the Fort Museum. She helped them do a lot of things other teachers wouldn't, and she wasn't a teacher, only a parent helper or something like that. Why didn't I know any of this?"

"Did you ask?"

"More times than I can remember. She said it didn't matter, her life was different now and she'd settled on that. But why, if she liked kids so much, did she choose not to be with me often?"

"The journals didn't tell you?"

"They end as of the day before I was born. It's rather offensive, really, since she felt the need to talk about the kids she worked with and not about her own. Nothing. There's a slight mention of being pregnant, but nothing more."

"Well, we're still sorting through stuff. There could be more we haven't found."

"Or she didn't bother."

"I don't know, Frannie. She was an odd woman, granted. But could be she was too wrapped up in taking care of you to bother writing about it. Either way, I'm sure as heck glad she had you." He stroked a large hand through her hair. "You're a mess. Have you done anything but read today?"

"I think I ate lunch."

"Well, that's a good thing." He stood and helped her up. "Guess you need something else to think about, then, while Lexi's whipping up her specialty, whatever that is this week."

Fran followed him out to the hall, smiled at Theo and his wife, and nearly pulled the baby girl from Theo's arms. "Come here, dear one. I haven't seen you in days."

She barely heard the baby's parents talking with George as she adored the sweet little face that looked so much like her grandpa it made her smile. Theo worried how the baby would do on the upcoming big family vacation to Colorado since she'd be scooting around the house by then. Carrie, his very young but capable wife who Fran still liked a lot, mentioned her new job as office assistant for her grandfather-in-law's construction company where Theo was apprenticing as the next family construction expert, that so far she could work around her daughter's needs while she kept her in the office, but she would need a sitter soon. They were looking for someone they could trust, which she said was scary...

"I'll keep her." Fran kissed the baby's cheek.

"Oh, but Fran, it's so much work..." Carrie looked both reluctant and expectant.

"Nonsense. I'll teach her how to paint. We'll be just fine, won't we, dear one? She might as well get used to me because I have all kinds of things planned for us to do together. No arguing. I get first dibs since it's my right as her grandma, and you can keep that babysitter money for her education."

George wrapped both of them in his strong arms and said she better count him in on some of those plans. Then he focused on Theo. "You will need someone to take over for three weeks in October. Just as a heads up."

"That's still months away, Dad. You have plans already?"

"Yep. Already booked. I'm taking Fran to Norway to visit her roots and then to the Netherlands to tramp around Van Gogh's old haunts for our fifth anniversary. Can't believe we're coming up on five years already. Seems like just yesterday when I married you." He kissed her head.

"Booked?" She stared at her husband. "You've booked it?"

"Surprise." He threw a grin. "Thought it might brighten your winter a tad. And I thought we should do it now, since you may have your hands full of grandchildren within a few years. You know, in case we haven't thrown enough chaos on you already."

"Non avrei alcun altro modo, il mio amore." She kissed his neck. "I wouldn't have it any other way, my love."

His eyes sparkled. "I understood you the first time."

"Just wanted to say it twice."

EllaMKaye.com

Acknowledgements and Author's Note

Dementia is a frightening thing.

I'll never (hopefully) forget that day I went back home to visit my family with my two children, sitting in Mom's living room while they ran around with their cousins. I was always Grandma's girl. I lived with her for some time during my college years. So when I sat next to her and she picked up my left hand, I wasn't surprised. When she looked at my wedding ring, puzzled, and said, "You got married?" though...

Um, yes, some time ago. Those are my children, Grandma. You don't know who they are? I said, finally, "Yes, a few years ago." She was there when I got married, but the look on her face said she didn't remember any of it, and she didn't know my children.

I suppose I never quite got over that moment.

Not only is it hard to realize you've lost, or partly lost, someone who is sitting right beside you, it's frightening. The fear of inheriting any disease is hard to shake. Knowing some day you could do the same to your grandchild isn't a funny thought.

With my penchant for research and natural remedies, I've at least made myself feel better that maybe dementia can be staved off. I'm not a health care professional, physical or mental. Anything I state within the story comes from some research and a good bit of hope, but I make no claims of effectiveness and accept no responsibility for what I've read elsewhere and shared here. The story is fiction and life is a crap shoot. We can only do what we can do, educate ourselves to our best ability, and hope for the best.

I want to shout out a big thank you to Robin Koster, who I found on social media while searching high and low for a good photo of Storm Lake, Iowa to use on my cover without copyright infringement. Robin was kind enough, not only did she *not* blow me off when I messaged her about a possible photo she maybe had that would work, but she took her camera on her next jaunt out around town and captured several images focused on my interests. As you can see from the cover, she found the perfect shot and was happy to allow me to use it. I'm very grateful. Robin, I hope you enjoy the story set in your hometown, which I've yet to visit but hope to do in the near future. I always fall a little in love with the places I use as settings.

Thank you, again, to my constant editor, Liz Ferguson. Her sharp eyes and witty comments about my drafts make them better reads. Every time. Every book. Such beautiful encouragement.

Thank you to my beta readers. I hope you'll be able to see the improvements you've helped to make.

Thank you, also, to my readers for tagging along on this journey, and to those who leave reviews anywhere. The author's part in creating a novel is only half the experience. To be a full experience, it must fall into a reader's hands, minds, and with any luck, their hearts. <3

Music Mentioned in the Story

Stevie Ray Vaughan: *Texas Flood, Love Struck Baby*
Buddy Guy: *Fever*
Maroon 5: *This Love, Moves Like Jagger*
Jimmie Vaughan: *Slow Dance Blues*
Buddy Guy and Bonnie Raitt: *Feels Like Rain*

About The Author

Ella M. Kaye uses her art and psychology background to create contemporary love stories with mental health issues set around the creative arts. Each of her novels and novellas fall under one of three series: Dancers & Lighthouses, Artists & Cottages, and Songwriters & Cities. Kaye has been writing romantically inclined literary fiction that branches into straight mainstream in both novel and short story form under the name LK Hunsaker for more than two decades. After many moves as a military spouse, she and her husband are settled in western Pennsylvania where she enjoys the abundant foliage, recreational lakes, and hilly vistas, as well trying to keep up with her hectic handful of gorgeous grandchildren.

EllaMKaye.com
LKHunsaker.com

Other Books by Ella M. Kaye

Pier Lights
Dancers & Lighthouses (2013)

Caroline was a relevé away from becoming prima ballerina when, partly due to her own actions, she was injured enough to end her ballet career. With a strong determination, along with some help and hindrance from her antisocial tendencies, Caroline returns to her beloved Folly Beach, finds a grittier dancing job, and makes up her mind to land on top.

Due to a disfiguring facial scar, Dio hides away on his South Carolina farm during the day, where keeping watch over his aging and mentally failing mother strains his time and energy. Venturing into Charleston only for his night job in a strip club allows him to keep needed contact with others while maintaining distance.

When the two collide amid the glow of the lights from the pier, their personal scars push them away, and pull them in, like the ebb and flow of the Atlantic.

Shadowed Lights
Dancers & Lighthouses (2014)

Delaney Griffin welcomed her sister's large family into her small home when they were displaced by Hurricane Sandy. With five noisy kids and an overbearing brother-in-law threatening her sanity, Delaney spends much of her free time cleaning up the wildlife refuge and helping at the local food bank. Still, the lack of privacy, along with having no space to dance, her only passionate release, causes her debilitating social anxiety to escalate.

Eli Forrester has come from small town Indiana to Barnegat, New Jersey with his company to help restore the coast. A high-rise worker who loves new people and new places, he fears nothing, except water. When he accidentally kicks one of the sea critters Delaney is trying to help rescue, Eli is drawn to the quiet New Jersey girl. Unwilling to take her cues to leave her alone, he is alternately put off and turned on by her odd behavior.

Pieces of Light
Dancers & Lighthouses (2014)

When her niece is diagnosed with autism, Emma Turner chooses to support her sister, a single mom, and is served divorce papers by her possessive husband who doesn't actually intend to let her go. Moving from Boston to Provincetown, Massachusetts, Emma teaches fifth grade during the week and takes care of Patty on weekends. That changes abruptly when her sister's health fails and Patty needs more than weekend care.

Fillan Reilly has taken a summer job on Cape Cod teaching ballroom dance. A Galway, Ireland native, Fillan uses the change of scenery to try to clear his head and decide his direction after his long-term girlfriend leaves him, unsure whether she'll return. With pressure to enter the family business and push his dancing to the sidelines, he expects an easy relaxed summer to think things over.

As fate brings them together, Emma and Fillan must determine whether joining their lifeboats will provide an even keel or throw them further off-balance.

Shadows of Blues & Echoes
Artists & Cottages (2016)

Gillian Hart has big ambitions while working as a reporter for a small circulation paper in Denver, Colorado. When her editor and friend assigns a story about some rich businessman who chucks it all to live in the woods alone outside Durango, she does her best to fight it. With no choice but to give in, Gillian determines to use it as a stepping stone.

Hank Dennison wants nothing but solitude while he recovers from a life-changing devastation he has managed to hide from the public. The last thing he wants is another nosy journalist badgering him, especially one who knows nothing about survival in the wilderness and taxes his waning strength. Noticing the darkness of depression that weighs her down, despite her attempt to hide it, Hank determines to keep her off the path that led him to his own illness.

Shadows of Rust & Reels
Artists & Cottages (2017)

By day, Holli Jacoby is a jewelry artist in her hometown of Williamstown, West Virginia. Abandoned by her family, Holli mainly stays to herself, preferring her potter's wheel to the risk of letting others see, and take advantage of, the uncontrollable effects of her bipolar disorder.

Isaac Bradshaw is a welder who spends much of his off time assisting his parents due to his father's declining health. While playing pool, he notices a fiery brunette eye him as though she knows him. He soon learns "fiery" is an understatement, and his buddy warns him against the girl, but something keeps him drawn to her.

Despite their earlier crossed paths and a shared love of adventure, Holli's roller coaster life might be more than Isaac is willing to handle. When the bottom falls out beneath her, their relationship hits a critical test.

A Melody in the Dark
Singers & Songwriters: a prequel novella (2017)
published by Fire Star Press as part of the *Music of the Heart* anthology.

Meladee Lerner, a single mom and struggling songwriter, moved to Pittsburgh to escape a marriage she didn't want. It's 1979, just after the big snow storm that paralyzed the city, when they run into Niall Dillon, a hard-working young Pittsburgher with strong Irish roots. Niall is making plans to travel the US on his own, but one eventful night gives him second thoughts.

~~ ~~ ~~

Watch for more Artists & Cottages books from Ella M. Kaye, as well as more from the Dancers & Lighthouses series, and the new Songwriters & Cities series, soon to come.

If you enjoyed this book, I would love a review at your favorite reader hangout or bookstore site. For private comments or inquiries, contact me at ellamkaye.author@gmail.com. Please allow a few days or so for a response, as the next book is always in the works.

www.ingramcontent.com/pod-product-compliance
Lightning Source LLC
Chambersburg PA
CBHW071140180726
48291CB00007B/2265